THE FAIRBAIRN GIRLS

Recent Titles from Una-Mary Parker from Severn House

The Granville Series

THE GRANVILLE SISTERS
THE GRANVILLE AFFAIRE
THE GRANVILLE LEGACY

ALEXIA'S SECRETS

ECHOES OF BETRAYAL

THE FAIRBAIRN GIRLS

Una-Mary Parker

This first world edition published 2013
in Great Britain and in the USA by
SEVERN HOUSE PUBLISHERS LTD of
19 Cedar Road, Sutton, Surrey, England, SM2 5DA.

British Library Cataloguing in Publication Data

Parker, Una-Mary.
   The Fairbairn girls.
   1. Aristocracy (Social class)--Scotland--Argyllshire--
   Fiction. 2. Argyllshire (Scotland)--Social life and
   customs--19th century--Fiction. 3. Domestic fiction.
   I. Title
   823.9'14-dc23

ISBN-13: 978-0-7278-8258-5 (cased)
ISBN-13: 978-1-84751-472-1 (trade paper)

All Severn House titles are printed on acid-free paper.

Severn House Publishers support The Forest Stewardship Council [FSC],
the leading international forest certification organisation. All our titles that
are printed on Greenpeace-approved FSC-certified paper carry the FSC logo.

MIX
Paper from
responsible sources
FSC® C018575

Typeset by Palimpsest Book Production Ltd.,
Falkirk, Stirlingshire, Scotland.
Printed and bound in Great Britain by
MPG Books Ltd., Bodmin, Cornwall.

This is dedicated to my family
with all my love

One

If only. The words reverberated again and again in Laura's head. If only she'd listened to her sisters. If only she'd not been so impulsive; she who was normally so careful, weighing everything up before she made a decision. Why had she rushed into it, when others had begged her to wait a bit longer? Why had her acute intuition utterly failed this time? Most of all, why had no one actually warned her?

A heavy crash from the floor above made her duck her head involuntarily. It was followed by another and another. Laura sank into a chair and buried her face in her hands. It was happening again and she didn't know how she was going to bear it. How long would it last this time? A few days? A week? Probably longer. And what about Caroline? Fear ran in icy rivulets down her spine and a feeling of utter despair washed over her. Then she drew herself up. This would never do. She must be strong. As she walked over to her bureau, a framed photograph on a side table caught her eye. It had been taken in 1891 when she'd been seventeen, at a family gathering to celebrate her engagement to Rory Drummond.

Grouped on the lawn in front of her family's imposing home in Argyllshire, she stood with her parents, her eight sisters, two brothers and a collection of dogs. All the girls wore long white lace and muslin dresses with large hats adorned with flowers and feathers. Papa looked so distinguished in the kilt with a velvet doublet while her mother, in a silk dress with a train, wore the biggest hat of all.

Laura studied her own likeness, taking in the girlish smile and wide, innocent eyes filled with joy, and felt a sudden stab of sadness. Papa had always claimed the family had been cursed by someone using the Rowan tree as an instrument of destruction. Superstition caused most Scotsmen to hold the Rowan in awe, for it held the power of good and evil. Laura no longer believed that. Over the years she had begun to fear that she might be the mistress of her own destruction. But as she stared at the photo she was lost in her memories of how happy she and her family had been in those days. How wonderful the future had promised to be. If only . . .

Two

Lochlee Castle, 1891

'Come along, girls,' the Countess of Rothbury urged. 'The guests will be arriving in a few minutes and we must be in the drawing room to receive them. It's getting cold out here, too. The little ones will catch a chill.'

Elegant in a pale lavender silk dress trimmed with velvet and a hat embellished with violets and roses, she tried to round up her children as she hurried across the lawn back to the castle. They were celebrating the engagement of their second daughter, Lady Laura, and to mark the occasion they'd had their picture taken, some sitting, others standing in a formal group.

The photographer, who'd been summoned from Edinburgh for the occasion, had taken longer than expected because he'd got carried away by the magnificent backdrop of a fourteenth-century castle with ramparts and turrets set amidst the mountains that rose from the stony edges of Loch Etive. It was said to be the finest castle in Argyllshire, and had been in the Fairbairn family for five hundred years.

'It's colder indoors than it is out here,' observed Lizzie, the eldest, in somewhat crisp tones as she grabbed Catriona, the baby of the family, and swung her up in her arms. The other daughters chatted as they moved in a drift of white lawn and lace, the flowers on their broad-brimmed hats quivering like a herbaceous border in the stiff breeze.

Meanwhile, the Earl of Rothbury strode ahead with his favourite Labrador, Megan, by his side.

'Hurry up, boys!' he shouted to his sons, but Frederick and Henry were watching the photographers packing up their bulky equipment and ignored him.

'I wish I had a camera,' Henry said, gazing longingly at the sturdy wooden tripod and the black cases holding glass slides.

'What would you take pictures of?' Freddie scoffed. He was thirteen and the heir to the earldom and the Lochlee estate. Freddie considered himself to be vastly superior to his brother, who was four years younger.

'The horses, of course. Especially Snowdrop,' Henry replied without hesitation.

'Oh, you and Snowdrop! You're as bad as Papa when it comes to horses.'

Henry, turning pink, looked enraged. 'What's wrong with that?'

'When I inherit I'll get rid . . .' But Frederick's voice was drowned out by a burst of laughter as his sisters jostled each other in their haste to get indoors as it suddenly started to rain. Their good-natured banter echoed across the lawn as they held on to their hats.

'Come on, Laura! It's you everyone wants to see today,' shouted Beattie, struggling with her frilled skirt up the steps.

'That's right, Laura,' Lizzie piped up. 'You're the centre of attention today and I'll never forgive you for getting engaged before me! I am the eldest, after all.'

Laura's hazel eyes were shining with amusement as she caught up with them. 'Only by fourteen months,' she retorted. 'I think that seventeen is the perfect age to get married. It's only Mama who says I've got to wait another year. If I had my way I'd get married next week.'

'Come on, you two lovebirds,' Georgie chided. 'I'm starving. When are we going to have tea?'

Overhearing her, Lady Rothbury glanced back at her plump daughter and spoke firmly. 'Tea will be served throughout the afternoon but you must make sure all our guests have everything they want before you go diving in, Georgie.'

Georgie's expression became sulky and her full mouth drooped at the corners. Well developed for a fourteen-year-old, she unsettled people with her knowing brown eyes, which gave her a rather bold look.

'I don't see why,' she muttered under her breath.

'It's a case of FHB,' Beattie pointed out. 'You know . . . Family Hold Back.'

Georgie looked rebellious. 'I'm not going to!' It was so unfair, she thought. All her sisters were willowy thin and they all ate as much as her, but she was the one who put on weight.

'You can eat as much as you like at my wedding,' Laura pointed out peaceably.

'Bags I actually get to the altar before you, though,' Lizzie insisted, puffing under Catriona's weight. 'By this time next year who knows what might happen between me and James?'

Laura looked at Lizzie, her eyes widening. 'You mean . . .? Has he . . .?'

Lizzie frowned. 'Shhhh!' she whispered, glancing in Beattie's direction. 'If *she* finds out the whole county will know about it by this evening.'

Laura nodded. Beattie was the big mouth in the family, incapable of keeping a secret.

Inside the great hall of Lochlee Castle, the butler and several footmen stood awaiting the arrival of over a hundred guests who had been invited to the afternoon reception. Excitement and expectation charged the normally uneventful atmosphere. Lord Rothbury strongly objected to having his own routine interrupted by people who cluttered up the place, chattering and expecting fuss and formality.

Today the large reception rooms were brightened by vases of flowers, and in the dining room the long refectory table was covered by a damask cloth, as white and smooth as snow. On the sideboard silver samovars gleamed in readiness to provide endless cups of tea.

The staff who worked at Lochlee, many of them since the age of sixteen, were aware that this was a special occasion: the first engagement of one of the Fairbairn girls. The house-keeper, Mrs Spry, had made sure everyone was up by dawn so that everything ran like clockwork as they polished the suits of armour that stood in the hall, cleaned and refilled the oil lamps and raked the gravel in the drive ready for the arrival of the horse-drawn carriages.

Down in the kitchen the activity had reached fever pitch as

the cook, Mrs Lyddon, and her assistant finished baking the last batch of macaroons, sponge cakes crowned with icing, muffins and savoy biscuits, which the maids arranged on great silver trays and the footmen then carried up to the dining room.

The engagement of Lady Laura Fairbairn to Mr Rory Drummond, son of Sir Hector Drummond, was the talk of the county. It was thought to be a match made in heaven by many and the gossip in the village was rife. Douglas Cameron, the local postman, was the first to air his opinion to all and sundry.

'I ken the Drummonds have a large estate in Hampshire so the wee gurril's no fool!' he said knowingly.

'Och, aye! But fancy, the second daughter getting engaged before the first!' observed Mrs McGregor, who lived next to the post office. 'It must be putting Lady Elizabeth's nose right out of joint. I bet the feathers flew when *that* engagement was announced.'

Now the hour had arrived when the gentry could meet the future bridegroom, and within hours their opinions of the forthcoming marriage would filter down to the working classes, who would have a fine time discussing them.

Lady Rothbury smoothed her white kid gloves and, although her heart was fluttering with anticipation, she looked calm and in complete control: a queen bee at the centre of a hive heaving with the activity of servants, who skimmed about doing their duty both inside and outside the castle.

In the vast drawing room where priceless tapestries hung on the walls and silk rugs covered the parquet floor, the family chatter was suddenly broken by the booming tones of McEwan the butler as he announced the first guests.

'His Grace the Duke of Melrose and Her Grace the Duchess of Melrose.' There was a pause and then more arrivals were announced. 'Lord and Lady Gargunnock.'

In her element now, Lady Rothbury greeted each guest as if they were the most important person to grace the reception, while her husband stood stiffly beside her, nodding a brief 'how do you do' as if they were the last person he was inter-ested in. Nearby, Laura stood proudly with Rory, as if she could hardly believe her good fortune, her eyes glowing with happiness and her face gently flushed.

Diana, hovering a few feet away, had never been to a grown-up reception before and she started trembling, overwhelmed by the occasion.

Beattie came up to her and put her arm gently around her sister's waist. 'It's only a tea party, Di, not a ball at Buckingham Palace,' she whispered gently.

'But what shall I say if someone talks to me?' Diana bleated.

'Reply politely but don't worry. Grown-ups find girls of our age boring. I bet they make a direct line for Freddie.'

'Why Freddie? He *is* boring.'

Beattie giggled. 'The Garunnocks have a daughter, Imogen. She's nine years old.'

Diana looked confused. 'But why . . .?'

'If she married Freddie she'd become Viscountess Fairbairn, and then one day when Papa dies she'd be the next Countess of Rothbury and live here.'

'But Freddie and Imogen are still children,' Diana protested.

Beattie smiled. 'That's the way it works, Di. Laura was lucky to meet Rory but I bet Ma already had someone in mind for her. Look how they've been cultivating James Fraser for years; he's just the right age for Lizzie.'

Diana's pale skin flushed pink. 'Well, I certainly hope they haven't got anyone lined up for me! When I'm older I intend to fall in love naturally.'

'What if they lined up one of the Queen's grandsons for you?' Beattie teased. 'Prince Albert, perhaps?'

'They *all* seem to be called Albert,' Diana grumbled.

At that moment Eleanor, the most timid of the Fairbairn girls, came up to them. She was small for eleven, and mousey-looking, unlike all the others, who were tall and distinguished with rich dark hair and cream skin.

'What are we supposed to *do*?' she asked, glancing nervously around as the room filled up with more and more guests.

Her father, overhearing her, spun round and glared down at her angrily. 'What do you think you're supposed to do?' he thundered. 'Swing from the chandeliers? Stand on the piano and do a jig? That's the stupidest question I've ever heard.'

Eleanor's eyes filled with tears and she tried to hide behind Beattie.

'She's shy, Papa,' Beattie protested, taking Eleanor's hand. 'Come along, sweetheart. There are some lovely cakes in the dining room.' Beattie led her gently away.

Frowning with irritation, Lord Rothbury watched them leave the room, and then he suddenly smiled and his cold grey eyes warmed with affection as his Labrador ambled lazily towards him. Bending down, he stroked her smooth black head. 'Come, Megan,' he whispered softly. 'You don't like this circus any more than I do. Never mind – we'll go for a run as soon as I can get out of here.'

'William!' Exasperated, his wife hurried over. 'It's a pity you don't treat your family and friends with the same fondness you lavish on your blessed dogs,' she whispered fiercely. 'For heaven's sake help me to welcome the guests. This is Laura's day and it's the least you can do.'

He shrugged. 'Damned waste of time and money if you ask me. It's not their wedding reception.' He glanced balefully around the now crowded room.

'Please try to look pleasant and welcoming, William. It isn't much to ask.' Aware at that moment of more arrivals, she turned swiftly with a beaming smile. 'Ah, my dear Lady Northope, how delightful to see you again. It's so nice of you to join us to celebrate Laura's engagement.'

For the next two hours Lady Rothbury continued to smile gallantly and greet new guests gushingly before working her way skilfully around the rooms to make sure that Lizzie, Georgie, Beattie and Diana were introduced to everyone, and most especially those who had eligible sons. With eight more daughters to get off her hands she reckoned one couldn't start soon enough to cultivate the right people.

Meanwhile, Lord Rothbury had decided he'd had enough. Making polite conversation to a bunch of people he had no interest in was for him like having to endure a form of torture. He signalled to the butler. 'McEwan, get Meads to saddle Megara for me and bring her round to the front.'

'Right now, M'Lord?' he asked, astonished.

'Well, obviously not tomorrow! Of course I want to ride

now. And tell someone to let the dogs out of the kennels. I don't see why they should have their afternoon ruined by a bunch of damned socialites.'

'Very well, M'Lord.' McEwan had worked long enough for the Rothburys to know that one didn't cross the master.

By the time his favourite chestnut mare had been brought round, Lord Rothbury was waiting impatiently in the drive, dressed in his riding clothes and with his beloved Megan by his side.

'Where are the others?' he demanded. At that moment a river of brown, black, white and grey fur belted through a gate that had been opened, and twelve dogs of various breeds and sizes were tearing around, barking and leaping about with excitement as they realized they were going out with their master.

'All right! All right! Let's get going.' His bad mood had vanished and his ruddy face was wreathed in smiles. Mounting easily in spite of his weight, he set off in the direction of the wild beauty of Beinn Larachan with the dogs racing ahead. Megara pricked up her ears and broke into a smooth three-beat canter. The rain clouds had parted and the sun was shining on the freshly showered mountainside. At that moment a golden eagle swooped and dipped then rose again, its wings spread wide in glorious freedom.

This was William Rothbury's world and it was all he wanted.

Rory put his arm around Laura's slim waist and led her into the garden, where the sun was now setting behind the distant blue hills.

The last of the guests had drifted away and the only sound was the rustling of leaves in the breeze that swept across the Loch. Laura shivered, suddenly feeling cold. This magical summer of falling in love with Rory was nearly over and a bleak, melancholy winter beckoned. With a pang she realized the happiest summer of her life was coming to an end and, as she looked down at her diamond and sapphire engagement ring, she felt for a moment like weeping.

'Peace at last!' Rory remarked lightly 'Shall we go for a little walk?'

'Could it be that you'd like to be alone with me?' Laura

asked, her eyes over-bright and her voice trying to strike a cheerful note.

His expression softened as he pulled her closer. 'Laura, this is agony. Do we really have to wait another year before we can get married?'

'I'm afraid we do, my love.' She reached up and stroked his cheek. 'Mama made it a condition of our getting engaged now.'

'I don't know how I'm going to get through twelve months without you.'

'I'll write to you, often,' she promised.

'Nothing's going to change between us, is it?' He looked wistfully into her hazel eyes.

Laura reached for his hand and held it between her own. 'Rory, a century apart wouldn't change anything between us. I love you so much and I'm longing to become your wife. You do believe me, don't you? I wish today had been our wedding day.'

He pulled her close with sudden passion and spoke as if in pain. 'I wish to God it was.'

Laura rested her cheek against his. 'Tell me about the life we'll have when we're married,' she whispered. 'I love to hear you tell me what we'll do.'

Rory smiled. 'We'll wake up in the morning and smell the roses that grow beneath our bedroom window. When it's fine we'll have breakfast on the terrace and then maybe we'll go for a walk in the orchard and pick some apples and dark juicy cherries. In the winter we'll sit by a log fire and I'll read to you. *"Let us sit upon the ground and tell sad stories of the death of kings . . ."* and then I'll lead the way up to our four-poster bed as the moon rises above the sea.' He broke off, unable to continue, his face buried in her dark hair.

'I'm not too sure about dead kings, though.' Irresistible laughter bubbled up in her throat. 'I never did much care for *Richard II*.'

Rory burst out laughing, the sudden sexual tension between them broken. 'Perhaps I should have gone for *Romeo and Juliet*?'

'Too sad.'

'What about *A Midsummer Night's Dream*?'

'Too whimsical.'

Rory looked at her with raised eyebrows. '*The Taming of the Shrew?*'

'Don't get ideas above your station!' she shot back with a wicked smile.

They were laughing so much they clung to each other for support, but then the laughter stopped as abruptly as it had started. Laura's eyes were filled with tears and her voice was thin and pained.

'I wish you didn't have to return to Sussex tomorrow.'

'I'll be back as soon as I can, my darling. I'm working on several litigation cases at the moment and the senior partner has been very understanding about my coming up here to see you as often as I do. If we both keep busy the time will fly. Before you know it we'll be married.'

Laura flung her arms around his neck. 'Oh, it's going to be so wonderful! Being married and having a home of our own!'

'And a family too, in time,' he said, looking deeply into her eyes.

A piercing dart of desire shot through her, leaving her weak and her heart hammering. *I want him now*, she thought as she leaned heavily against him.

Rory wrapped her in his arms and buried his face in her neck. 'My darling girl,' he whispered, 'I want us to be together as much as you do.'

Rory left at dawn the next day and Laura and some of her sisters stood on the castle steps, waving him off in a horse-drawn brougham.

'When will he get to his home?' Diana asked, waving her white handkerchief energetically.

'Late tomorrow.' Laura quickly wiped away a tear. Their mother had instilled in them that it was bad to break down in front of the servants because it would embarrass them.

Little Eleanor frowned anxiously. 'Won't the horses get tired?'

'Don't be such a goose,' Georgie remonstrated robustly. 'He's going on the new train from Glasgow to London.'

'But won't the horses get tired before they reach Glasgow? It's *miles* away.'

'They'll probably change the horses when they reach Fort William or Rannoch.'

Eleanor's mouth drooped. 'But what will happen to the tired horses?' she persisted. Eleanor worried about everything but most especially the welfare of animals.

'They'll sleep in nice warm stables,' Beattie assured her, taking her hand. 'And they'll be fed and watered.'

'And someone will tuck them up and read them a bedtime story,' Georgie cut in with acerbity.

Laura gave her a disapproving glance. 'Don't be so mean. Eleanor is sensitive and very caring. Unlike you.'

'She's a wimp!' Georgie declared. 'She needs toughening up.'

Eleanor shrank inside her cotton shift, miserable at being picked on and the centre of attention.

Beattie, always the calm peacemaker, led the way back into the castle. 'Let's have breakfast,' she suggested brightly.

'I'll be with you in a minute,' Laura said, hurrying away across the great hall. Up on the first floor she flew along the wide corridor with its family portraits and heavy Jacobean furniture smelling of beeswax polish until she came to the guest wing. A moment later she entered the room where Rory had slept for the past few nights. It was just as he had left it, with the bedding pushed back and the pillow indented where his head had rested.

Lying down where he had lain and slipping her hand under the bedding which was still faintly warm, she caught a whiff of the sweet, clean smell of his skin. Breathing deeply, she sidled further down the bed, pulling the blankets up over herself while imagining him lying beside her. Then she closed her eyes and a deep wave of longing washed over her. His warmth and his scent was making her feel dizzy and she wished with all her heart that he was lying beside her now. Desire flowed through her like a heavy ache and she felt intoxicated by the thought of their love-making one day. But how was she going to bear the long wait before it was so?

Alone in her own bed that night, she recalled the first time she'd met Rory, when he'd been brought to Lochlee by friends of her mother, who were interested in buying a nearby property. He was their lawyer and a trustee of a fortune they'd recently inherited, and the moment Laura saw him she'd realized there was something special about him. It was as if she already knew him, and he'd felt the same. That first meeting had been overshadowed by the business in hand, but then he'd written to her – this handsome, dynamic man who was ten years older than her. She still had the letter. And this time next year they would be man and wife. She could hardly wait.

Downstairs in the breakfast room Lord Rothbury was chucking scraps of ham from his plate on to the floor as he laughed at the way the Highland terriers and poodles were quicker and more efficient at nabbing the titbits in mid-air than the Great Danes and Labradors who blundered clumsily around. Meanwhile, the basset hounds sat watching morosely, unable to compete in the chaos.

'Here, Megan. Here, girl,' he whispered softly. He fed her a special bit of ham and then stroked her as gently as if she'd been a human baby. Dark liquid eyes filled with devotion gazed back at him. His wife had never looked at him like that in the nineteen years they'd been married, he reflected sourly. Megan didn't rattle on about money or domestic issues either.

Lady Rothbury, sitting at the other end of the table, had long since learned to ignore what she considered to be her husband's deplorable table manners and his insistence that all the dogs should be free to roam around indoors during the day. When she'd first had a baby she'd been shocked and hurt at his cavalier manner towards her whilst he'd hovered nervously nearby over one of his bitches who was whelping at the same time. He'd summoned the vet although there was no need, yet had asked her crossly if she really needed Doctor Doughty to attend her as well as the midwife?

Then, when Lizzie was born he said, 'A girl is it? Huh!' and walked out of the room, but when the puppies arrived he joyously announced the news to all and sundry and ordered that all the workers on the estate be given a pint of ale. Then he'd gone out shooting with the ghillie.

Something died in Margaret Rothbury's heart then and, as the years passed and their family grew in size, sometimes she wondered if it was her fault that she'd produced nine girls and only two boys? On the other hand, she figured it might be God punishing William for no longer caring for her, although at the beginning he'd sworn passionately that she was his love and his life.

Breakfast over, the Fairbairn family scattered in different directions with great purpose and without saying a word to each other. Lord Rothbury was the first to stride from the room and go straight out where the ghillie was waiting for him with Megara, ready saddled, bridled and raring to go. For the next three hours they'd ride around the estate and talk about the coming shooting season when grouse, pheasant, widgeon, woodcock, plover and snipe would be brought down. Then there were leverets to be shot before they became fully grown hares, and then stalking would follow. Only one thing clouded William's pleasant expectations for the coming months: a large number of guests were always invited to Lochlee Castle for a few days at the end of each week. The men were fine. They were his friends. It was the frivolous wives who drove him mad; sometimes he wished he could shoot them, too.

Meanwhile, Margaret Rothbury had gone up to her private sitting room to give orders to the housekeeper, Mrs Spry, before sitting at her desk to see to her correspondence. She was an avid writer of letters and believed in keeping in touch with even the merest acquaintance.

'You never know,' she pointed out on one occasion, 'when they might come in useful.'

'They're not a damned pair of boots!' her husband had growled back.

'Come along, children,' called Susan the nursery maid, whose job it was to 'give the girls a good run in the garden' as Nanny ordered, as if they, too, had been a pack of dogs. Bundled up in tweed coats, woollen hats and scarves and little buttoned-up boots, Alice, Flora and Catriona trotted up and down the garden paths with sticks and hoops, seeing who could keep the hoops bowling along the longest.

Alice, who was six, was highly practised and her hoop rolled along merrily, but four-year-old Flora was wild with her stick and her hoop kept crashing down on to the lavender borders.

Only three-year-old Catriona ran up and down, gripping her hoop firmly in one of her tiny hands while waving her stick above her head and yelling, 'Look at me! Look at me!'

Susan watched them absently, her mind on the dashing new footman who'd arrived the previous week. She half hoped he was watching her now from one of the castle windows, and she raised her dainty chin so that he would see her pretty profile.

In the west wing, Freddie and Henry sat at a long table with glum expressions as Hector Stuart, their tutor, lectured them about the vast extent of the British Empire on which the sun never set.

By the window a globe of the world stood on a walnut stand. 'Take a close look at it,' he told them, rising to his feet. 'I want each of you to write a list of the countries that make up our great Empire.'

Freddie's groan was audible and Henry's gusty sigh made the sheet of paper in front of him quiver.

'Come on, lads! Buck up!' Mr Stuart said bracingly.

Freddie gave him a withering look. 'A stable boy is a "lad"; I'm Lord Fairbairn,' he said coldly.

Mr Stuart eyes glinted with amusement. 'Your father has given strict orders that titles do not exist in the schoolroom. You are plain Freddie and Henry is Henry. Your sisters are not referred to as "Lady" this and that when they're in the schoolroom or the nursery.'

Freddie raised his chin rebelliously. 'I'm Viscount Fairbairn everywhere I go.' There was a defiant swagger in the way he spoke.

Henry gave a sweet smile. 'Well, I don't mind being called just "Henry".' There was a thoughtful pause. 'I'm only the Hon. anyway.'

Mr Stuart gave an approving nod in his direction. It had been obvious to him from the moment he'd set eyes on the brothers that Henry was a good-natured soul, kind and even-tempered, while Freddie was an obnoxious little bully who was far too full of himself. In fact, if he'd been a betting man, Hector Stuart would have put a few sovereigns on Freddie turning out to be a complete and utter rotter.

In the north wing a governess, Miss Napier, was endeav-
ouring to educate Diana, Georgina, Beatrice and also Eleanor,
who had recently, at the age of ten, been considered bright
enough to be with her older sisters.

'I believe she just needs encouraging and being with the
others will help. She lacks self-confidence,' Miss Napier told
their mother.

'Not too much encouraging, I hope,' Lady Rothbury retorted
briskly. 'Men do not like clever girls. Don't bother teaching
her arithmetic or anything like that. She'll never need it. I'd
rather you concentrated on getting her to read good books
and maybe do a little sketching.'

Laura had gone straight to the library, where she settled herself
at the round table in the centre. This was the warmest, most
welcoming room in the castle, lined by oak bookcases holding
six thousand books. Thick green velvet curtains masked the
icy draughts from the windows and brown leather chairs were
arranged for comfort near the big stone grate where logs fizzled
and blazed.

She opened a notebook and, after sharpening a pencil, started
to write, wanting to pin down on paper all her memories of
the past few days while they were still fresh in her mind. It
had been six weeks since Rory's last visit, when he'd proposed
and given her a diamond and sapphire engagement ring, and
she'd felt quite sick with excitement when she heard his carriage
draw up in the drive four days ago. On seeing him again
sudden shyness had overwhelmed her for a moment, and she
was glad they weren't alone as her mother and sisters gathered
around to welcome him back, but then they'd gone for a walk
in the gardens on their own and suddenly she knew without
a shadow of doubt that she was deeply in love with him.

How happy they'd been during the past few days, she thought
as she scribbled in her notebook. She was missing him already,
even though he'd only been gone an hour. If only she could
have gone with him, she reflected, to his home in the south
of England where it was warmer and the landscape was gently
undulating and green instead of rugged.

Only now, as she sat alone in the library, did she realize

with a sense of shock how empty and incomplete her life was without him.

Lizzie came barging into the room at that moment, full of purpose. 'What are you doing?'

'I was thinking . . .'

'That can be dangerous, you know. Are you missing Rory already?'

Laura nodded, her eyes over-bright. 'Don't you long to leave here?'

Lizzie sat down opposite and leaned her elbows on the table. 'Yes, sometimes,' she agreed.

'We're missing so much by being cooped up here miles from anywhere,' Laura complained. 'I'm longing for the bright lights of a great city like London where there's so much to see and so many things to do. If it wasn't for the fact that when I'm married to Rory we can nip up to town whenever we like, I think I'd go mad.'

Lizzie looked thoughtful. 'I think we all want to escape south. Especially Freddie. It's because we're young. We want adventure. We want to see the world. I expect we'll be quite happy to settle here again when we're as old as Mother and Father.'

Her sister looked appalled. 'I hope I won't end up here when I'm old. I don't think Rory would like it either.'

'I don't think James would mind. Eventually, you know.'

'Do you think you'll really marry him?'

Lizzie smiled smugly. 'Yes, definitely. He's just waiting for the right moment to propose.'

Laura spoke eagerly now. 'When Rory and I are married we'll be in a position to invite Georgie, Beattie and Di to stay with us, and we'll introduce them to Rory's friends. Young men who live in London, too,' she added impressively.

'What? Not county, you mean?'

She shrugged. 'Maybe no one who is listed in the peerage, but Rory knows masses of people through his work, including an actor. They all seem to be making a lot of money.'

There was a shocked pause before Lizzie spoke. 'Goodness!'

'Most of the really rich young men are in trade, or at least their fathers are,' Laura continued defensively.

'Goodness,' Lizzie repeated. 'Don't you think we might frighten them off with our titles?'

'I'm seriously thinking of dropping mine when Rory and I are married.'

'Whatever for? You've always been Lady Laura and I'm certainly not going to stop being Lady Elizabeth for anyone.'

'I don't want to overshadow Rory by being Lady Laura Drummond while he remains plain Mr Drummond.'

Lizzie's eyes narrowed shrewdly. 'Hasn't it occurred to you that having a titled wife might raise his standing amongst his clients?'

Laura flushed angrily. 'What a horrid thing to say.'

'I'm not saying that's why he's marrying you, I merely meant . . .'

Laura jumped to her feet. 'I know what you mean. You think we're defined by our titles and the fact that we're women. Thank God Emmeline Pankhurst formed the Women's Franchise League two years ago. Soon women will be equal to men and allowed to vote, and it's about time too. We've been regarded as appendages to our husbands, with not an original thought of our own, for too long. It's time we stood up for ourselves,' she added forcefully.

Her sister looked askance at her. 'Here we go! Does Rory know you're a secret suffragette?'

Laura burst out laughing. 'Of course he does, and it's no secret. That's what he likes about me. Times are changing. Do *you* want to be like Mama? Letting Papa make all the decisions? At least we've now got a Married Women's Property Act, but we need much more recognition.'

'I'm happy with the way things are. I don't want the responsibility of having to make all the decisions.'

'So you're content to live your life as a second-class citizen? A "Yes Woman" who does what her husband says?' Laura countered swiftly, her hazel eyes glinting with intelligence.

Georgie, Beattie, Diana and little Eleanor came into the room at that moment and looked at them with curiosity.

'What's going on?' Beattie asked.

'What are you arguing about? We could hear you from the hall,' said Diana.

Laura looked amused. 'We weren't really arguing. We were having a discussion about a woman's role in the future. I believe we should have the same rights as men.'

'How boring,' Georgie exclaimed in disappointment.

'Would you give up your title to make your husband feel less inferior?' Lizzie demanded.

'As my future husband will have a title already it won't arise,' scoffed Georgie airily.

At that moment they heard their father's voice coming from somewhere outside the castle, yelling furiously at someone. Laura and Lizzie both rose to their feet and rushed to open the window, along with their younger sisters, so they could hear better.

'If you come here again,' the Earl was raging, 'I'll personally see you are flogged with a horsewhip, damn you! Do you understand? Keep away from here if you know what's good for you!'

Then they heard another man's voice, this time low and menacing. 'As the Rowan tree is my witness, I curse the Fairbairn family from here until eternity.'

'Go and be damned!' yelled their father in response. 'Get out of here or I'll set the dogs on you.'

There was a skirmish of horses' hooves followed by the clip-clop of someone riding away down the drive. Then they heard Lord Rothbury speak again in a calmer voice to the ghillie. 'Linton, that man is not to be allowed on my land again. Call the police if you see him and have him arrested at once for trespass. On no account must he be allowed to come anywhere near me or my family. Now take Megara back to the stables. I won't be going out again today.'

'Yes, M'Lord.' Linton sounded utterly quenched and unlike himself.

A moment later they heard their father cursing loudly as he stomped up the stone steps of the castle and into the great hall. 'That *bastard*! I'd like to kill him.'

'I'm going to find out what's happening,' said Laura.

Lizzie looked perturbed. 'Do you think you should?'

'I'm not afraid of Papa.' Opening the library door, she stepped into the hall. 'Papa? What's the matter? Who was that you were shouting at?' she asked calmly.

He shot her a furtive glance. 'Mind your own damn business.' Then he brushed roughly past her, almost knocking her down.

At dinner that night Lord Rothbury sat at the head of the long table, drinking heavily and refusing to speak. Only his wife's ceaseless prattle broke the heavy silence and, as usual when there was trouble, she appeared as if she was unaware of it – that was her armour.

'You haven't forgotten, girls, that Mrs Armitage is arriving tomorrow?' she asked brightly.

The sisters all perked up immediately and started talking at once.

'What time is she arriving?'

'How long is she staying for?'

'Mama, I need a new coat . . .'

'Two winter skirts . . .'

'A smart day dress and . . .'

'She can make my wedding dress, can't she?' Laura's voice was the loudest. 'And my going-away suit. I want a sapphire-blue velvet skirt with a matching jacket with satin revers.'

Lady Rothbury threw up her hands with a girlish gesture. 'Goodness me! You'll work the poor woman to death. She's only staying for three months. May I also remind you that before she does anything else she has to make *my* winter wardrobe.'

Georgie immediately looked rebellious. 'We can plan what we want, though, can't we?' she asked defiantly.

'You're way down the pecking order,' Lizzie observed bossily. 'I'm the first who needs new clothes, then Laura and then Beattie. Anyway, you're not going anywhere special.'

'Then when do I get new things?' Diana wailed. 'I want to have a new jacket.'

Suddenly Lord Rothbury rose to his feet; his face ruddy and bloated, his height and breadth dominating the room and making Diana cower back nervously. He raised his crystal wine goblet in his hand and then with great force threw it down into the fireplace. There was an explosion of glass splintering as it hit the old bricks, causing the dogs to jump to their feet with fright.

'Let me remind you,' he boomed above the din of screeching

daughters and yelping dogs, 'that "I want" doesn't mean "I
get".' With that he turned and stormed out of the room with
Megan at his heels, her tail between her legs.

Little Eleanor couldn't get to sleep that night. Something
strange was happening below her bedroom window, where
an ancient and rather magnificent Rowan tree grew. She'd
always loved its scarlet leaves and the bright red berries that
hung in the autumn like magical rubies from the branches.
Nanny had once told her that the berries were the blood of
the tree, and those who shed its blood would be for ever
cursed. That was why no one was allowed to cut branches
to bring into the house to enhance an arrangement of flowers.
It was also why everyone regarded the Rowan tree with awe
and great respect.

So why was someone standing under its branches with a
lantern in the middle of the night?

Eleanor managed to open her window a little wider so she
could see better. Nanny had also said the Rowan tree was the
protector and guardian of the family, and if anyone harmed it
the tree would become malignant, harnessing powers of evil
it would use to harm the family for eternity.

Shivering in her thin nightgown, as if the wind coming
from the west was ice-laden, she peered down, trying to see
what was happening. A sudden movement below startled her
as she saw a man in a long black cloak raise the lantern up
among the jewel-laden branches before putting it on the
ground. Then she saw his hands, pale in the dim light, resting
on the trunk of the tree.

She heard the man's voice, low and rumbling and full of
vengeance. It filled her with fear, for she knew instinctively that something terrible was about to happen, something
fatal that she wished with all her heart she could prevent
but knew she couldn't.

The voice rose threateningly. 'May God desert you. May
each and every one of you suffer as I suffer. May ruin beset
you and destruction fall upon your heads for the injustice you
have shown me.'

The voice had risen higher, full of anger and anguish, spite and venom. 'Damn you all in the name of the Almighty. May you rot in hell.'

The lantern went out. The empty silence that followed was even more frightening than the cursing. Eleanor blinked into the darkness but she could see nothing now. Trembling, she closed the window tightly and crept back to bed and pulled up the blankets. Her head ached and she'd never felt so cold. Most of all, she was filled with terror.

'Mrs Armitage, can I have long, tight sleeves with smart cuffs, please?'

'I'm *dying* for a pin-tucked blouse, like this one in the magazine.'

'I've drawn a picture, Mrs Armitage, of the jacket I need so badly. Please can you make it for me?'

Lizzie and Laura with Beattie, Georgie and Diana were quietly driving the dressmaker mad. They were all talking at once and they all wanted their new garments to be made first. They reminded her of a flock of hungry birds, all trying to peck at one morsel of food.

Mrs Armitage's tired face broke into an indulgent smile as she looked at the Fairbairn girls, who were renowned for their beauty, their slender figures and long legs. She enjoyed their creative input and stylish ideas, but there were moments when she felt overwhelmed by their demands.

'I think it would be a good idea if you each gave me a list of what you require, then I can show it to Her Ladyship. I'm sure that once I've completed her winter wardrobe I'll be able to start on yours,' she said diplomatically.

'When will that be?' Georgie asked impatiently.

A glint of annoyance flickered in the dressmaker's eyes. Georgie was her least favourite. 'I believe we should do what we always do,' she replied smoothly. 'I will start with the eldest of you and work my way down to the youngest.'

Georgie's scowl deepened. 'I need new things more than the others,' she grumbled.

'No, you don't,' Diana argued. 'You and I don't need much. Lizzie, Laura and Beattie need things more, especially Laura.'

Mrs Armitage turned to Laura, her favourite in the family.

'I hear you are to be married, Lady Laura? May I wish you every happiness.'

'Thank you.' Laura flushed with pleasure and her eyes shone with excitement. 'You will make my wedding dress, won't you?'

'It would be a great honour and nothing will give me more pleasure. Have you thought about what fabric you'd like?'

Laura nodded, running her fingers through her long dark hair, which she still wore hanging down loose on her shoulders. 'I'd like it to be made of ivory duchess satin. Mama says I can wear her Brussels lace veil and she'll lend me a diamond tiara.'

'How splendid. I imagine the rest of you will be bridesmaids?'

The girls all nodded, with the exception of Lizzie. 'Laura isn't getting married until next year so I may well be getting married first,' she announced importantly.

'You're not even engaged yet,' Georgie protested. 'Talk about counting your chickens.'

Lizzie raised her chin. 'I shall most likely become engaged any minute now.'

'Oh, rubbish, Lizzie! You've been talking about marrying James Fraser since you were fifteen!' Beattie mocked good-humouredly. 'Has anyone told James what's expected of him?'

'They are practically childhood sweethearts,' Diana pointed out loyally.

Mrs Armitage rose to her feet. Any moment now hostilities were about to break out, and from experience it was better to be out of the way when that happened.

'I must go to Her Ladyship now. There's a lot of work to be done and I must attend to your mother's needs first.'

Beattie looked over at Eleanor, who'd been sitting silently in the corner, her presence unnoticed by the others. 'You've been very quiet, sweetheart? What's the matter? You want some pretty new clothes too, don't you?'

Eleanor had dark shadows under her eyes and she looked troubled. 'I suppose so,' she replied listlessly, 'but what's the point?'

'What do you mean?' Lizzie demanded. 'You'll soon be eleven and able to wear almost grown-up dresses.'

Eleanor shook her head. 'You wouldn't understand.'

'I could try.' Beattie spoke gently. It was unlike her younger sister to be so withdrawn.

'Forget about her – let's get on with making lists of the clothes *we* want,' Georgie intervened. 'If only there weren't so many of us. When I get married I'm only going to have one daughter and I'll make sure she gets *everything*.'

Freddie pushed his chair away from the dinner table. 'I'm not staying with a bunch of empty-headed girls who talk about nothing but clothes,' he said rudely. 'Come on, Henry. I'll give you a game of Whist,' he added, as if he was bestowing an honour on his younger brother.

'You need four people for whist,' Henry pointed out as he slid from his chair.

Freddie's tone was lofty. 'I'll rope in Hamish and Joe.'

Lizzie looked shocked. 'You can't play with the stable lads,' she protested. 'Mama, tell them they can't do that.'

Lady Rothbury smiled indulgently at her beloved son and heir. 'You don't gamble for money, do you, dearest?'

'With marbles,' he replied rather too swiftly. 'We gamble with marbles. What's the harm in that?' Then he swaggered out of the dining room and Henry followed sheepishly.

'You shouldn't allow it, Mama,' Georgie said.

'It's just boys being boys.'

'It's more than that,' Lizzie pointed out. 'For one thing it's not fair on Joe and Hamish. They're not in a position to refuse Freddie anything, and I don't believe they only have marbles for betting any more than I believe it when he says they're drinking a pint of water! Freddie is only thirteen, for goodness' sake! And Henry is just nine. He ought to be in bed by now.'

Her mother looked pained. 'You must allow your father and I to decide how to bring up the boys,' she replied stiffly, although everyone knew William couldn't control his dogs, far less his sons.

Laura remained silent, lost in her own rainbow thoughts. It wouldn't be long before she finally left Lochlee as Rory's wife, and the rest of her life would be with him, in their own home, doing only what they wanted to do as they created their own family in the happiest of atmospheres.

How she longed for it all. It was cold and gloomy in the castle and the only fun they had was of their own making, such as playing croquet or following the guns or reading. Once she was married to Rory she vowed never to return.

'Rory says he'll often take me up to town,' she confided to Diana during one of their evening chats when they crouched by a log fire, rubbing their hands to keep warm. 'We'll go to concerts at the Royal Albert Hall which Queen Victoria has named after her late husband. Then we'll dine at the famous Café Royal in Regent Street where the cuisine is French. Apparently Oscar Wilde goes there a lot. Oh, we're going to have such a marvellous life, Di! I'm counting the days until we get married.'

She spread her left hand to look for the thousandth time at her ring, a symbol of Rory's love and her key to the future.

As the days dragged on Laura's longing to get away increased and out of boredom more than anything she started to sit in Mrs Armitage's suite of rooms to watch her making clothes for all the women in the family. At first she enjoyed their conversations, but gradually she became fascinated by the way the dressmaker cut the cloths and tacked the seams for the first fitting. Then she watched, spellbound, as Mrs Armitage worked at a machine that did the stitching for you, saving hours of work – and the result was neater, too.

'Can I have a go?' she asked excitedly one day. She'd watched how Mrs Armitage used a foot pedal to turn the wheels that made a special needle do the stitching, and it didn't look difficult to work.

'Certainly, Lady Laura. I'll give you a piece of flannel to practise on,' she replied, amused.

After a few false starts Laura suddenly shrieked, 'The machine's running away! How do I stop . . .! Oh, goodness, this is fun.'

It wasn't long before she'd mastered the machine and learned to control how much pressure to apply to the pedal. Then Mrs Armitage showed her how to refill the spool with cotton thread. Laura was enchanted.

'One could do pin-tucking by machine,' she exclaimed, 'and hemming, couldn't one?'

Mrs Armitage nodded. 'It cuts the hand stitching I used to do by eighty per cent, too. To be a really good dressmaker there are three things it's vital to do.'

Laura looked at her curiously. 'And they are?'

'Press. Press and press again. As soon as you've done a seam it must be thoroughly pressed, or the seam will show when the garment is worn. If the sewing machine is a dressmaker's best friend, then a hot iron is her *very* best friend.'

Laura looked thoughtful for a moment. 'Do you suppose . . .' she hesitated, then the words came out in a rush. 'Will you help me make my own wedding dress? I mean, really make it? I'd design the style. Cut the cloth. Tack and stitch it, although you'd have to help with the fittings?'

The dressmaker smiled. 'I don't see why not,' she said slowly. 'I've always thought you had a talent for design and you've just proved you're willing to learn. It would be a real novelty for a bride to design and make her own dress.'

Laura's face glowed with delight. 'Thank you. I'll work on some designs right away and you must tell me how many yards of satin I'll need.'

Mrs Armitage laughed. 'Lady Laura, you'll be doing me out of a job if you're as talented as I think you are.'

'Can I be your apprentice, then? Can you give me simple things to do on all the others' clothes? Please say yes. It would help me pass the time until I get married.'

'It would be a pleasure to have such a willing student.'

'You're going to do *what*?' Lizzie asked when she heard the news. 'It's a bit *infra-dig*, isn't it? Wearing home-made clothes?'

'We're already wearing home-made clothes,' Laura retorted.

'Yes, but made by a professional seamstress! Running up your own wedding dress is an appalling idea. I'm sure Mama won't let you.'

'How can she stop me? It's my wedding and my dress, and I'm sure Rory will approve when he knows.'

'Don't think you're going to be allowed to even put a pin in *my* wedding dress when I get married,' Lizzie said loftily.

'I'll be living it up in England by the time you get married so I'll be far too busy.'

Lady Rothbury came into to room at that moment. 'What's going on? What are you quarrelling about?'

'Laura's got the ridiculous idea that she can make her own wedding dress and I'm just telling her she's going nowhere near mine.'

'Since when are you getting married, Lizzie?' her mother demanded sarcastically. 'To my knowledge no one has so far asked your father for your hand.'

'I'm sure James Fraser is going to marry me, Mama. I love him and I really want to marry him.'

'The man you fall in love with isn't necessarily the man you should marry,' Lady Rothbury said firmly.

Laura flushed with anger. 'Mama! That's a terrible thing to say. Of course you must marry the man you love. I wouldn't be marrying Rory if I didn't love him madly.'

Lady Rothbury remained serene. 'You've been very lucky in finding the right man, Laura, especially as you're so young. His father is a baronet. He has wealth and a good career. Your sisters may not have the same good fortune.'

'I'm sure I will,' Lizzie retorted. 'I've known James since I was fifteen. It's not a question of if we'll get married, but when. You've cultivated all the right people for our benefit and we're very grateful, Mama,' she added slyly.

Her mother beamed, taking it as a compliment for her parenting skills. 'I want you all to be happy, my dear, and a young woman is doomed if she marries a man who does not belong to the same religion, the same political party and the same class as herself. He must be a man of means, too, of course. Marriage is about suitability, compatibility and eligibility. It's got nothing to do with love.'

The silence that followed spoke volumes of the dashed dreams held so dear by Lizzie and her sisters, who imagined they would all be swept up by their very own Prince Charming and carried off to a magical place where love and passion would last for ever.

'When poverty comes in at the door love flies out of the

window,' their mother intoned with a final flourish as she turned to leave the room.

Laura burst into silent laughter. 'So now you know,' she murmured. She had no doubts Rory would always be there for her, looking after her and loving her until the end of time, and she thanked God for her good fortune.

For the next two months Laura worked under the supervision of Mrs Armitage, being taught everything from how to take measurements to cutting, pinning, tacking, pressing, machining and finally finishing off by hand. She learned to cut the lining for coats and jackets a size larger than the actual garment and how to make buttonholes. She was taught how to hemstitch, frill and pleat and edge a garment with piping. Soon she was able to emboss a silk bodice with lace and embroider it with crystal beads. Mrs Armitage was amazed at how quickly Laura learned and how dedicated she was to the craft of dressmaking.

Laura herself was in her element and the hours flew by as she dedicated herself to this new skill with a sense of growing excitement at what one could do with a length of fabric.

At last it was her turn to make her own wedding dress and, as she worked on every stitch, she had visions of the expression on Rory's face as she came up the aisle towards him. In her mind's eye he'd be full of love and admiration, longing for the moment when they'd be man and wife with the rest of their lives ahead of them.

When it was finished the only person who was allowed to see it was her mother. Mrs Armitage went to fetch her and as Lady Rothbury entered the room she stopped in her tracks, overwhelmed for a moment as she gazed at her second daughter. Then her eyes brimmed with tears which she didn't attempt to hide. 'Dearest girl,' she said softly.

'Do you like it, Mama?' Laura turned slowly, showing all the little buttons down the back of the close-fitting bodice and the cleverly cut skirt that flowed into a train.

'You look beautiful. You really made it all by yourself?'

'All by herself, M'Lady,' Mrs Armitage vouchsafed. 'I only did the fittings.'

Lady Rothbury shook her head in wonderment. 'It's quite marvellous. I love the way you've swathed the lace around the shoulders and on the bodice and as for the bead work . . . don't tell me you did that, too, Laura?'

'Yes, I did. I had to use the finest needle in the pack and it was quite a strain on the eyes. Do you think Rory will approve?' she asked eagerly, longing to hear more praise.

'There's no doubt about that.' Lady Rothbury turned to Mrs Armitage. 'You must be very proud of your pupil?'

'Yes, M'Lady. Lady Laura has a natural aptitude for design and dressmaking. It took me years to acquire the skill she's shown. I was telling her she'll be doing me out of a job if I'm not careful.'

They all laughed at the absurdity of a future where Laura would become a seamstress, but she still blushed with pleasure at the compliment.

'You look beautiful, my dear. Rory is an extremely lucky young man.'

They were the nicest words Laura had ever heard from her mother.

When she'd changed back into her own clothes she and Lady Rothbury went downstairs together to be met by Lizzie, who was standing at the bottom in a state of great agitation.

'Laura's wedding dress really is wonderful,' Lady Rothbury announced, not noticing her eldest daughter's distraught manner.

'Damn her wedding dress!' Lizzie exclaimed wildly. 'Something *terrible* has happened.'

Lady Rothbury froze. 'Not Papa?' she breathed in terror.

Lizzie burst into tears as she sank on to the bottom step, bent over with sobbing.

'What is it?' Laura's features were sharp with fear. Their father was a reckless rider, taking his horses over fences and dry walls that were treacherously high. He'd already had some bad falls and broken bones but the older he got the more risks he seemed to take, as if to prove he was still young and active.

'Lizzie, tell me,' Lady Rothbury spoke angrily. 'Pull yourself together, girl, and tell me what's happened.'

Lizzie drew in a long, shuddering breath and raised her

tear-stained face. 'I've just heard that James Fraser has announced his engagement to Araminta Maclean.' She started sobbing again. 'I was so sure it was me he loved.'

A subdued atmosphere pervaded over Lochlee Castle for the next few days. No one could comfort Lizzie, who looked upon James' engagement to someone else as an act of hideous betrayal.

'Poor you,' Diana sympathized as Lizzie wallowed in bouts of weeping between reading passages of Longfellow poems.

'Perhaps Araminta MacLean is prettier than Lizzie,' Georgie suggested unhelpfully.

Beattie looked scandalized. 'That's a horrid thing to say,' she snapped as Lizzie dissolved into a fresh bout of crying. 'Araminta probably seduced him and maybe he's been forced to marry her.'

Lizzie stopped mid-sob and looked up, her face stricken. 'You mean he might have made her pregnant?'

Diana frowned disapprovingly. 'I think we should be careful what we say, especially when the servants are around. We don't know anything about Araminta and you know how gossip spreads.'

Lizzie was not to be comforted. For the past few years she'd harboured the thought of marrying the handsome James Fraser, known as Jamie to his friends, but now the realization that she'd woven his friendly attitude towards her into something far deeper hurt most of all. Her fantasies were shattered. Her dreams gone. There was no way now she was going to be his fiancée, his bride, his wife and the mother of his children.

There was no hope of her getting married before Laura. The empty void that she gazed heart-brokenly into spoke of failure. She also looked stupid for so badly misjudging his intentions.

So her sisters' words of sympathy fell on barren ground where no green shoots of hope for the future were ever likely to appear.

Three

The stumbling thumps were coming down the stairs now. Laura heard a framed picture being knocked off the wall and landing with a shuddering crash in the hall below. Then the sudden howl of a maddened dog barking furiously rent the air. Only it wasn't a dog.

She clasped her hand over her mouth to stifle a cry of fear. Then she hurried, half-staggering on legs weakened by terror, across her sitting room. She must lock the door. Every room in the house had a key on the inside lock. The drawing room. The dining room. The library. Her bedroom. Oh, God! Especially her bedroom. Fumbling frantically with trembling fingers, she groped for the cold metal key but it wasn't there. Where was it? God in heaven, where was it? Who had removed it?

She dropped to her knees, scrabbling around on the carpet and all the while the heavy thuds and crashes and bellowing roars were coming closer, reverberating through the house.

Clambering to her feet, she rushed to the sash-cord window on the opposite side of the room and reached for the snib to open it. Then she pushed up the bottom half as far as it would open. The gap was only wide enough for her to lie on her stomach on the window sill then wriggle out feet first. A moment later she tumbled down into the thorny rose bushes that surrounded the house.

She lay there for a moment, bruised, scratched and shaken. Then she heard it. The sickening sound of splintering wood as her sitting-room door was being kicked in.

Struggling to her feet, although the soft, damp earth seemed to cling and pull her back down and her dress got caught on the sharp thorns, she managed to stand up and run across the lawn, where at the far end Greg the gardener kept his tools in a sturdy little wooden shed. The key was kept under a nearby log. Once inside she locked herself in and, sitting on a bundle of old sacks, watched through a small window and waited as darkness started to close in.

The house was pitch-black. She'd purposely given the servants the day off. The previous evening she'd sent Caroline to stay with Diana because this was no place for a two-year-old child.

Now there were just the two of them. In combat. In a war zone that could last all night. Closing her eyes, she leaned back against the comforting solid feel of wood and breathed in the earthy tang of seedlings growing in recently watered soil. She could still hear bangs and thumps coming from the house but she refused to think about the damage being inflicted on their home.

The garden was in darkness now, the house no more than a large shadow among the trees. For the past hour there had been silence and, exhausted, she had dozed off for a few moments – perhaps even a few minutes – but now she felt alert, as an animal intuitively senses an impending unknown danger.

Gazing into the blackness towards the house, she saw a flicker of light through one of the windows. The silence hung heavily in the still, cold night as she watched and waited.

Then there was another flicker, coming from another room this time. Was an oil lamp being lit? Was a match being struck to light a cigar? She watched unblinkingly. It was a large three-storey house with many windows and it stood silent now as if it, too, was waiting for the inevitable crisis to happen.

Then she saw it. The light came from a candle held by a hand, moving from room to room as if searching for someone. The other hand was also raised and in its clenched fist was an axe.

The next morning Laura discovered that the portrait of her which hung in the drawing room had been slashed, the canvas hanging in ribbons over the gilt frame.

Four

Spring had arrived after a long, dark, cold winter, and Lord
Rothbury strode into the dining room for breakfast with a
spring in his step because the ground was perfect for riding
and the dogs were jumping around his feet, eager for a good
run.

Placing the morning's post on one side, he helped himself
to porridge from the sideboard before sitting down and ripping
open the envelopes with a knife.

'Bills! Bills! Nothing but damned bills!' he muttered to no
one in particular. Then he paused. 'Dear God!' he groaned
loudly, and the room fell silent.

Lady Rothbury looked nervously at him. 'What's happened,
William?'

Laura, entering late for breakfast, sat down at that moment
just as he was answering his wife's question. Suddenly the room
turned into a long, dark tunnel; it was freezing cold and
someone was screaming. Laura found herself clinging to the
dining-room table as if it were the side of a fishing boat and
they were out on choppy waters. There were more screams
and she heard a voice asking from somewhere, 'What happened?'
Then she realized the person who was screaming, 'No! No!
Please God, no!' over and over again was herself.

From a thousand miles away her father was reading aloud
from a letter he'd opened. '*There was a sudden storm. Rory
was out riding. A terrible gale blew up. Nothing anyone could do.
Trees were being blown down. A branch fell. He didn't stand a
chance.*'

He didn't stand a chance. The words were lodged in her
brain, going round and round, and she couldn't stop them no
matter how hard she said *no*.

★   ★   ★

In the days that followed, Diana and Lizzie and Beattie clustered around her, patting and stroking her, desperately anxious to ease her pain.

Beyond accepting comfort or compassion, Laura simply wanted to die herself. Without Rory what was the point of anything? She believed that no one would ever understand how much she'd lost. The moment he'd died he'd taken with him the rest of her life. She felt desolate and nothing and no one could console her.

She would never be his wife now. Never be embraced by the gentle surroundings of a country house in the south of England. Never enjoy the excitements of going up to London for a trip to the theatre and dinner in a restaurant. All her hopes, all her plans had been demolished in a single moment when she'd heard the words *he didn't stand a chance*.

Most of all, beyond everything else, she bitterly regretted that she'd never let him sleep with her and that they'd never made love.

Feeling cheated now, her first wave of grief turned into a deep, raging anger. She'd been denied the greatest emotional experience of all because of the teaching of the church and other people's principles. If only she could turn the clock back to when he'd last stayed at Lochlee. She'd desired him then as much as he'd wanted her as he held her in his arms and pressed himself against her body. Then he'd released her with a long, deep sigh because he was an honourable young man.

'Oh, God, why didn't I let him!' she burst out, oblivious of Lizzie's presence beside her in the drawing room. 'At least I'd have that to remember,' she sobbed.

Lizzie's eyes widened in understanding. 'Would you really have dared? Think of all the warnings Mama has given us. Supposing you'd got . . .'

'I wish to God I had,' Laura retorted angrily. 'Then I'd have had something of his. Now I've got nothing. Nothing.'

Lizzie sat in silence. Her loss, which she now had to admit to herself was more a case of being piqued because she'd been scorned, was nothing compared to the death of Rory.

'You're such a lovely person, Laura, and so beautiful. I know you'll find someone else before long,' she said comfortingly.

Laura rose to her feet, shaking with fury. 'I don't *want* anyone else!' she cried shrilly. 'Now leave me alone.' Bent over like an old woman, she stumbled to the door and slowly and painfully made her way up the wide oak stairs to her room.

Lady Rothbury watched her from the landing above. 'Come, dear girl. You need to lie down,' she said gently, putting her arms around Laura. 'You need to rest. Get some sleep, perhaps.'

Laura allowed herself to be treated like a child as her mother helped her take off her dress and then tucked her up in her four-poster bed, before seating herself nearby so she could keep vigil. It was obvious that the last thing Laura needed at the moment was to be exhausted by the well-meaning attempts of her sisters to try to console her.

For ten days Laura stayed in bed, with Nanny, who had looked after her since she'd been born, bringing her bowls of broth and home-made lemonade. Listless and disorientated, she finally came downstairs in a valiant effort to get back to normality. For the first time in her life, though, she was no longer sure what her place was in the family. For seventeen years she'd been the second daughter, a supposed role model with Lizzie for her younger siblings. She'd felt the need to be a good example in everything she did. Her mother's lists of do's and don'ts had to be learned like a catechism.

Recently she'd moved on to become the 'engaged daughter' of the family and that meant the first big step into being Grown Up: the one stage in her life she'd been longing for since she'd been twelve. It meant more than that to her. It meant getting away from home, from the bleak dullness of Lochlee which she'd come to hate. Now she was stuck here. Swept away by the terrible catastrophe was the life she'd never have. A husband she loved passionately. The Queen Anne house in Kent she'd never see now. The children that would have filled the nursery, and the knowledge that when they grew up and left home she would still have the love and companionship of a husband. All gone. It was unlikely anyone else would want to marry her either. An old maid on the shelf nursing her grief. It made Laura also realize she didn't even have the dignity awarded to a widow. She'd be known as the Fairbairn girl whose fiancé was tragically killed in an accident.

★   ★   ★

'I'm worried about Eleanor,' Diana remarked as she and Beattie walked in the grounds of the castle. Wrapped up against the freezing wind, they wore fur hats and big fur collars on their long tweed coats, and they tucked their gloved hands into fur muffs that hung from gold chains around their necks. Before them lay sweeping lawns that led to a fast-running river. Crossing it on the large, flat stepping stones that led to the far side, where pine trees flourished along the water's edge, they sat to rest on the rocks.

'*Eleanor?*' Beattie asked in surprise. 'Why Eleanor? What about Laura?'

'We all know that poor Laura has good reason to be suffering, but haven't you noticed how Eleanor has been creeping around the place as if she's worried about something? She's always looking out of the window, too. For hours, sometimes, as if she's expecting someone to call.'

'She's probably shocked by what's happened to Rory and she can see how distraught Laura is.'

Diana frowned as she pulled her fur collar tighter around her neck. 'I think it's something else. She looks more worried than sad. I asked her recently what was wrong but she turned scarlet and said nothing. Then she scuttled out of the room. I think she was scared I was going to probe.'

'She's never been outgoing like the rest of us.'

'I know, but this is different. Watch her, Beattie. See if you can get anything out of her.'

'Are we going to the top?' Beattie asked, rising to her feet.

They looked up at Ben Lossie, with its peaks dusted with snow.

'Not today,' Diana replied.

'You *always* say that.'

'It's too cold.'

'You always say that, too. Even when it's summer.'

Laughing and jostling each other, they started walking back to the castle which stood strong and proud, its great stone walls and ramparts gleaming like polished marble in the winter sunlight. Once a mighty fortress, it had been tamed into being a domestic abode, filled with children and dogs. Surrounded by vast open areas of grass and heather and a history of belonging to the Fairbairn family for the past five hundred years, it struck Diana that anyone seeing it for the first time would think it was like something out of a fairy-tale book. Her father might adore living in his ancestral home, but to Diana and her siblings it was always cold and dark, even during the brightest day, and one had to walk what seemed like miles to get to the bedrooms, along acres of draughty corridors and passages with walls hung with gloomy tapestries and family portraits. The misery didn't end there. They had to bathe in tin baths which the servants and the watermen brought up to the bedrooms and filled with hot water. The water always chilled quickly and drying oneself in front of a log fire still didn't prevent one from getting chilled.

'I can see why Laura's so heartbroken, apart from losing Rory,' Diana said thoughtfully as they made their way back up the drive.

'Because she's stuck here, you mean?' Beattie replied knowingly.

'We *all* are unless we get married. Only Freddie and Henry can leave to do something interesting.'

'I wish there was something interesting we could do. I'd like a proper career.'

Diana looked at her in surprise. 'What could we do, though? We're completely unemployable, unless we got jobs as maids in someone else's house. Actually, I don't think I even know how to clean a house. Isn't that dreadful?'

Beattie laughed. 'I bet we'd miss Lochlee if we ever had to leave.'

'That's not going to happen in a thousand years! Even when we're all married with dozens of children we'll always come back home for Christmas.'

Eleanor knew she'd aroused her sister's suspicions by keeping a watch, but she wanted to make sure that the horrible man with the low, menacing voice who had threatened Papa and who had come back to cast a terrible curse on them all by the Rowan tree hadn't returned.

Wracking her brains, she tried to think of something she could *pretend* was worrying her if Diana questioned her again.

What about her fear of burglars? Or poachers? Maybe even ghosts?

Instinctively she knew that if she told anyone what she'd really seen that night then something terrible would happen. Then it struck her with a fearsome blow that two terrible things had already happened. Could a curse work so quickly, though? Or was it just coincidence?

Sick with worry that more terrible calamities were going to befall them all, she tried to keep watch. Maybe if the man returned again she could throw something heavy from her bedroom window and frighten him off?

There had been no sign of him since that evening but she couldn't sleep for thinking about it, and she kept getting out of bed in the night to make sure he wasn't lurking below her window casting his evil spells. At dawn she'd fall into a heavy sleep, exhausted by her vigil, and then Mama would be cross because she was late for breakfast.

At times, feeling quite desperate with anxiety, she'd slip into their private chapel, which was down a spooky corridor leading off the great hall. There she'd kneel and pray, and if anyone came along and found her she'd decided to say she was praying for Rory's soul. They'd believe that, wouldn't they?

Most of the time she also felt too worried to eat. Then she was struck by an idea. Maybe she could break the spell he'd cast? It would require her to be tremendously brave, but after another night thinking about it she decided it was the only way to prevent the family being for ever cursed.

Laura was up and about again but a strange state of calm had enveloped her in the past few days. She longed to cry to wash away her pain, but she couldn't. She wanted to rage at the Almighty for taking the rest of her life away from her, but not even the mildest anger came to the surface. It was as if all her emotions had been locked in an ice box and nothing was ever going to make them thaw again.

'It's shock, dear girl,' her mother told her. 'I was the same when my father died. I didn't feel sad but I didn't feel remotely happy either. I just went about my business in a sort of limbo.'

'How long did it last for, Mama? It's a terrible thing to say and I can't believe I feel like this, but it's, well, it's sort of a relief to feel absolutely nothing,' Laura admitted, almost ashamed by her lack of open sorrow.

'It's nature's way of helping you cope. Your grief is still intense but your brain is saying enough is enough for the moment.'

'How long will I feel like this?'

Lady Rothbury smiled gently. 'The deeper your feelings are for someone the longer you'll feel numb, my dear.'

The tragedy had brought mother and daughter closer together than they'd been since Laura was a child, and she in turn was glad because she hadn't felt this close to her mother for years; partly because there were so many of them.

'How long did you feel numb when Grandpapa died?'

'About six months. I loved him dearly.'

'Six months? Goodness! Will I really feel like this for six months? It's better than feeling the other way, I suppose.'

'When I was myself again,' Lady Rothbury continued, 'I'd come to terms with what had happened. I remember your papa saying to me, "Welcome back; you've been away a long time". In a way I suppose I had, and thank God for it.'

She reached out to take Laura's hand. 'I'll still be here to welcome you back when it happens to you.'

'The skirt is too tight,' complained Georgie as she tried to pull down the long, dark green woollen dress which Mrs Armitage had made for her on her last visit. 'Why does she always make everything so tight?'

'She doesn't. It's you who's putting on weight,' Lizzie pointed out, amused.

'I haven't put on weight. I eat like a bird,' Georgie retorted angrily.

'Yes, a little fat hen that pecks away all day long,' joked Beattie. 'You know you do, Georgie.'

Georgie turned scarlet. 'I don't peck all day long. I'm bigger boned than the rest of you but I'm not fat.' Tears of vexation sprang to her eyes. 'Why are you always so mean to me?'

'Give it to me – I can probably alter it for you,' Laura suggested, putting down the newspaper she was trying to read while her sisters squabbled around her. It was February and there was a blizzard blowing, so they sat clustered around a log fire in the morning room which spat and sizzled but gave out little heat.

'Could you really?' Georgie looked doubtful. 'You might spoil it and then I wouldn't be able to wear it at all.'

'You forget that Mrs Armitage taught me how to sew,' Laura pointed out. Six months after Rory's death, she seemed impervious to snubs and criticism. The strange numbness that had frozen her feelings shortly his death still shut her off from the rest of the world.

'Well, I suppose you could try,' Georgie replied ungraciously.

The room Mrs Armitage always used still had a chest of drawers full of leftover sewing things, different coloured threads and a spare packet of needles.

'I'll have to do the alterations by hand as we don't have one of those marvellous sewing machines, but that's all right,' Laura said as Georgie struggled out of the skirt and handed it to her. 'At least Mrs Armitage has left some pins and a measuring tape. I wonder if there's any green thread?' She opened another drawer.

Then Georgie heard a howl of pain. 'What is it?' she asked but Laura couldn't speak. She stood with her hand clapped to her mouth and her body wracked with sobs. Carefully folded in the drawer was the wedding dress she'd made for herself.

The ivory damask satin gleamed in the cold light from the window and the crystal beads encrusting the lace glistened like frost. Someone had put it away knowing it was no longer needed and most likely would never be worn.

'Are you all right?' Beattie asked anxiously, putting her arms around Laura, who had crumpled to her knees, leaning over the drawer so her face almost touched the dress while her tears melted into the lace, adding to the glitter of the crystal beads. A nerve had been touched and in a second the comforting numbness that had spared her for the past months had vanished, exposing her to uncontrollable emotional pain.

The door opened at that moment and Lady Rothbury came hurrying into the room. 'I'll look after her,' she whispered to Beattie and Georgie. Then she guided Laura to a nearby sofa and made her comfortable with cushions while

she murmured sympathetically and with great understanding.
After a while the storm passed and Laura looked up, her
expression bewildered.

'When I saw the dress . . .' she whispered brokenly.

'I know, my dear. I know. You've been away for a long time.
Welcome back,' she added softly.

Eleanor was in a state of growing agitation, fearful that Laura
would have a complete breakdown and never recover. Her
elder sisters insisted her grief was normal under the circumstances and she would eventually get over it – something they
themselves weren't sure of in spite of their mother's assurances,
but Eleanor was not convinced.

One of her father's dogs had recently died in its sleep, causing
him profound grief and, although the Labrador was twelve
years old, Eleanor was certain he'd been cursed. Otherwise,
why would he seem perfectly fine one day and dead the next?

The following morning she walked round to the stables, and
while the grooms were busy she stole a long length of rope.
She'd seen it being used for breaking-in foals. One end was
attached to a light harness while the groom held the other,
letting it out slowly until the foal was trotting around in ever-
widening circles. Gathering it up in her arms, she smuggled
it into the castle without anyone seeing. Then she hid it under
her bed. There was one more thing she had to get before she
could put her plan into action.

After lunch, when her father had gone out, her mother was
reading aloud to the younger girls and there was no noise from
the nursery or the schoolrooms, she slipped into the private
chapel. Two candles always burned on the altar, kept alight by
McEwan the butler night and morning. Between them stood
a big brass crucifix. There was also a cross by the font where
they'd all been Christened. It was very old and carved in dark
wood. She slipped it into her pocket and, unseen, tore up to
her bedroom where she placed it carefully under the rope. No
one would know it was missing, and afterwards she'd return it
to the chapel. Satisfied, she set about planning what she was
going to say.

★   ★   ★

'I shall never marry now,' Laura said pragmatically during one of her calm spells that came between bouts of grief and despair. 'I could never find another Rory. Not in a million years.'

'Won't you miss having children?' Lizzie asked carefully. She never knew when her sister was to be overcome by grief again and the slightest thing could set her off.

'Frankly, no,' Laura replied candidly. 'Rory and I had never planned a big family. There are far too many of us. Mama does her best but how can she stretch herself to spend lots of time with eleven children?'

Lizzie looked shocked. 'Everyone has big families, though. Of course, you've got to marry a rich man so you can afford lots of nannies and nursery maids and . . .'

'And never have time to look after them yourself,' Laura cut in. 'That's my point. I'd want to spend every minute with my child. Teach it things. Watch it grow. Be a part of its life.'

Lizzie grinned. 'It? You sound as if you're talking about a plant, not a boy or a girl.'

'You know what I mean. What's the point of having masses of children if you barely have time to see them all?'

'A large family ensures there will be plenty of people to look after you in your old age,' Lizzie protested.

'Well, it's not going to happen to me,' Laura said lightly.

Lizzie looked thoughtful. 'I suppose in some ways you're right. I spoke to Mama about Eleanor yesterday. I told her we were all concerned because she's been behaving strangely and Mama agreed to talk to her, but then Cook wanted her to look at a menu for tonight's dinner party and I just know that Mama's forgotten all about Eleanor.'

'There's no use asking Papa, either.'

'Oh, he's hopeless with children. Now, if one of the dogs had a problem he'd be frantic!'

Laura smiled wryly. 'I'll *never* have any of those either.'

Lying in bed that night, Eleanor recited to herself what she was going to say while pressing the crucifix against the trunk of the Rowan tree. She'd composed a special prayer and written it down so that she could memorize it.

Please, dear God, it began, *tell the Rowan tree not to curse us any more. I know it can prevent bad things happening to the family but a wicked man has told it to do bad things to us, and only you, dear Lord, can change its mind.*

Was that going to be enough? Should she say the Lord's Prayer as well? Just to make certain God understood? It would be awful to go to all this trouble and find God didn't know what she was talking about. So she decided to say the Lord's Prayer too, to be on the safe side.

Eleanor knew she couldn't do this in broad daylight. There were too many servants and gardeners and too many of them in the family to do anything private during the day. She was going to have to exorcize the Rowan tree under cover of darkness, but her plans were all in place and tonight was the night she was going to lift the curse.

Every now and again she crept out of her room on to the landing, waiting for her parents' dinner guests to depart. Then McEwan would make sure the house was locked up and bolted for the night and all the candles blown out except for the two in the chapel.

At last, and it was after midnight by the chimes of the church bells, Eleanor knew everyone in the castle had gone to bed. For security reasons they were all safely locked in, and would remain so until the castle was opened up at six the next morning.

Climbing out of her bed, she groped under it for the rope, uncoiling it until it stretched across the room. Then she wound one end of it around the carved post of her bed and tied it in a double knot. Pulling on it with all her strength until she'd made sure it would hold her weight, she then opened her window and silently dropped the other end. It uncoiled and slid like a snake down the castle wall. Leaning out as far as she could, Eleanor waited until there was a gap between the clouds as they scudded across the moon. Suddenly the terrace below was bathed in faint light, confirming that the rope was long enough to reach the ground.

Now she just had to collect the little wooden crucifix from under her bed. How hard and strong it felt in her hand, she thought, as she jammed it into the pocket of her dressing gown.

Eleanor's heart was racing now with part excitement and part terror. She gave a final glance at her prayer, which she'd left on the dressing table, and then she decided the best way to climb down the rope was to sit on the window sill with her legs dangling while she got a good grip by wrapping it around one of her wrists before gripping it with both hands.

At that moment the moon disappeared behind another cloud and she looked down into the pitch darkness with alarm. Beneath her was nothing but blackness. She couldn't even see the Rowan tree, although it was only a few feet away from the castle wall. She sat still, breathless and frightened. She couldn't back out now, though. The curse had to be broken before anything else dreadful happened in the family. If she gave up now she'd never forgive herself if someone else died. Supposing it was Papa or Mama?

Galvanized into action and petrified of the consequences if she didn't act quickly, Eleanor got a tighter grip of the rope and then eased her body out of the window. Her bare feet found the rope beneath her and she held it between them to steady it. Inch by inch, hand over hand, she began to descend, although her shoulders became agonized by the strain and her wrists and hands burned as if they were on fire. Biting her bottom lip, she edged a few more inches down but it was taking much longer than she'd expected and it was far more terrifying than she'd realized.

'Please, God . . . help me do this,' she prayed. 'Oh, please, God . . . help me . . .'

Suddenly she was bathed in a pale light as the moon momentarily slid out from behind a cloud. Encouraged, she lowered herself a few more inches. Then she glanced down again. The terrace must still be thirty feet away and she didn't know how much longer her thin arms could take the strain of her weight.

'Oh, God, I *must* do this,' she whispered in desperation.

At that moment she was plunged into darkness, followed a moment later by a vivid flash of lightning which illuminated the land all around, followed by a deafening crash of thunder. Startled, she gave a loud scream and lost her grip on the rope.

★　★　★

Laura sat up with a start. The violent storm must have awakened her, she reflected sleepily. Through her curtains flashes of lightning kept penetrating the room and she turned over in bed, wondering vaguely how long it would last. She thought she'd been awakened by the sound of a scream but that must have been part of the dream she was having. Listening to the rain and hailstones which sounded as if someone was flinging gravel at her window, she could tell the storm was right over the castle by the speed with which the thunder followed.

After a while it faded away and all was quiet again. Laura closed her eyes and fell into a deep sleep.

Shrill screams and a man's voice yelling and blaspheming broke the tranquil silence of another cold dawn. Laura woke again, startled. This time she wasn't having a nightmare. Flinging on her dressing gown, she ran barefoot into the corridor and looked down over the banister to the great hall below. Servants and footmen were standing still as if stupefied, while her mother clung to Beattie and Georgie, in obvious distress. At that moment Diana and Lizzie shot out of their rooms, still in their long white flannel night robes.

'What's happened?' Diana asked in a frightened voice as she rushed ahead, followed by Laura and Lizzie.

Their mother suddenly collapsed and Georgie and Beattie were helping her to a chair. Then Laura saw her father standing in the entrance of the castle. He looked like a broken man, his face white and gaunt and his expression wracked with grief.

In his arms lay the soaked and frozen body of Eleanor.

Laura stared in disbelief, unable to speak.

'*Why* . . .?' Diana whispered. No one was able to answer and the only sound in the great hall was the soft sobbing of the kitchen maids.

Then the sisters turned and looked at each other, almost accusingly.

'We *knew* something was troubling her, didn't we?' said Lizzie.

'She insisted there was nothing the matter,' Beattie whispered.

'She's been acting strangely for weeks,' Laura said despairingly.

'Then why didn't you tell us?' their father suddenly bellowed in a rage. They hung their heads, overcome, as he glared at them with his bloodshot eyes. 'You should have told me or your mother instead of standing idly by.' He looked down into Eleanor's face as if he couldn't believe he was holding her dead body. 'Poor little girl,' he groaned. 'Poor child.'

McEwan stood two paces behind him. He was staring straight ahead, then he raised his right hand and they saw he was holding the small wooden crucifix. 'This had fallen out of her pocket. It was lying beside her body on the terrace.' He sounded bewildered, light-headed almost, a lifetime of training in etiquette forgotten.

'Christ! Why did she jump?' asked Freddie angrily.

His younger brother stood beside him, trying very hard not to cry. 'Why did she want to die?' Henry asked in a quivering voice, but nobody was listening to either of them.

As if aroused from a coma, Lady Rothbury suddenly looked up from where she was sitting and spoke. 'Will someone tell Nanny not to let the young ones come downstairs.'

Mrs Spry moved swiftly forward. 'I've already given those instructions, M'Lady.' Then she turned to the kitchen maids. 'This way, please,' she commanded in a quiet but firm voice as she opened the green baize door.

Her professionalism instantly made them shuffle back towards the kitchens, some of them wiping their eyes with their aprons. Then she ordered the footmen to fetch brandy and the maids to light the fires in every room.

Leading the way, Lord Rothbury carried Eleanor's body into the chapel. 'Bring something to lay her on,' he commanded, his voice gruff. A long oak table was hurriedly fetched and a silk Turkish rug was laid on it. As he placed the little broken body of his daughter on the table, he let out a bellow that sent shivers through all those who heard him.

'May God forgive me, for this is all my fault,' he moaned. 'The sins of the father . . .' His voice broke and he covered his face with his hands as he slumped down by Eleanor's body.

His wife went to him and laid her hand on his shoulder. 'You mustn't blame yourself, William.'

'Why did she jump?' persisted Freddie in a loud voice.

His father turned on him in a burst of savage rage. 'She didn't jump, you fool! She fell from her window.'

Freddie's mouth dropped open. 'But why . . .?'

'Stop asking questions,' his mother begged.

Laura and her sisters looked at each other again. It didn't make sense. Eleanor believed in God. She would never have taken her own life. Laura turned to Lizzie and they both started running back up the stairs.

As soon as they entered Eleanor's bedroom they froze and stood still, shocked by the sight of a rope still tied to the carved bed post. It hung from the bed to the window like a washing line.

Laura pressed her hand over her mouth as she walked unsteadily to the window and looked out. Then she flinched. 'It's a terrible drop!' she whispered as she looked down at the bloodstained flagstones far below.

'Do you think she was trying to run away?' Lizzie whispered.

'No. There are a hundred other ways she could have run away if she was that unhappy. Why choose this dangerous method in pitch darkness? It doesn't make sense.'

'I'd never have had the courage to try and climb down that rope,' Lizzie said brokenly. 'What in God's name was she trying to do?'

Laura leaned against the window frame, feeling sick and dizzy as terrible thoughts filled her head. Had Eleanor died instantly? Or had she lain injured on the freezing terrace, alive but unable to move, knowing it would be hours before anyone would find her?

'Are you all right?' she heard Lizzie ask. She shook her head, unable to speak. Now she knew, with terrible certainty, it had been Eleanor's scream she'd heard in the night as the storm broke. And she'd turned over and gone back to sleep. Her anguish became laden with guilt. Maybe Eleanor would still have been alive if she'd raised the alarm?

'I can't bear it.' She pulled herself away from the window and turned to run from the room but something caught her eye: a sheet of white paper lying on the dressing table. She instantly recognized Eleanor's childish handwriting. 'Look, Lizzie! She's left a note.'

Lizzie peered over her shoulder. 'It's a prayer,' she exclaimed in surprise.

They hurried downstairs again to find their mother had retired to her bedroom, overcome with grief, while their father had just given orders for the family doctor and the police to be called.

'Papa,' Lizzie said urgently. 'We have something to show you.' They led him into the study and closed the door.

He read the prayer in silence and as the tears flowed freely down his ruddy cheeks he murmured again, 'The sins of the fathers . . .' Then he dashed out of the room and ran up the stairs, still muttering.

'He'll have gone to see Mama,' Lizzie observed bleakly.

Mrs Spry appeared, walking briskly along the corridor. 'Ah, Lady Elizabeth, Lady Laura,' she said when she saw them standing huddled in the middle of the hall, still in their nightgowns. 'Can I get you anything? Some beef tea? Or something to eat?' She spoke under her breath as if they were in a church.

They shook their heads. Lizzie asked, 'Where is everyone?'

'Her Ladyship has requested not to be disturbed; I think Lady Georgina, Lady Diana and Lady Beatrice are also in their rooms; all the younger ones are upstairs, the boys with their tutor and the little girls with Nanny. So far the girls haven't been told what's happened.'

Laura suddenly felt deeply sad. Families were supposed to stick close together in a crisis, like they did in the cottages in the village when something happened. Why did the upper classes have to grieve alone? she wondered. Was it to maintain their dignity? She looked at Lizzie, who was biting her bottom lip to prevent herself weeping in front of a member of staff, and she suddenly wished she belonged to a very ordinary family.

At that moment Beattie, Georgie and Diana came downstairs, already wearing an assortment of black clothes.

'We thought we'd sit in the chapel,' Beattie explained. 'We can't leave Eleanor alone. Why aren't you two dressed yet?'

Lizzie told them about the prayer they'd found.

'What did it say?' Diana asked.

'I can't remember it word for word,' Laura pointed out, 'but she was asking God to tell the Rowan tree not to curse us any more. She said a bad man was making the Rowan do bad things to us.' Her voice trailed away.

'What tosh! What was she talking about?' Georgie said scornfully.

Beattie understood at once. 'Remember the fierce argument we overheard when Papa and a man were fighting? They were cursing each other. I remember Eleanor was with us and we all wondered what it was about? Papa was very angry and ordered the man to leave and never come back.'

'Yes,' Diana butted in. 'I clearly remember the man shouting, "As the Rowan tree is my witness, I curse the Fairbairn family from here until eternity".'

They looked at each other, shocked and appalled as the words sank in and they realized that Eleanor had tried to save them all.

'Dear Lord, I feel sick,' Diana whispered.

'Why didn't she tell us what she was planning?' Beattie exclaimed. 'We could have helped her and done it properly.'

Georgie, for once aware of her own acerbic shortcomings, spoke humbly. 'She'd have been afraid we'd laugh at her, and the awful thing is we probably would have done.'

There was a long silence, and then Lizzie spoke. 'You have to admit it's a strange coincidence that since Papa had that fight with that man I lose James, Rory is killed, one of Papa's dogs mysteriously dies, and then Eleanor is killed as she is about to take a crucifix down to the tree and pray to God to lift the curse.'

'Maybe that's what Papa meant when he said Eleanor's death was all his fault. Why was he fighting with that man in the first place?'

Beattie suddenly jumped to her feet, startling the others. 'Don't! That way lies madness. We all know Eleanor was a fanciful little girl and very impressionable. It was obvious she was worried about something. We should have forced her to tell us then none of this would have happened.'

'We didn't because we didn't want to face the fact that something might be really wrong,' Laura pointed out. 'Looking back, Papa has been much grumpier since that man came here. What did he want? Why did Papa send him away like that?'

'I wish I knew. What are we going to do?' asked Diana. 'I don't want to go through life with a curse on my head.'

'You won't be the only one,' Georgie remarked succinctly.

Five

Lasswade Hall, 1907

Caroline came hurtling across the lawn to where her parents were having afternoon tea. Pretty in a white lawn dress and bonnet, the three-year-old was smiling with excitement at being home again.

'Mama! Dada!' she shrieked, waving her arms. 'Look what Aunt Di gave me.' She was clutching a doll in her tiny hand. Her nanny came hurrying after her, trying to catch up.

'I'm sorry, M'Lady. Sir. She's that thrilled to be back and there's been no stopping her since dawn,' she panted apologetically.

Laura and Walter smiled as their child threw herself into Laura's arms.

'Hello, my darling. I believe you've grown,' Laura exclaimed, settling Caroline on her lap. 'Did you have a wonderful time with Aunt Di? And did you have fun playing with Nicolas and Louise?'

Caroline nodded vigorously as she pulled off her bonnet, revealing long, flaxen hair which fell into curls down her back.

'I saw Punch and Judy!' she squealed. 'And I sat on a pony.'

'What a busy little girl you've been,' Walter observed warmly.

Caroline looked around. 'Where's Neil, Dada?' He was her six-year-old half-brother by Walter's first marriage; his mother had died five years ago.

'He's been away too, staying with his aunt,' Laura said quickly, flashing a knowing look at Walter.

'That's right,' Walter agreed. 'You've been staying with your aunt Di and he's been staying with his aunt Rowena.'

'Why doesn't she ask me to stay with her? Doesn't she like me?' Caroline's eyes, so dark like her father's, looked fretful.

'She will when you're a bit older,' Laura assured her soothingly. 'After all, Neil is six, nearly seven.'

Tears sprang to Caroline's eyes and her mouth drooped at the corners. 'I don't want to be three.' A dry sob caught in her chest. 'Mama, I want to be seven!'

'You will be but how about a slice of cake first? Shall Mummy cut you a piece?'

The child nodded sulkily.

Laura spoils her, Walter thought. *Probably to compensate.* Neil was rather spoilt, too. It was what parents did when they felt guilty.

'Shall I push you on the swing when you've had your cake?' he asked gently.

Caroline jumped down from Laura's lap, her cheeks bulging with sponge and jam cake.

'Finish your cake first,' Laura said, grabbing her by the arm and attempting to wipe her mouth with a table napkin, but the child was off, running defiantly on her little legs to where Greg the gardener had hung a home-made swing from one of the branches of a tree near his hut.

Laura watched her with anxious eyes.

'Is everything all right?' Walter asked.

'Yes.' What else could she say? Her voice was flat, though, and she sounded desperately tired. 'Is Rowena bringing Neil back this evening?'

'I suggested she might come to luncheon tomorrow and bring him with her. I thought that would give Caroline time to settle down.'

Laura looked at him directly. 'Neil is going to ask questions, you know. He's getting too big to have the wool pulled over his eyes any more. What are you going to tell him, Walter?'

'Leave him to me, my dear,' he said quietly.

'This has been the longest time you've been . . . away,' she pointed out.

'I know.'

A silence hung over them like a poisonous cloud, stinging their eyes and breaking their hearts so they could scarcely breathe.

How much longer can I bear this situation? Laura reflected bleakly. *As long as you have to,* answered the voice in her head.

'Dada! Come on. I want to swing.' The little girl's childish voice floated across the sunny lawn.

Laura turned to look at Caroline and at that moment knew she was going to have to continue to do her best at playing Happy Families.

Rising, she slipped her hand through Walter's arm and as they strolled towards their daughter, she said, 'We should start entertaining again. Why don't we have a house party next month? Say we invite a dozen friends from a Saturday morning until after lunch on Monday? We used to do that at home before Papa died and it was good fun.'

'As long as it's not too much for you I think it's a great idea,' Walter enthused.

What's too much for me is being cooped up in the house with you and the children, holding my breath and wondering when the next episode is going to be sprung on me when I'm least expecting it.

Aloud, she said, 'It won't be too much for me at all. I enjoy entertaining.'

'They used to be known as the Fairbairn girls, you know,' Celia Brownlow chattily informed her husband Hugo as they were driven in their carriage to join a house party just outside Edinburgh given by Laura and Walter Leighton-Harvey. Keen on social climbing, Celia had nurtured this friendship for some time, taking advantage of when they met at the school attended by Laura's stepson and Celia's son.

'You know she's the daughter of an Earl, don't you?' she continued excitedly. 'Now remember to address her as Lady Laura, not Lady Leighton-Harvey, because her husband hasn't got a title.'

Hugo nodded patiently. He didn't have a title either and never having met this Lady Laura he hoped she was kinder to her husband's lack of nobleness than Celia was to him. 'The world is yours if you have a title', Celia always said and it was obvious she deeply regretted her husband's lack of being listed in the peerage. His fortune, self-made by manufacturing terracotta chimney pots, went some way to alleviating her desperation to 'arrive', but he knew it would never be enough.

'Who else has she invited for the weekend?' he asked, to humour her.

Celia turned to stare at him, her large blue eyes registering shock.

'You must never call it a "weekend",' she whispered, although the coach driver was unlikely to have overheard.

'But it is a weekend? Saturday morning to Monday morning is certainly the end of the week in my world.'

'I know, but it's common to call it a weekend. Lady Laura specifically invited us to spend a couple of days with them at the end of the week. Those were her exact words in her letter.'

'I wonder what her husband – the one without the title – calls it then,' Hugo retorted sarcastically.

'Now don't be like that, Hugo,' she said sharply. 'Don't go letting me down. This could lead to lots of things. She might even invite us one day to stay at her ancestral home, Lochlee Castle.'

He smiled, amused now that he could score a point. 'I doubt that very much,' he said smugly.

'Why?'

'It no longer belongs to the Fairbairn family.'

'Come and meet the others,' Laura said in welcome when they arrived. 'We're having drinks on the lawn before luncheon. Thank goodness it's stopped raining.' She led the way, an elegant figure in a long, dark red skirt and a cream high-necked lace blouse with long sleeves puffed to the elbow. Ropes of priceless pearls hung to her waist, and drop pearl earrings quivered when she moved. Celia, covertly admiring the rings on Laura's fingers, noted her aristocratic hands and well-kept nails. The hands of someone who had never scrubbed floors, she told herself, resolving to keep her gloves on for as long as possible.

'We have rather an invasion of family today but they're not all staying because we don't have enough rooms,' Laura continued gaily. 'This is my sister, Diana, and her husband,

Lord Kelso, and this is another sister, Lizzie. That's her husband over there, Sir Humphrey Garding. Have you met Mary and Theo, the Duke and Duchess of Melrose? Well, come along and meet them too. They're mad about dogs. Do you have dogs? Here's another sister of mine, Beattie and her husband, Andrew Drinkwater.'

Laura prattled on, the perfect hostess, busy introducing everyone to each other, and Celia thought this is what Paradise must be like. She'd never met so many titles in the space of twenty minutes and she couldn't wait to tell her mother all about it.

Bursts of laughter coming from the far end of the lawn where some of the men had congregated attracted Hugo Brownlow's attention and he realized the revelry was due to Laura's husband, who seemed to be recounting some amusing incident.

Hugo strolled over to join them, leaving Celia in animated conversation with Sir Humphrey, who looked exceedingly pompous and boring.

Walter stepped forward to shake his hand. 'You must be Hugo Brownlow – my wife told me you were coming today. How very nice to meet you. Do you know . . .?'

Hugo found himself being introduced to some more people but then Walter didn't move on as Laura had done. He turned to Hugo and spoke with genuine charm. 'How was your journey? You've come over from Glasgow, haven't you? Has Laura shown you where you and your wife are sleeping or were you just flung to the wolves?' His dark eyes twinkled good-humouredly. 'Laura is the most marvellous hostess once you've pinned her down, which is about as easy as nailing a butterfly, but it really is most good of you to have come all this way just for a couple of nights.'

Melting under Walter's personable manner, Hugo reflected that Celia would have been prepared to travel the length of Britain just to be in a room full of people like this.

'It's our pleasure. You have a lovely place here.' Hugo glanced around at the large garden.

'Yes. I'm very lucky. Laura is the most wonderful woman, too.' He spoke with such depth of feeling – almost sadness

– that Hugo raised his eyebrows, wondering if this splendid house and all that went with it was Laura's dowry. Yet Walter had a confident, prosperous air about him.

Curious to know more, he asked, 'So, are you in business?'

'I was in the army,' he replied briskly. 'Now I've got a couple of directorships. Keeps me busy, you know.'

'Do you have children?' It struck Hugo there was something missing in Walter Leighton-Harvey's life, although he looked like a man who had everything.

'A son by my first wife and Laura and I have a daughter,' he replied briefly before turning to greet some new arrivals. The moment of intimacy was over, leaving Hugo vaguely puzzled, pondering on his enigmatic host.

At dinner that night twelve guests were seated around the beautifully laid table and Celia was in a fever of excitement and nerves as she took her seat next to Lord Kelso. 'So you're married to Lady Laura's sister?' she gushed.

'Yes. Di and I got married a few years ago. Just before the Boer War, actually.' She found him to be a mild-mannered man with kind eyes and a quiet voice. 'How long have you known Laura and Walter?'

She longed to say, 'Oh, ages . . .' but fear of being found out forced her to admit, 'Not that long. We met at the Children's Aid Society to discuss raising funds for orphans. Lady Laura said she'd write to our local MP. She thinks he should tell the Prime Minister that they should do more for orphans.'

Robert Kelso smiled and glanced at the head of the table where Laura was talking animatedly to the Duke of Montrose. She was wearing a purple chiffon evening dress which showed off her smooth white shoulders and diamond drop earrings that quivered when she moved her head. Whatever she was saying was causing the Duke and those sitting near her much laughter, but Robert detected an undercurrent of desperation in her manner that worried him. Her gaiety this evening was brittle, which was unlike her, and her smile too brilliant to be genuine. Diana had been shocked by the way Laura had run off and married Walter, whom she'd barely known. She'd seemed genuinely happy at first but tonight she was showing signs of strain, as if she was covering up something, though he'd no idea what.

'She's very beautiful, isn't she?' Celia remarked.

'Yes. Have you met her other sister, Lizzie?' he asked conversationally. 'They're the image of each other but their characters are completely different.'

Celia looked intrigued. She longed to know all about the famous Fairbairn girls of whom she'd heard so much. 'In what way?'

'Laura is more resilient. Stronger. She's a great survivor.'

Celia blinked. She wouldn't have thought Laura had anything to survive, what with her money, her status and her position. Then she glanced across the table to where Lizzie was sitting in cream lace, talking quietly to the man on her left. 'They do look alike,' she agreed. 'Quite fascinating.'

'Lizzie is probably the most pragmatic one. My wife Diana is the most sensitive of them all.' There was a pause, then he spoke again, thoughtfully this time. 'Some have risen above the tragedies that have fallen on their family . . . and some haven't.'

Celia stared at him. Was he referring to the loss of Lochlee Castle? Rather than appear ignorant she nodded sadly, as if in understanding.

'That's what happens with large families,' he added with finality. Then he raised his head, a look of alarm in his eyes. 'I can smell burning. Can you smell something?'

Celia sniffed the air like a busy little terrier. 'Yes, I can!' she exclaimed, wide-eyed.

One of the parlour maids came running into the dining room at that moment. 'Fire!' she shrieked. 'Fire!'

Walter bounded to his feet, pushing his chair back roughly. 'Where's the fire?' he demanded.

'Upstairs,' she wailed, pointing with a trembling hand.

Hobbs, the butler, appeared. 'I think your bedroom is alight, sir,' he blurted out, panicked.

A commotion broke out, with people jumping to their feet, all talking at once; some running into the hall, others going into the garden through the French windows.

'Call the fire brigade!' Walter shouted to Hobbs above the din.

'Everyone into the garden,' Laura told the guests. Then she ran from the room into the hall. 'Help me bring down the children,' she said to Walter, but he was already racing ahead of her up the stairs. She followed, picking up her long skirt so as not to trip.

The first-floor landing was filling up with smoke seeping from under their bedroom door.

Walter yelled, 'Stay there, Laura! I'll get them.'

'No, I'm coming with you!' she replied. The night nursery was on the floor above and as they ran up the second flight of stairs they met Nanny. She was carrying Caroline with one arm and holding Neil's hand with the other.

'Well done, Nanny,' Walter said, grabbing Caroline.

'Quick, the smoke is getting worse. Are you all right, Nanny? Can you manage?'

'I'm all right, M'Lady.' She covered her nose and mouth with her starched apron. By the time they arrived in the hall they were all coughing and their eyes were stinging.

'Take Caroline, will you, Laura?' Walter said breathlessly. 'Stay in the garden well away from the house. Don't let Neil out of your sight.'

Then he dashed off to find out if the fire brigade were on their way. The acrid smell of burning was everywhere now, filling the air with smoke and dangerous burning particles. Everyone stood huddled together at the far end of the lawn, watching in horrified silence as flames licked the curtains of Laura's bedroom window, shattering the glass which exploded in a shower of fragments, landing on the terrace below.

'Keep well back!' Walter shouted.

'I hope to God it doesn't spread,' Robert observed in a low voice.

Diana stood close beside him, her eyes filled with tears. 'This is too wretched for Laura. Her bedroom was so beautiful. What on earth could have caused it?' she said in a low voice.

'The fire brigade are on their way,' Walter announced thankfully. Then he turned back to Hobbs, who was hovering helplessly. 'Have you any idea what caused this?' he asked abruptly.

bicycle and I've managed to close the drawing-room door 〈to〉 prevent the fire spreading into the hall.' Her eyes were 〈re〉d-rimmed and Diana wondered if it was due to the smoke 〈or〉 tears.

Walter strode over and looked into her face. 'Are you all 〈ri〉ght, my dear?' he murmured. 'For a moment I feared . . .'

'I'm all right, Walter,' she replied, although she was obviously 〈ve〉ry shaken. 'We just have to pray the fire brigade come 〈qu〉ickly.'

Caroline whimpered, 'Muzzie' as she stretched her small 〈ar〉ms towards Laura.

'It's all right, darling,' she replied, taking her gently from 〈D〉iana.

The servants came pouring out of the house now, led by 〈H〉obbs.

'Everyone to the far end of the lawn,' Walter commanded. 〈W〉e don't want anyone struck by flying glass.'

Pale and shaken, the sisters sank down on to their chairs 〈ag〉ain while Laura cuddled Caroline.

'How did it start?' Diana exclaimed, leaning closer while in 〈th〉e distance the firemen were getting the flames under control. 〈T〉his is the second fire you've had, isn't it?'

'The third.' Laura's voice broke.

Diana stared at her as if she couldn't believe what she was 〈h〉earing.

'*Third?*' she repeated. 'What's the cause? Is it your oil lamps? 〈Y〉ou know they need regular cleaning and the wick trimmed.'

Laura looked immensely tired. 'The lamps weren't lit in the 〈ro〉oms where the fires started.'

'Why didn't you tell me before? Someone must have a 〈g〉rudge against you and Walter and you should tell the police.'

Laura closed her eyes, not answering. 'I'm almost at the end 〈o〉f my tether,' she murmured eventually.

'You're keeping something from me. What is it?'

'No, nothing. I'm just tired. The thought of having the 〈in〉surance people here again, wanting me to write out a list of 〈e〉verything that has been destroyed, then there's the business 〈o〉f getting new curtains and rugs and furniture. Not that we 〈c〉an replace the antiques.'

'I don't know, sir. All the staff were working downstairs, attending to your dinner guests, but then I was aware of smoke . . .'

'I know. I know.' Walter frowned worriedly as he went over to Laura, who stood with Caroline still half asleep in her arms. 'Have you any idea what started the fire? You did put out the oil lamps, didn't you?'

Laura looked at him in surprise. 'You know I did. You saw me do it.'

He still looked puzzled. 'That's what I thought.'

At that moment they all heard the clanging of the fire engine's bell as it came tearing up the drive. Everyone stopped talking and watched as the crew started uncoiling a long hosepipe while the chief shouted, 'Back away please, everybody.'

From where she was standing on the lawn Celia could see the fire was worsening. 'Will they be able to put it out?' she asked her husband as she clung to his arm. 'Supposing it spreads?'

'They'll contain it,' Hugo replied reassuringly. 'These new internal combustion engines carry much more water than the old engines. Look, they're putting up a ladder and they're going to tackle the flames through the window.'

Celia's head was in a spin. She could dine out on the experience for months to come. The most remarkable thing to her was seeing how calm Laura seemed to be. Her lips were pressed together and her eyes were filled with anxiety, but her emotions were under control and that, to Celia, was a sure sign of good breeding.

'We must leave and go home first thing in the morning,' Hugo said.

'What?' she spun round to glare at him. 'Go home? But we've been invited to stay until Monday morning!' she squealed in horror, thinking of all the new clothes she'd bought for this visit and all the new friendships she was about to acquire.

Keeping his voice low, Hugo spoke sharply. 'How would you like it if people you hardly knew remained as house guests when your home had been wrecked by fire and water damage? Of course we must leave. It's one thing for her sisters to stay on if they want to, but we must certainly depart. I'm sure their other guests will also leave under the circumstances. And without question,' he added vindictively.

It was, Celia was to later recount to her mother, one of the greatest disappointments of her life to be denied the chance of forging a friendship with the Duke and Duchess of Melrose.

An hour later the fire was out, leaving Laura's bedroom a charred and blackened ruin. Waterlogged and still steaming, nothing had been spared. The silver-backed brushes she'd had since she'd been a child were now twisted and blackened pieces of metal, while the oil paintings now hung on the walls like torn rags. Even the antique *armoire* where she kept her clothes had been utterly destroyed.

Lizzie put her arm around Laura's shoulders. 'I'm so sorry, my dear. This is a dreadful shock for you, especially with all these people staying. Do you know how it started?'

Laura shook her head. 'I can't understand it. I know I turned off the oil lamps. Isn't the smell terrible? And have you seen the state of the hall? The firemen took their hoses into the house as well as through the window. Oh, God, it's such a mess.'

'Why don't you all come back and stay with us?' Diana suggested, joining them at that moment.

'No, thank you, Di. I must stay here. There will be such a lot to do,' Laura replied, hitching Caroline on to her other hip. 'I don't want the children's routine disturbed more than necessary.'

It was a while before the firemen left, as they stayed to make sure there were no smouldering embers. Meanwhile, the guests were allowed back into the unaffected wing of the house so those who wanted to could go to bed.

'I'm so sorry.' Laura kept apologizing to those who lingered downstairs in the drawing room because their rooms were considered unsafe. 'This is not quite the weekend I'd planned for you all, so please come and stay again.'

It was obvious, even to Celia, that the correct thing to do was to depart. She and Hugo were just about to say goodnight

to their hosts when the fire chief came over to w_ and Walter were now sitting in the hall.

'Are you off now?' Walter asked.

'Yes, sir. We'll return tomorrow to carry out furth_ gations but we can be sure of one thing.' He pause_ still flushed and smeared with soot and sweat. 'Th_ started deliberately.'

'Not again, for heaven's sake!' Laura jumped up fr_ she was sitting in the garden talking to Diana _ watched their husbands playing tennis. 'Di, can you_ Caroline?'

'What's the matter?'

Laura didn't answer but, picking up her long, _ skirt, she ran towards the house in obvious pani_ moment a sudden breeze swept across the lawn _ could smell it, too. The pungent, acrid smell o_ Gathering Caroline up in her arms, she raced o_ tennis court. 'Walter! I think the house is on fire _ shouted.

The soft *plop plop* of tennis balls hitting racke_ immediately. Then she saw Robert, tearing up the_ led to Lasswade Hall, followed by Walter, who was_ to keep up with the younger man.

The sudden crack of shattering glass as a gr_ window burst with heat made them halt with sho_ saw flames were flickering around the window fram_ cream brocade curtains were already hanging in bl_ Smoke came pouring out, spreading across the gar_ breeze grew stronger.

'Laura! Laura!' Walter roared, terror in his voice. _ God's sake, where are you?' He turned in desperation_ 'Where did she go?' he shouted.

'I'll go round to the front of the house,' Robe_ speeding away.

At that moment Laura appeared from the other s_ house, breathless and with her hair tumbling dow_ usual smooth bun.

'I've sent the boot boy to fetch the fire brigade_

'Why don't you come and stay with Robert and me for a bit? Bring Caroline and her nanny too, if you like. There's plenty of room at Cranley Court.'

'Maybe in a while. I need to see to things here first.'

Diana knew her elder sister so well she could read her like an open book. Something was wrong and Laura was either too proud or too scared to tell her what it was. She leaned closer and talked in a low voice.

'Are you having trouble with Neil? Stepchildren can create havoc in a family.'

'I can't help feeling sorry for the boy. When he was two years old he was the one who found his mother's body, you know. She was lying at the bottom of the stairs and her neck was broken. I don't think he'll ever get completely over his loss. I think he resents me being here but Walter and I hope he'll come to terms with it when he's older. He is only nine and all we can do is reassure him that he's much loved.'

'Poor little mite. That explains a lot. It must have been terrible for Walter, too.'

'I think he was quite broken-hearted at the time. Priscilla was a sweet woman but desperately stupid.'

Two hours later the fire had been extinguished, although the firemen were keeping watch in case there were any hidden embers, but the room had been gutted and blackened by smoke and what remained of the contents was steaming dankly. Worse was the destruction of all the antiques which had been saved from Lochlee Castle. They were her only dowry.

After Nanny had come to fetch Caroline for her bath and bed, Laura burst into tears. The collection of furniture and family portraits, familiar objects she'd known and loved since she'd been small, had been wiped out in one afternoon. It felt like she was saying goodbye to her youth and the happy childhood she'd had. Now there was nothing but the pungent, acrid smell of destruction. The tears flowed silently down her cheeks and she suddenly felt afraid. Who hated them so much . . . or was it only she who was hated? Someone was intent on some sort of mad revenge and they had to find out who it could be. Next time they might not be lucky enough to escape with their lives. With deepening concern, Laura decided she could no longer bury her head in the sand. It was time she faced her hidden fears.

Nanny came hurrying into the room, bustling with bad tidings.

'What is it, Nanny?' Laura noticed the nurse's hands were shaking and she was visibly upset.

'I hardly like to tell you, M'Lady.'

Laura's heart gave a painful lurch. Had the nightmare started again? It was more than a year since the last occasion but she would never forget the night when she'd hidden in the gardener's hut and seen, in the darkness, a hand holding a lit candle as he searched the house, with an axe in the other hand.

'Please, Nanny, tell me,' she said faintly.

'On the way to the night nursery I passed Neil's room. The door was open and I saw something sticking out from under his bed.'

'And . . .?' Laura frowned. 'What was under his bed?'

'I found a bottle of methylated spirit.' She paused painfully. 'And a box of matches that was almost empty.'

Laura looked stunned. Her first emotion was one of relief; the nightmare hadn't started again. Then she was flooded with anger.

This was worse in many ways. It was Walter's son who had put all their lives in danger, and somehow she'd always known it.

Walter put his head in his hands and groaned when Laura told him. Diana and Robert had returned to their home that morning and he was trying to make sense of what had happened.

'Is it my fault?' he asked in a choked voice. He raised his head to look into Laura's face as if searching for something. 'Is it because . . .?'

'That may be part of the problem but I think you should take him to see the doctor.' Laura spoke carefully but earnestly. 'We can't go on like this, Walter. Neil needs to be watched all the time now but supposing he starts a fire in the middle of the night when we're all asleep?'

Walter suddenly looked enraged. 'I'm not having him sent
to some institution or mental home. That really would unbal-
ance him and make him feel we'd rejected him, which is the
last thing I want.'

'Oh, my dear, I didn't mean that. I was thinking of a child
specialist, who might be able to prescribe something that
would calm him down. I've heard Bromide is very good.
There's also the problem of . . . when you're not here. You
know, when . . .'

'I might have known you'd bring that up sooner or later,'
he snapped. 'It won't happen again, I promise you.'

Laura looked hard at him. 'You always say that but it's no
good. You're unable to keep a promise. Neil is also angry with
you because you married me. I really try not to behave as if
I was his own mother but he does resent me being here and
he won't do anything I ask.'

Walter seemed to crumble and she realized for the first
time how old he looked, although he was only fifty-two.

'Why don't we get a nice tutor for him? A young man he
can trust and who can keep an eye on him at the same time.
A tutor who could take Neil on educational trips and they
could go and see things like Edinburgh Castle and have fun
climbing Arthur's Seat, for instance. I don't believe he's happy
at school anyway. Isn't that a good idea, Walter?'

He nodded. 'Neil may just have been larking around, you
know. It was probably only a bit of fun and he didn't mean
any harm. He's lost his mother and I think he must be shown
a degree of leniency. One has to remember he's still only a
child,' he added, 'and too young to think things through.'

'A very dangerous child,' Laura replied tightly.

Six

'Your father has been a broken man since Eleanor's death,' Lady Rothbury told Laura sadly. 'I'm at my wits' end trying to cheer him up but nothing works. It's nearly two years now and life has to go on for the sake of the younger children, but he doesn't seem capable of putting his grief behind him. For some reason he seems to think the accident was all his fault, although I can't think why.'

Laura remained silent. There were moments when she felt tempted to tell her mother about her father's fight with some man who'd been unwelcome, but instinctively she felt it might make things worse. Her father must have had good reason for keeping quiet about it and a lot of other things, too. The question was, who was the stranger and what was the fight about?

'Papa has this crazy notion that we're all doomed,' her mother continued. 'He now says Rowan trees bring bad luck. Why should he think that?'

'I know Papa's superstitious but so are a lot of people,' Laura pointed out. 'Any crofter will tell you that you need to treat a Rowan tree with respect.'

'Ignorant people believe such rubbish but not people of our standing, my dear. Ignorant and uneducated lower-class people also tend to believe in witches and spells.' Then she looked thoughtfully out of the window. 'I've a good mind to get that tree cut down. Then your father might come to his senses.'

Laura looked at her in alarm. 'Don't do that, Mama. It would upset a lot of people.'

It was true that her father, usually so ebullient, had become silent and withdrawn. When he wasn't out riding with the ghillie he locked himself in his study these days, surrounded by all his dogs lying in a close pack around his desk, as if they sensed something and were protecting him. And at night he slept in his dressing room with the ever-faithful Megan slumped at his feet.

Sometimes his wife heard him shout abuse during the night at some phantom figure in his nightmares and he'd yell, 'Go away! Leave me alone.' But the next morning he denied even having dreams.

'I'm at my wits' end,' Lady Rothbury repeated, 'I've spoken to Doctor Andrews and he says Papa is just depressed and it's nothing to worry about, but I *am* worried. How can we entertain when he refuses to meet anyone? He won't even come to the table when it's just the family dining.'

Laura thought back to when Eleanor had died. The verdict at the inquest had declared her death was accidental and her mother had accepted it, because Lord Rothbury had destroyed the prayer Eleanor had written begging the Rowan tree to lift the curse, and he'd also removed the rope from her bedroom window before Dr Andrews and the police had arrived. It was Dr Andrews who strongly put forward the suggestion that Eleanor had been sleepwalking when she fell from her window and Papa had agreed with him at once. Then he'd turned and glared at Laura and her siblings. 'That explains everything, doesn't it?' he'd demanded with chilling ferocity. 'Eleanor was a somnambulist.'

None of them had the courage to argue, not even when they were questioned. They all stuck to the same sad little story.

'I'm sure,' Lizzie said later, 'that he's saying that to avoid a scandal.'

They all nodded. The alternatives were either to say she'd tried to get rid of the curse placed on the Fairbairns or that she had committed suicide while the balance of her mind was disturbed. This way everyone would have compassion for a family who had tragically lost a daughter while she was sleepwalking.

'I don't think it's right, though,' Beattie said robustly when they were all out walking in the grounds where no one could overhear them. 'She was a brave little girl even if her efforts to save us from being cursed were foolhardy and unwise. It was a gallant thing to do.'

'I agree,' Diana said at once. 'I feel with this silly sleepwalking story she's being denied the glory of her endeavour.'

'But she was crazy,' Georgie said, her voice heavy with criticism. 'Why didn't she just walk up to the tree and recite her prayer in broad daylight? Who would have seen her? And as long as they didn't know what she was saying, who would have cared? She was always so dramatic. I think she was trying to be the centre of attention, myself.'

Laura turned on her angrily. 'What a nasty thing to say! You're just jealous because everyone is talking about Eleanor and not about you.'

Georgie's face flushed scarlet. 'That's not true. I wouldn't be so stupid as to try and climb down a rope in the middle of the night. There are plenty of other ways of getting attention, if that was what she wanted.'

'You really are horrid, Georgie,' Lizzie exclaimed coldly. 'You think you're so superior to everyone else and we should all worship at the shrine of Georgina Fairbairn. Well, let me tell you something: you're jealous and spiteful and if you say one more obnoxious word about poor little Eleanor we'll all refuse to talk to you for one week.' She turned to Laura, Beattie and Diana. 'Do you all agree?'

There was a chorus of agreement.

Georgie tossed her head defiantly. 'You'll regret being so foul to me! Just you wait until I'm a duchess with a husband who's a millionaire and we live in a palace while the rest of you stay old maids.' Then she strode off back to Lochlee as the gales of laughter from the others carried on the wind.

Laura smiled with amusement. 'She's quite childish for seventeen, isn't she?' she murmured.

Lizzie was laughing but her eyes looked suddenly worried. 'We should get a move on, though,' she said with sudden seriousness. 'None of us are married yet and I'm already twenty-one.'

Laura's smile faded and a shadow crossed her face. 'I'm twenty but I'm never going to get married. How could I? I'll never find anyone like Rory,' she added quietly.

'You will, dearest,' Beattie said, giving her a hug. 'You're such a lovely person lots of men will want to marry you.'

'I might not want to marry them.'

'Well, I needn't start worrying yet,' Diana remarked smugly. 'I don't think you're allowed to get married when you're fifteen, are you?'

'Don't worry, Di. We'll leave a few Earls and Viscounts for you to marry once we've taken our pick,' Lizzie teased.

April arrived in a flurry of rain with brief snatches of sunshine and the promise that 1894 was going to have a good summer with bumper harvests. For the Earl of Rothbury, however, it spelled the doom and disaster he'd told everyone was blighting his family.

A loud roar from his study startled the family as they came out of the breakfast room.

'What on earth . . .?' exclaimed Lady Rothbury. The strangulated bellows continued and Lizzie rushed forward and flung open the study door. Her father was standing at his desk, holding an open copy of *The Times*.

'William! What on earth is the matter?' his wife scolded, sounding shocked. 'The servants will hear you.'

'Damn and blast the servants,' he raged, purple in the face.

'What on earth has happened?'

'Have you seen this?' He shook the newspaper at her. 'Have you seen what's going to happen? Then will you believe we're doomed?'

'William, please,' she remonstrated. 'Compose yourself!'

Laura watched her father's face crumple like an overtired child.

'Let's sit down quietly and you can tell us, Papa,' she coaxed.

He flashed a look of contempt in her direction. 'It doesn't bloody matter whether we're standing or sitting – this is going to ruin us,' he said. Then he looked at the newspaper again, as if he couldn't believe what he'd read.

Lady Rothbury seated herself by the fireplace while the five elder sisters sank into the chairs around her. The atmosphere bristled with tension as Lord Rothbury paced up and down.

'Tell us what the paper says, Papa,' Laura said softly.

He cleared his throat. 'This is a total calamity,' he began.

'In the House of Commons yesterday Sir William Harcourt delivered the budget and he's introduced a new tax, dammit! In fact, it's five new taxes. Death duties, they're called, and you'll find out all about them when I die, because the government is going to demand thousands of pounds from you.'

Lady Rothbury froze. 'From me?' she repeated as if she'd been personally insulted.

'From the estate,' he retorted impatiently. Looking down at the newspaper he read aloud, '"The five duties present an extraordinary specimen of tessellated legislation. The Probate duty, which began life as a stamp duty in 1694 . . ."' He flung the paper down in disgust. 'It goes on and on,' he continued, 'and by the look of it, you'll have to sell most of our land to pay these new death duties. Have you ever heard of anything so outrageous?'

'Has the government passed this bill?' Laura asked.

'They will if they haven't already. They are a bloody lot of scroungers.'

Lady Rothbury looked dazed and vacant. 'What exactly will it mean?'

'It means,' he replied with a vengeful glance in her direction, 'that when Freddie inherits Lochlee Castle and its valuable contents plus one-hundred-and-forty-five-thousand acres, a huge amount of money will have to be raised in order to pay this tax.'

'That's so unfair,' Diana exclaimed. 'Why should they pick on us?'

'Dear God.' Her father groaned at her stupidity.

Laura stepped in quickly. 'Not just us, Di. Tax will be based on a percentage of the total value of a property and its contents. Every landowner in the country will be affected. The Duke of Atholl, the Duke of Northumberland, the Duke of Westminster, the Earl of Fife. They'll all have to pay up when the head of the family dies,' she added as her eyes skimmed the newspaper.

'Then it's got nothing to do with our family being cursed?' Georgie asked.

Lady Rothbury looked stern. 'I've told you, that's a lot of nonsense. Of course we haven't been cursed.'

Her husband started pacing around the room again. 'For five hundred years my family has owned Lochlee and we've spent our hard-earned money filling it with beautiful furniture and paintings and a mass of silver, and we've farmed the land and provided employment for hundreds of people and now, when I'm gone, some snivelling little Inland Revenue clerk is going to go around valuing every bloody thing. It's criminal! It's the beginning of the end for landowners like us. Farming will be ruined, especially small holdings.' He shook his head in despair. 'By the time my great-grandchildren inherit this place there'll be nothing left for them except a few sticks and stones.'

Lady Rothbury looked at him in distress. 'You mean each time the head of the family dies, the tax man comes back for more?'

'What do you think it means?' he demanded with renewed anger. 'All the grand estates will eventually be whittled down to next to nothing.'

'Stop, William! It's too depressing. It will be years before you die so there's no point in worrying about it now. Freddie will look after everything when the time comes.'

'We shouldn't grumble,' Beattie said earnestly. 'We'll never be poor like some people. I read that in the East End of London most children go barefoot and sometimes only have a crust of bread to eat. Can you imagine it? We're fretting about having to sell some of our land one day while those families are sleeping six in a bed, in rat-infested hovels.'

Her mother glanced at her frostily. 'I hope you're not thinking of getting involved in good works?'

'It would make a change from husband-hunting,' Lord Rothbury remarked scathingly. 'Now that Freddie is sixteen it's time he learned how to run this place. I'll talk to his tutor tomorrow. He must be taught exactly what to do when I die. He'll have to have his wits about him then.'

Freddie, bored by his studies, sauntered over to the stables while his father was out riding. 'Hamish?' he called out.

The stable lad came running; his red hair was ruffled and his freckled face had a wary expression. 'Aye, M'Lud?' he replied in a broad Scottish accent.

Freddie nodded. As Viscount Fairbairn, heir to the Earl of Rothbury, he tried to insist that all the staff both inside the castle and out address him properly, although his parents had countermanded his order.

'Get me some more whisky,' he demanded, flicking a sovereign into Hamish's grubby hand. 'I want tobacco, too.'

'Aye, M'Lud.' Hamish did not dare object to being treated like a messenger because refusal to oblige in the past had led to a beating and the threat of dismissal. 'I'll tell my father you're a thief and not to be trusted,' Freddie had warned.

'Shall I be leaving it hidden in the usual place, M'Lud?'

'Where else?' Freddie turned and swaggered off arrogantly. 'And don't be long about it.'

Hamish didn't reply but raised two fingers and grimaced angrily at Freddie's receding figure. 'Scum,' he muttered under his breath. He swore he'd swing for him one day if his young lordship kept pushing him for favours – and they weren't always just for whisky and baccy. He recalled with a shudder how he'd realized some time ago that the young master was never going to be interested in girls. More than once he'd tried to grab Hamish, making the lad blush scarlet with fury and embarrassment. At the time Hamish had pretended that he didn't know what Freddie wanted, but if it happened again he swore he'd teach him a lesson.

'What have you done to your face, Freddie?' Lady Rothbury asked as they sat down to dinner two nights later.

He touched the deep graze on his cheek and his speech was slightly slurred. 'I tripped over one of Papa's damned dogs. It was wandering about on the drive,' he growled angrily.

'Don't swear, dear,' she said reprovingly. 'Are you all right? You sound funny.'

'I think I accidentally bit the inside of my cheek,' he replied swiftly.

'How could you be so clumsy?' Georgie protested.

'Was Papa with you?' Lizzie inquired.

'No. Why should he be?' Freddie's brow glistened with sweat and his hands shook slightly as he took a gulp of water.

'Because the dogs never leave Papa's side,' Laura explained in a reasonable voice. 'I've never seen any of them wandering around on their own.'

He shrugged extravagantly. 'What the hell does it matter?'

'Kindly stop swearing.' His mother spoke severely this time. 'Where are your manners?'

Lord Rothbury charged into the dining room at that moment. His wife looked critically at him. 'You're late for dinner, William.'

'Something dreadful has happened.' He sounded distressed as he took his place at the head of the table. 'They've just found Hamish, the stable lad, dead in one of the stalls.'

'Dead? Oh, his poor mother!' exclaimed Lady Rothbury, holding her table napkin to her mouth. 'Had he collapsed or something?'

Lord Rothbury shook his head. 'He'd been terribly badly injured, especially around the head.'

Henry, who had been listening in shocked silence, spoke croakingly. 'Had one of the horses kicked him? Juniper was lashing out a bit today when he was being saddled up but I've never known him to kick anyone before.'

Lord Rothbury's words hung heavily in the air, changing everything. 'Hamish was beaten to death by someone with a riding crop. Dear God! What will go wrong next? And you say we're not cursed?'

Lizzie sat on the edge of the bed as Laura lay propped up on pillows, discussing the latest tragedy before they went to bed. 'Hamish was such a nice lad and so good to his mother. Do you think someone had a grudge against him?'

Laura shook her head. 'No. He was popular with everyone. Good at his job, too.'

'The police will no doubt get to the bottom of it but what a tragedy! Poor Papa really does believe we're cursed, doesn't he?' said Lizzie.

Laura raised her arms and put her hands behind her head. 'Don't you think Freddie behaved very strangely at dinner?'

Lizzie looked at her sharply. 'In what way?'

'I'm sure he was drunk.'

'Where could he have got alcohol from? You know Papa makes sure none of us can get hold of even a glass of wine.'

Laura spoke as if she hadn't been listening. 'That yarn about tripping over one of the dogs? I don't believe a word of it.'

Lizzie looked shocked. 'What are you saying?'

'I'm sure there's more to this than meets the eye. I'm scared, Lizzie. How did he get that graze on his cheek?'

Lizzie shrugged. 'I think you're getting carried away. Whatever the outcome Mama will insist on the truth being kept secret to avoid a scandal and she'll make sure Hamish's mother is well looked after in case she tries to make trouble for us.'

'Lizzie, you're so cynical.'

'No, I'm just being realistic.'

'Have you heard what's happened?' Diana exclaimed, rushing into the library where her sisters were writing letters.

They looked up expectantly.

'Papa has been told the inquest held on poor Hamish found that he had been most severely beaten by a riding crop and then kicked in the head several times by a boot.'

Laura's eyes widened in shock. 'Do you mean he was murdered?'

Diana nodded. 'The police will be returning any minute now to examine the riding crops in the stables. I suppose they're looking for blood or something.'

'I can't believe it!' Lizzie exclaimed. 'Who on earth would want to kill Hamish? He was such a gentle lad, and only a year older than Freddie. His poor mother – what can she be feeling now? It's one thing if someone is kicked by a horse, but to be murdered is terrible.'

'Does Mama know?' Georgie asked.

'Yes. She's in a terrible state. I afraid she's more worried about the scandal than anything else and how it will affect the family.'

'She can't be,' Diana said sadly. 'It's got nothing to do with any of us.'

'You know what boys are like. He must have got into a fight with one of the other lads. Or maybe someone tried to break into the stables and steal a horse and he tried to stop them?' Georgie commented.

'This is terrible,' Beattie wailed as she listened to the others. 'What is Papa going to do about it?'

Lizzie spoke calmly. 'There's nothing we can do except look after his mother. She's the one who must be in a terrible state. Imagine! Your child – your son – is murdered while he's at work.'

'But we will be the centre of attention and gossip,' Beattie pointed out. 'The police will want to interview everyone on the estate, I suppose.'

Laura and Lizzie looked at each, thinking the same thought but fearful of giving voice to it.

The little ones had been put to bed and Lady Rothbury came to kiss them goodnight, as she did every evening.

'Mama! Mama!' Alice, Flora and Catriona clamoured, reaching out to her with eager little hands. They reminded her of little angels with their long, dark brown hair and sweet faces. Dressed in white flannel nightgowns to their feet they put their arms around her neck, kissed her cheeks and wanted to sit on her lap. She felt a pang of sadness that they couldn't stay like that for ever. Little children were so easy to please, so charming and obedient, and then they grew up and everything changed. The closeness was gone. She worried about her older children all the time. Would the boys do well with their studies? Would the girls make good marriages? None of them were married yet; Lizzie was already twenty-one and she feared that Laura had decided she'd never marry because there'd never be another Rory.

Sighing nostalgically, she gave her little angels another kiss as they snuggled under their eiderdowns. 'Goodnight, my darlings. Sleep well.'

As she passed the schoolroom and the boys' rooms she called out, 'Freddie, Henry – I hope you're getting ready for dinner?'

'Yes, Mama,' Henry answered obediently. She particularly loved her younger son. He was affectionate and yet respectful and she secretly wished he'd been William's heir. Then she hurried to her own quarters to get changed for dinner.

★   ★   ★

'William! William!' Lady Rothbury's voice echoed loudly along the wide picture gallery as she ran out of her room. 'William! Come quickly!' she shrieked in panic. Several bedroom doors were flung open. Beattie, Laura and Diana were the first to rush to her side.

'Mama! What's happened?' asked Laura. Their mother looked demented and she was wringing her hands.

'Get your father! Make him come quickly,' she said, her voice breaking.

'What the devil's going on?' Lord Rothbury boomed as he came up the stairs towards her.

'Something terrible,' she exclaimed.

'What's happened?' He'd turned pale. 'For God's sake! Tell me what's happened!'

'They've gone! Everything's gone!' Lady Rothbury shrieked as she hurried along the corridor, followed by her husband. 'Someone has been in our bedroom.'

Doors were flung wide open along the corridor and Lizzie was the first to reach her mother.

'Mama, what is it?' she asked as she and her sisters gathered around. They'd never seen her in such a state.

'Everything's gone!' she repeated, and her face crumpled as she started to weep.

'*What's* gone?' Diana demanded, while her father strode on down the corridor to the master bedroom.

'All the family jewels!'

'You mean they've been stolen?' Beattie asked, aghast. 'But I thought you kept them in a locked chest in your bedroom?'

'Yes, but it's been broken into. The tiara, the diamond necklace, your great-grandmother's emerald and diamond stomacher! Oh, God, this is a calamity! There's nothing left.'

'It's not your fault,' Diana said soothingly.

Lady Rothbury wiped her eyes with a small lace-edged handkerchief. 'Papa always said I should keep the jewellery downstairs in the strong room with the silver but it's such a business getting it out every time and I do like to choose what I want to wear every day.'

A minute later Lord Rothbury came charging back, looking

enraged. 'How did this happen?' he roared. 'The jewel case is empty.'

'I don't know what happened.' She raised her tear-stained face. 'I'm sorry, William. Please don't be angry with me . . .' She stopped, unable to continue.

'Someone must have broken into the castle during the day,' Georgie said bluntly.

He turned on her with fury. 'How could anyone have broken into it when our bedroom is on the first floor and the whole place is crawling with people?' He strode back down the corridor again and they all followed in shocked silence. When they entered the room they stood still, trying to take in what had happened.

On the far side the large stout oak chest stood in front of a wall hung with a large tapestry. The lid was flung open; the four layers of fitted trays which were covered with green felt had been thrown to one side. The awful emptiness of what had once held magnificent jewels appalled them all and for a moment they could only stand and stare.

'Who could have done this?' Lizzie exclaimed at last.

Laura looked at the empty trays with deep sadness. 'Everything *has* gone,' she murmured while Lady Rothbury sank down on to her carved four-poster bed, unable to stand any more.

'When did you last open this chest?' her husband demanded.

Lady Rothbury looked at him with agonized eyes. 'This morning. I wanted to wear my pearls today and I know that I locked it afterwards and hid the key in the usual place.'

'Who else knows where you hid the key?'

'Only you, William.'

'Where did you hide it?' Beattie asked curiously.

'In that cubbyhole behind the sliding panel by the bed. No one knows about it except Papa and me.'

'Quite obviously someone else *did* know,' Lord Rothbury fumed.

Laura turned to her father. 'Do you think it may have something to do with Hamish's death? Perhaps someone did this as an act of revenge on our family?'

'Hamish only had a widowed mother,' Beattie pointed out.

'The servants would have noticed a stranger so it's obviously someone in the castle who did this. The question is, who?'

'Stop prattling on, girl,' William bellowed. 'That lad's death had nothing whatsoever to do with anyone in the family, so let's have no more stupid ideas. We must get the police at once.'

Lizzie had a sudden thought. 'Should we check the silver in the strong room, Papa?'

Her father looked horrified. 'I'll go and see but McEwan keeps the keys on his person at all times.' He sighed gustily. 'God Almighty. When will it ever end?'

After the police had been, strongly suggesting that at first glance it looked like an inside job, they left, saying they'd be back in the morning.

'Don't let anyone touch anything in the bedroom,' the chief constable warned as he left.

It was late when the family sat down to dinner; the beef had been overcooked and so had the vegetables, which put His Lordship in a worse temper than ever.

'Where is everyone?' he demanded, glancing down the table.

Henry hurried into the dining room, apologized for being late and sat down quickly. 'I'm afraid I lost track of time,' he confessed.

'Where's your brother?' Lord Rothbury demanded.

'I don't know, Papa. I've hardly seen him all day.'

'What do you mean, boy? You don't know?'

Henry shook his head. 'I don't know where he is.'

'You'd think all the commotion this evening would have brought him out of his room. Freddie is getting lazy, Margaret,' he said, addressing his wife as if it were all her fault. Then he turned to the butler. 'McEwan, send someone up to Lord Fairbairn's room to tell him to come down to dinner immediately.'

'Yes, M'Lord.'

'Are the police going to take all our fingerprints tomorrow, Papa?' Beattie asked.

'Don't be stupid. Why should they take the fingerprints of anyone in the family? We didn't steal our own jewels,' he added mockingly.

'Of course not,' Lady Rothbury murmured as she toyed with her poached salmon. Her heart was actually aching as if she'd been punched in the chest, and she felt cold and shivery. Her jewellery – her beautiful jewellery which she so loved, especially the pieces that were of sentimental value – had all been taken and she was literally heartbroken. How could anyone have done something so cruel? May God forgive his sins, she said to herself, but I for one will never be able to.

A few minutes later McEwan came back and there was something urgent and yet reluctant as he spoke to the Earl in a low voice. 'M'Lord, it might be better if you came into the hall,' he murmured.

'What's that? Speak up, McEwan.'

'One of the chambermaids has been up to His Lordship's room. She has something to tell you, M'Lord but maybe not in front of the ladies.'

'What is happening, William?' his wife asked from the other end of the table.

'God knows,' he groaned, rising to his feet. 'If he's got a girl in his room I'll kill him.'

The sisters looked at each other with a mixture of interest and alarm, while Henry remained impassive.

Ruby the chambermaid was standing in the middle of the great hall, looking terrified. Her hands were trembling and she was trying not to cry.

'Tell His Lordship what you've just told me,' McEwan commanded.

She gave a loud sniff. 'Pardon, M'Lord.'

'It's all right,' Lord Rothbury said with unusual kindness. 'Just tell me what you found in my son's room.'

She spoke in a low voice. 'His clothes are all in a heap in the corner and his boots too, and they are all covered in blood. There's no sign of him and it looks like he's gone away, M'Lord.'

There was something akin to fear in His Lordship's eyes. 'What do you mean, gone away?'

'Left 'ome, M'Lord. His wardrobe was all open and it looked like 'e's taken some things with him.'

Lord Rothbury stood stock still for a moment, then without

another word he strode off across the hall to his study. A moment later he opened the bottom left-hand drawer of his vast mahogany desk. It took just another few seconds for his worst fears to be realized. Freddie's passport was missing.

'Dear God!' Lord Rothbury groaned. 'I always feared Freddie was a wild card but not in a million years did I think he'd do a thing like this!'

'You *can't* tell the police, William!' Margaret Rothbury pleaded.

'How the hell can we keep it a secret?' he raged. 'Everyone on the estate will know by tomorrow morning about the death of Hamish, the stolen jewellery, the bloodstained clothes and then Freddie's disappearance; how can we possibly keep it a secret?'

'How could he have done this to us?' She'd aged ten years in the last few hours as she tried to take in the appalling tragedy that had enveloped her family.

Sleep was impossible. At three o'clock in the morning she and her husband lay close together in their vast bed and yet a million miles apart in other ways. She could see no plausible way out of this appalling mess and yet reporting what had happened to the police seemed to be an unforgivable option.

'The sins of the fathers . . .' the Earl quoted as if he was talking to himself.

'Your father didn't commit any sins, William.'

'No, he didn't. He was a good man.'

'Well then, who?'

He didn't answer but pretended to have fallen asleep.

Lochlee Castle stood defiantly against the tsunami of scandal that engulfed it and the Fairbairn family in the ensuing months. Freddie had not been traced and it was reluctantly assumed he'd fled the country, although every shipping line had been on the alert to look out for him. One of the photographs taken of Freddie standing with the rest of the family in the garden at the time of Laura's engagement had been circulated to all the newspapers. The report that the 'young Viscount Fairbairn is being hunted by the police in connection with the murder of a stable boy at his Family Seat' made sordid reading in the downmarket newspapers, accompanied by further reports that he'd also stolen the family jewels.

For the first time in five hundred illustrious years shame was being heaped on their heads, besmirching their reputation for ever. From the moment Freddie's bloodstained clothes were found abandoned in his room, it was obvious to everyone that he'd killed Hamish, then stolen the jewellery and scarpered. After the initial shock the whole family had reluctantly come round to accepting Freddie's guilt. Even his mother.

As howling winds swept across the now-frozen grouse moors the atmosphere inside the castle was no warmer. Lady Rothbury had retired to her own quarters since the disappearance of Freddie, refusing to join the rest of the family for meals and sitting by the fire in a deeply distressed state of mind.

Meanwhile, her husband's depression took the form of being angry one moment and wallowing in guilt the next, although he refused to admit it. He talked more than ever about the family being doomed and how he only expected the worst.

'I know it's to do with the fight we overheard him having with someone,' Lizzie insisted. 'I tried to get it out of him but he refused to talk about it. If only we could find out who it was we might be able to get to the bottom of things.'

Alice, Flora and Catriona were saved from the gloom and constant sense of anxiety that pervaded the castle because they were all under six years old and looked after entirely by Nanny and her two nursery maids. Their only contact with their mother was when they were taken to her private sitting room after tea every day. Lady Rothbury found it hard to play with them and usually resorted to reading them a story before Nanny collected them again to get ready for bed.

Henry was also rather withdrawn and even his kindly tutor was unable to get much out of him.

'Did you have the faintest inkling that Freddie was going to do a runner?' Mr Stuart asked one day, knowing that Henry had told the police he neither knew nor had suspected anything.

Henry shrugged and averted his gaze. 'We weren't that close,' he replied vaguely.

'You must miss him, surely?'

'Not really. He was always putting me down.'

Mr Stuart remembered very well how Freddie, whom he had never liked, would taunt Henry about being 'bookish' and told everyone Henry was 'soft' because he didn't particularly enjoy 'the slaughter on the moors', as he described the shooting season.

Secretly, Mr Stuart shared the view of all those who worked at Lochlee that Freddie would never come back. To him personally it was a case of good riddance.

The five older sisters now depended even more on each other and spent most of their time together endlessly talking about the tragedy.

'I wonder where Freddie is now?' Laura surmised as they sat huddled around the library fireplace one evening.

'Perhaps he stowed away on a ship,' Diana said.

Beattie frowned, thinking. After a moment she declared triumphantly, 'I've just remembered something. I read in a newspaper about a new ship owned by the Nourse Line called the *Clyde*. It was launched from the Clyde Side near Glasgow earlier in the year. I think it was in July. He could have got away on that! He ran away at the beginning of July, didn't he? I bet he used a bit of jewellery as a bribe to get on board. A member of the crew might have agreed to let Freddie be a stowaway, and if the jewellery was sold in a foreign country who would know?'

'Isn't that a bit too convenient?' Georgie asked critically. 'It's more likely Freddie disappeared down to London, sold the jewellery there and then caught a ship from Southampton, perhaps to America?'

'I have a feeling they'll never catch up with him no matter where he is,' Lizzie spoke seriously, 'and I don't think any of us want him caught, including Mama and Papa. He can never come back now. Not after killing Hamish.'

'If he did return, would he really be hung at the gallows?' Diana asked in a horrified voice.

Beattie shuddered. 'Of course he would.' She gave a loud sigh. 'How could he have done it? Why did he want to hurt Hamish in the first place?'

Laura looked at her sister and her eyes had a haunted expression. 'Knowing Freddie, if he didn't get his own way there was always trouble. We'll never know what happened between them but whatever it was, Hamish paid with his life and I can never forgive Freddie for that.'

Diana said hopefully, 'Perhaps Freddie was acting in self-defence?'

'I doubt it.' Lizzie's voice was as brittle as an autumn leaf. 'I heard Papa say the same as what you told us, Di – that Hamish had died from an unmitigated beating with a horse whip and several heavy kicks to the head.'

'Don't!' Diana begged.

'It's a tragic waste,' Georgie agreed. 'Freddie had everything he could ever have wanted and he's thrown it all away.'

'Maybe if they do catch him,' Lizzie suggested, 'he'll say it was a case of mistaken identity, but he panicked and fled the country because he was scared of being accused.'

'I doubt if even the best barrister would try and take that line,' Laura protested. 'I believe they had a fight and Freddie lost his temper. I also think he'd secretly watched Mama take the key to her jewellery chest from behind the sliding panel in her room. Otherwise how did he know where it was hidden? I'm afraid he's as guilty as hell and I don't think a jury would find otherwise.'

'What went so wrong?' Lizzie asked. 'I remember when he was born. I was four at the time but I distinctly recall Papa thanking God he'd had a son at last. I was quite put out at the time. I thought, what's so special about having a boy? But he was such a sweet baby I wouldn't have imagined in a hundred years that he'd turn out like this.'

'I remember feeling the same when Henry was born,' Georgie admitted. 'Now Papa has only got one son.'

'Freddie's still Papa's heir, though, isn't he?'

The others nodded. 'If Freddie doesn't reappear in the next seven years he'll be legally declared dead. Then Henry can inherit everything.'

'Except the family jewels.' Lizzie sounded bitter. She'd always hoped to wear one of the diamond tiaras when she got married.

'I'd like Henry to inherit,' Laura admitted.

'I think we all would, including Mama and Papa,' Lizzie agreed quietly. The others said nothing. The enormity of what had happened had cast a blight over the whole family.

Seven

Lasswade Hall, 1909

It had started again, but this time the nightmare was worse. It had escalated so quickly and unpleasantly that Laura had not had the time to give the staff a few days off as she usually did when the rampaging began. More importantly, Caroline was still up in the nursery with Nanny and the last thing she wanted was for her child to witness the horror . . .

Still in her *peignoir* because the disturbance had started at dawn, Laura rushed down to the hall where they'd recently installed a new and marvellous invention – the telephone. Unaccustomed to using it, she gingerly took the earpiece off its hook before leaning towards the mouthpiece, which was screwed to the wall.

'Can I help you?' she heard an operator enquire.

Laura rapidly told them in a low voice so she wouldn't be overheard the telephone number of Diana's house, which was some thirty miles away. All the while she was watching the door to the study where thumps and bumps and blaspheming growls could be heard. Fearful that the door would suddenly burst open she gripped the earpiece tightly and prayed the operator would connect her quickly.

Then she heard the butler's voice. 'Lord Kelso's residence.'

'I'd like to speak to Lady Diana Kelso, please. It's rather urgent. This is Lady Laura Leighton-Harvey speaking.'

A few minutes later she heard Diana's still-girlish tones. 'Is that you, Laura, darling?'

'Di, I've got to be quick. I'll tell you later but I can't talk now. Listen, if Nanny brings Caroline over to your place could you put them up for a few days?' Laura's voice shook and she kept looking nervously at the closed study door across the hall where the noise was increasing.

'Are you ill?' Diana queried in alarm.

'No, but things are rather difficult here at the moment. I don't want Caroline to be in the midst of it.'

Diana sighed. 'Oh, Laura! Is Neil at it again? I thought he'd been all right since you got that nice tutor for him?'

'Neil's fine. This is something different.'

'Poor you! Staff can be a real problem, can't they? Of course she can come and stay. It's no problem and Nicolas and Louise would love to have her as a playmate. Tell Nanny to bring play clothes for the garden. We've just had a climbing frame made for the children and they adore it.'

'Thank you, Di. I'm really grateful.'

'Are you sure you're all right?' Diana asked in concern. 'You sound really rather desperate.'

'I'll tell you later. I've got to go now.' Laura hurriedly hung the receiver back on its brass hook and then fled as she heard the handle of the study door being opened. There was not a moment to be lost. Running up the two flights of stairs to the night nursery, she spoke to Nanny who was giving Caroline her breakfast.

'Muzzie!' the child said in delight, clapping her hands together.

'Hello, my darling.' Laura planted a kiss on her child's head then turned to Nanny, who was already familiar with the 'problem', as Lady Laura so euphemistically called it. She'd begun to hope there would be no more 'problems' in the household, for everything had been fine for over two years now, but obviously the devil had struck again. The only thing she didn't understand was Lady Laura's refusal to admit to her family what she had to endure from time to time. It was no secret among the servants, although they were sworn to secrecy. Was it pride that prevented Lady Laura telling her family that something was seriously wrong?

Laura now spoke quickly without making eye contact. 'My sister, Lady Diana, has invited you and Caroline to stay with them for a few days at Cranley Court, so I'm getting Gordon to drive you both over right away. She said to pack play clothes for Caroline. Is that all right, Nanny?'

'Yes, M'Lady. That will be very nice.' Nanny had never been in a motor and, although it was a chunky-looking thing called a Stanley, she rather fancied the new chauffeur so perked up at the thought of the journey.

Laura then went down the back stairs where she found Hobbs in the silver pantry. She took a deep breath and spoke bluntly. 'The problem has started again. Lock up all the drink, please.'

'I'll see to it right away, M'Lady.' He took pains to avoid making eye contact.

'I'd also like you to tell Gordon to bring the motor round to take Nanny and Caroline to stay with Lady Kelso,' she added.

'Very well, M'Lady.'

At that moment they heard the study door burst open and a voice shrieked, 'Hobbs? Where the devil are you?'

Laura swiftly climbed the back stairs again to return to her bedroom, knowing Hobbs wouldn't respond. He knew better. All the staff knew better. They'd all slip away from the house in an hour or so and not return until the crisis was over. Only Hobbs would remain to fulfil his duties and stand guard if necessary.

This was the moment when she felt the most alone. Her sisters had begged her not to marry Walter, saying she knew nothing about him, and they accused her of rushing into marriage because she was twenty-nine and this might be her last chance.

If only she'd heeded their caution. If only she'd waited a bit longer as they'd advised. Instead she'd seen the other side of his Jekyll and Hyde character as it lurched from a charming, loving and compassionate man into a raging alcoholic who ended up in hospital every time. Laura had even learned that in the past he'd been detained more than once in an asylum whilst suffering from delirium tremens.

Looking back, Laura remembered how Priscilla Leighton-Harvey had looked very strained at times when she'd come to have a dress fitted and had remarked that her husband was 'away on business again' so had been unable to escort her to some social functions. Only later, after they were married, did Laura realize that Walter had never been in business in his life. Yet she still couldn't let her sisters know the private hell she suffered from time to time. They had all made such happy marriages to such successful men, and being the second eldest she felt she and Lizzie had to be good examples to the younger sisters of what a loyal and loving wife should be.

Yet at moments like this she wondered how much more suffering she could endure without their knowing and without their support. When Walter didn't drink he was a perfect husband and she treasured the times, always hoping they'd last for ever, but then he'd have a drink – one small drink – and be unable to stop as he crashed around the house, knocking things over and causing fearful destruction. Most damaged of all was Neil, who was spending more and more time at his Aunt Rowena's, who could ensure the child had a peaceful routine.

It was a long day and Laura spent it in her bedroom listening to the yells of fury and the screams of rage as Walter searched for alcohol and tried to break down the wine cellar door.

Then there were long silences which she found almost worse as they gave vent to her vivid imaginations. At one point she left her room and went on to the landing to listen but all was still. After a bit she returned to her room and lay down on the bed, exhausted. Then she heard a dog barking and howling as if in distress and she sprang to her feet, shaking all over. They didn't have a dog. She'd sworn never to keep dogs after a lifetime of being surrounded by them. The hideous noise was coming nearer. Then she heard scratching on her bedroom door and the handle shook. Too late, she realized she'd forgotten to lock it. Picking up the little mahogany chair by her dressing table, she held it with its legs, pointing to the door which had now sprung open.

Laura barely recognized the blind-looking man who was on his hands and knees growling like an animal. Dishevelled and bloated, his filthy clothes were stinking of methylated spirits while from his swollen mouth a trickle of black ink dripped down his chin on to the carpet.

'Walter!' Her voice was filled with despair as he slumped unconscious at her feet.

'I always knew something was not quite right,' Georgie claimed robustly as soon as she arrived at Lasswade Hall, where she and her siblings had turned up on hearing that Walter was desperately ill in hospital and might not survive.

'Well, I didn't,' Lizzie said comfortingly, placing her hand on Laura's arm. 'I know I was against you marrying him at the time but whenever I saw you together I thought you looked very happy.'

'We were . . . we *are* happy. Except when he starts drinking,' Laura protested, determined not to cry but thankful she didn't have to pretend in front of her family any more that everything was perfect.

'How long has this been going on?' Beattie enquired. 'Had you no idea at all that he was a drunkard when you got married?'

'Of course I didn't know,' she retorted. 'Something triggers his need for alcohol and he can't help himself.'

'Then he must be weak,' Georgie said disparagingly.

'No, it's not like that.' Laura spoke angrily now. 'The doctor explained the difference between people who like the occasional drink and people who have a compulsion to drink until . . .' Her voice faltered.

'You must be so worried about him and I know how much you really love him,' Diana said sympathetically. 'Will he be in hospital for long?'

'I don't know. He's very ill.' For once she sounded defeated. Walter had been unconscious when the ambulance had taken him to the nearest hospital. They'd told her to go home and said that they would let her know when he regained consciousness. This was the worst 'attack', as she called it, that he'd ever had and she worried desperately about the future. He was no longer a young man with the stamina to cope with vast quantities of alcohol, not to mention poison like methylated spirits and bottles of ink.

'Oh, Laura, darling.' Diana stroked her arm. 'I'm so sorry and I think you've been wonderful the way you've coped for the past few years. I don't know how you've done it. Why didn't you tell us before? You know we'd have helped if you needed anything.'

Beattie, pregnant with her first baby, echoed Diana's sentiments. 'It must have been agonizing for you. No wonder you always had to send Caroline away when it happened.'

'You were a friend of Walter's first wife, weren't you?' Lizzie asked. 'Did she never mention his drinking?'

'Why should she? I expect she was as ashamed as I've been, although I now realize it's an illness and not an indulgence on Walter's part.'

'Tell us what you're going to do, Laura?' Diana said peaceably.

'What can I do? He's Caroline's father and I still love him. I wish someone had really warned me, though. His sister could so easily have said something but I suppose she wanted him to get married again so Neil would have a stepmother. John Osborne could have warned me, but I suppose as he's Walter's best friend and they were at Fettes College together, his loyalty to Walter came first.'

'Are they still friends?'

'Yes. John is an accountant, though not Walter's accountant. He's an unofficial advisor on stocks and shares and all that. Whenever Walter falls apart from drinking, John keeps an eye on his finances. Arranges the bills to be paid and makes sure I get the housekeeping allowance. I don't know how I'd manage without him.'

'He's lucky to have a friend like that,' Lizzie remarked.

Laura nodded. 'John is wonderful and so nice.'

'Walter ought to go around with a warning label hanging from his neck,' Georgie complained. 'Even you, Laura, weren't desperate enough to marry a raging alcoholic.'

'Unlike you, I wasn't desperate at all,' Laura retorted coldly. 'I already had a life of my own and a successful career, which is more than you have.'

Eight

Lochlee Castle, 1895

Laura flung her arms around Lizzie. 'I'm so happy for you,' she exclaimed. 'Humphrey is one of the nicest men in the world.'

'I know.' Lizzie beamed, looking once again at her ruby and diamond engagement ring. 'I can't believe how lucky I am. Who would have thought we'd meet lying on our stomachs in the middle of Dumfrieshire whilst deer stalking? I didn't even want to go and stay with the Buccleuchs but Mama insisted and now thank goodness she did.'

'You were obviously destined to meet.' Diana sighed. 'It's just so romantic.'

'Don't tell me Lizzie didn't know what she was doing,' Georgie scoffed. 'Mama and Lizzie have a natural born instinct, like bats in the dark, to head for men with titles. He's only a Bart but you will be Lady Garding and aren't you going to love it!'

Lizzie flushed with annoyance. 'I didn't know he was Sir Humphrey when we were introduced. I don't suppose he knew I was Lady Elizabeth either. You're the one in this family who is fixated on titles, Georgie. We've got our own. Why should we need to marry for someone else's?'

Georgie shrugged and tossed her head angrily. She knew she'd inherited her father's heavy jaw and she was also painfully aware of her plumpness compared to the slender elegance of her sisters. Beside the others she was clumsy and ungainly but she couldn't help it. The only satisfaction she got in life was trying to pull her sisters down a peg or two but it rarely worked. She was the one who always ended up feeling inferior.

'When are you planning to get married?' Beattie asked Lizzie.

'Humphrey suggested October. That gives us six months to get everything organized.' Lizzie's face glowed with happiness.

'We'd better get Mrs Armitage to come earlier this year because she'll have to make my wedding dress.'

Laura's heart lurched painfully and she looked away. This was what she'd been saying nearly four years ago when she'd been about to marry Rory. By now they'd probably have had a couple of children and be having a lovely life dividing their time between his house in the south of England and London. They'd made so many lovely plans and her longing to be married to him had consumed her at the time.

She clenched her fists now and dug her nails into the palms of her hands to prevent the upsurge of tears that threatened to spoil the happy occasion for Lizzie. Oh, but how desperately she still missed Rory and the closeness she'd never experienced with anyone else. They'd had so many mutual interests and likes and dislikes, but most of all she missed the laughter that ran through their relationship like a sparkling stream. Gone. All gone. She was no longer the light-hearted and vivacious girl he'd proposed to four years ago and she missed that part of herself as much as she missed him.

Knowing what she was thinking, Diana flung her arm around Laura's shoulders in silent sympathy.

To lighten the moment Laura said jokingly, 'We'll never speak to you again if you don't invite us all to be bridesmaids.'

'Mrs Armitage is going to have her work cut out this year and Mama is going to want a special outfit for the wedding, too.'

The girls all started babbling merrily, knowing their parents would lay on a splendid wedding for their eldest daughter, each of them wondering who would marry next. Except for Laura. For she knew it would never happen now.

The loud *tock* of the mallet hitting the wooden ball through the iron hoop in the grass until it hit the peg was followed by a cheer from Henry, while the girls clapped in approval. Croquet had become the rage in the Fairbairn family that spring ever since Sir Humphrey Gardin had presented Lord and Lady Rothbury with the game as a thank-you present for inviting him to stay most weekends at Lochlee since his engagement to Lizzie had been announced.

'Let's have another match, old feller,' Henry exclaimed excitedly.

'We could play against Lizzie and Laura this time.'

'Aren't you afraid of being beaten?' Laura asked spiritedly.

'We don't mind allowing you girls to win occasionally,' Humphrey teased.

'*Allow?*' Lizzie mocked. 'Such cheek!'

The two girls threw off their capes and picked up the mallets.

'We'll slaughter you,' Laura challenged.

'This I've got to see,' Beattie chortled from the iron bench where she and her mother were watching.

Lady Rothbury laughed indulgently. After the horror of the past year and still no sight or news of Freddie's whereabouts, it was a relief to sit in the sunshine again and watch her family playing happily together, especially with her future son-in-law.

Diana and Georgie came out of the castle a few minutes later, glad to see their mother joining in the family activities once more.

'We should get the tennis court mowed so we can start playing again,' Diana suggested.

'We don't usually have such lovely weather in April,' Lady Rothbury pointed out. 'I do hope it doesn't mean we'll have a wet summer.'

'Why should we?' Georgie said. 'The weather in Scotland is sometimes better than it is in England.'

'Not often.'

'Oh, Mama! Don't always look on the dark side. What we really have to hope for is a fine October for Lizzie's wedding. I love it best in the autumn when everything turns gold,' exclaimed Laura.

Lady Rothbury smiled serenely for once. 'I'm sure it will be a golden autumn.'

McEwan came hurrying across the lawn towards them looking flustered. 'M'Lady,' he said breathlessly. 'His Lordship has had an accident. A bad one, I'm afraid.'

Everything stopped at that moment. They all looked at him and Lady Rothbury started trembling. 'What's happened?'

'His Lordship has been thrown from his horse. They're bringing him home on a stretcher.'

Before he'd finished speaking Henry and Humphrey had dropped their mallets and were racing towards the castle entrance, followed by the girls.

Lady Rothbury got to her feet with difficulty and nearly stumbled, but McEwan managed to catch her by the arm.

'Allow me, M'Lady. Someone has gone to fetch Doctor Andrews. I'm sure he'll come as fast as he can.'

As soon as she saw his face and the strange angle of his body as he was laid carefully on their bed her worst fears were realized.

'William,' she whispered brokenly.

'I'm done for,' he whispered, his eyes closed.

'Where does it hurt?'

There was a long pause between his words. 'Nowhere. Nothing.'

'I think he's broken his neck,' Sir Humphrey whispered, leaning forward. Henry was holding his father's hand while Laura and Lizzie with Beattie, Georgie and Diana clustered around the bed, their faces white and drawn with concern. The Earl, normally so strong and domineering, so powerful and formidable, lay broken as he drifted in and out of consciousness.

When Dr Andrews arrived he quickly examined Lord Rothbury and confirmed their worst fears. Drawing Lady Rothbury to one side, he spoke in a low voice. 'I think the wee girls should be brought down from the nursery to say their goodbyes,' he suggested.

Lady Rothbury nodded, unable to speak. Of all the horrors she'd had to face in the past, this was the worst thing that had ever happened to her. 'Get Nanny to bring down Alice, Flora and Catriona,' she whispered to Lizzie, whose eyes flew wide open with shock.

'Is it as bad as that?' she asked hoarsely.

Her mother nodded, unable to speak before returning to her husband's side again.

As if he'd sensed her presence, he opened his eyes and tried to speak.

'I'm here, William,' she whispered.

'Alone.' His voice was faint but urgent.

'Do you want to speak to me alone?' she asked.

He made an effort to move his head but then his face screwed up in agony and he let out a groan.

Sir Humphrey stood on the other side of the bed. 'Would you like us all to wait outside for a few minutes?' he whispered.

'I don't want . . .' Lizzie began.

He put his arm around her and said softly, 'I think your parents would like a few minutes alone, darling. Then you can all come back.'

She nodded and the family trooped out on to the landing while Henry quietly closed their bedroom door. Then he turned to Sir Humphrey.

'He's not going to make it, is he?' His voice shook but he did his best to be brave in front of all his sisters, who were now openly weeping.

Sir Humphrey whispered, 'I fear not.'

Alone with William in their big bedroom where she'd conceived and given birth to eleven of their children, Margaret Rothbury lay down beside him for the last time. Looking into his face, she laid her hand on his shoulder. 'We're alone now, William.'

His eyes opened again and he spoke slowly and with obvious effort. 'I have a son, Margaret. He was born a month before Freddie.'

Her eyes widened and she frowned. 'You have two sons, William. Freddie and Henry.'

'Yes. Yes.' He sounded agitated now. 'I have another son born out of wedlock. You mustn't let him seize Lochlee. D'you understand? His mother is Dolly Kirkbride from the village. I was drunk one night and she . . .'

Margaret felt cold and sick, not wanting to believe it was true and that William was confused.

'Don't worry . . .'

He rallied angrily. 'Listen!' His voice was harsh and guttural as he made a desperate attempt to speak again. 'He cursed us all, Margaret, when he was here a few years ago. That's why we're doomed. Everything has gone wrong ever since.' His voice faded to a whisper. 'You must stop him when I'm gone.'

Her throat was dry and the beating of her heart was suffocating her. 'Where is he?' she managed to ask.

'He lives in a bothy on the banks of Loch Lorne. His name is Douglas Kirkbride and I fathered the Devil himself.'

There was silence. William's eyes were closed again and he lay still now, deathly pale.

'I've always loved you,' she murmured, with her lips close to his. There was no answer. Struggling to get off the bed, she called out urgently, 'Lizzie! Laura!'

They came rushing back into the room with the others, followed by Henry and Sir Humphrey.

'Is Papa . . .?' Laura asked fearfully.

'No,' Lizzie replied, bending closely over him to feel a faint breath on her cheek. 'Fetch all the others. They ought to be here.'

The family clustered around the bed and the older girls held Catriona and Flora in their arms while Alice, who was ten, sat on her mother's lap. Lying by Lord Rothbury's feet, faithful to the end, was his favourite dog, Megan.

No one spoke as they kept watch until the local church bell chimed four on this spring afternoon in 1895, when William Angus Henry Fairbairn, seventh Earl of Rothbury, finally slipped silently away into the next world.

'It has to be said,' Georgie remarked in her usual blunt way, 'that it's a pity Papa didn't die two years ago. Then we wouldn't have had to pay all these ruinous death duties.'

It may have been what a lot of people were thinking in the tumultuous weeks that followed Lord Rothbury's funeral, but in front of his grieving family it was met with horror and cries of 'How can you say such a thing!'

Although Freddie had now officially succeeded his father as the eighth Earl, Henry, in his brother's absence, had taken over the complications of dealing with lawyers and accountants, helped and guided by Sir Humphrey who, being older, was more experienced in such matters, while Lady Rothbury retired once more to her room, unable to face the difficulties that lay ahead.

'Once probate has been granted, and as your late husband's will is very straightforward, there are no problems there,' Sir Humphrey assured her. 'Now it is a matter of valuing his assets;

that is the castle and its contents, the land and the houses on it, the grouse moors, the home farm – everything your family possesses, in other words. Only then will we know how much you will owe to the Inland Revenue.'

'Will it be many hundreds of pounds?' she asked fearfully.

He looked startled, realizing she knew nothing of the value of either the land or the works of art that were hung on the walls of Lochlee Castle.

'It will,' he replied carefully, 'be in the region of many thousands of pounds.'

'We're ruined then!' she exclaimed in distress. 'How can I pay for your and Lizzie's wedding? Oh, this is the most terrible calamity!' She covered her face with her hands, wracked with the horror of her position.

Sir Humphrey laid a calming hand on her shoulder. 'My dear Lady Rothbury, please don't upset yourself. It would give me the greatest delight to provide the wherewithal so that Lizzie and I can be married in style.'

'That would never do,' she said, scandalized. 'What would people think?'

'No one will know. Not even Lizzie,' he replied swiftly. 'Remember, it's going to be months, if not years, before the tax actually has to be paid, so please don't worry about it now.'

Once he'd placated his future mother-in-law he told the lawyer in charge of the Fairbairn affairs that whilst he should advise the family to cut back on their usual extravagant expenditure when it came to entertaining and clothes for the eight sisters, he should not worry the widowed Countess with all the details until they were a *fait accompli*.

'That doesn't mean we can't have Mrs Armitage as usual for three months, does it? What about my wedding dress?' Lizzie asked when she was told about the cutbacks.

'Mrs Armitage will be the first person to go,' Georgie said with a touch of spite. 'Mama can't afford her any more so we'll all have to wear last season's clothes.'

Lizzie's eyes brimmed with tears of disappointment. 'But my wedding . . .?' she exclaimed. 'I have to have a wedding dress.'

'Have you forgotten that Mrs Armitage taught me how to make dresses?' Laura said. 'Remember the beautiful wedding dress I made for myself?' she added poignantly.

'Yes, but . . .' Lizzie began, then stopped. 'I'd forgotten that. Could you really make one for me, too?'

'If we can buy the new Singer sewing machine that has been written about in the newspapers, which can apparently do everything from piping to pin-tucking, then of course I can make your wedding dress. In fact, I'll be able to make clothes for all of us, even Mama, and it's something I'd really enjoy doing.'

Georgie frowned doubtfully. 'There's a lot more to dress-making than just having a machine to do the stitching for you,' she pointed out. 'Who's going to do the designing? And cutting? Not to mention fitting? Remember how Mrs Armitage used to take all our measurements? And then make a *toile* in plain cotton before she cut out the actual dress out?'

Laura nodded, not in the least put out by her sister's doubts about her capability. 'I know it's not straightforward,' she replied, 'but who sat watching her hour after hour, taking in everything she did? Asking her questions all the time? Asking if I could help?'

'We must let Laura have a go,' Diana insisted. 'She knows theoretically about dressmaking and I'm sure she's clever enough and artistic enough to put it into practice. I'd certainly love for you to make me a dress, Laura,' she added warmly.

'Me too,' Lizzie agreed. 'And I'd like my wedding dress to be made of white taffeta edged with lace and decorated with white satin bows.'

Beattie was also quick to give her approval to the plan. 'We can concoct original designs,' she said enthusiastically.

As Laura sat listening it struck her with sudden force that she'd unwittingly created more than just an economical solution for them all to have new clothes for the season; there was also a future for herself that could one day make her financially independent. She'd never marry. Rory could never be replaced, so was she going to remain at Lochlee for the rest of her life? A spinster looking after her widowed mother while all her sisters married and had their own families? Was she condemned to living off the estate and never having her own money to spend as she liked?

Deep inside her was a longing and a need for independence. It was one thing to be financially cared for by a loving husband and quite another to be 'looked after' by her parents' money. This way, perfecting her skills as she went along, she'd be able to carve out her own business, in much the same way as Mrs Armitage had done. She rose to her feet, an exultant expression on her face. 'I'll do it!' she told the others, but whilst they were thinking about next season's clothes, she felt charged with ambition as she thought about what she could do with the rest of her life.

Nine

Lasswade Hall, 1910

Laura had arranged vases of flowers in every room and she had made sure the cook bought the best beef to roast for dinner that night to go with the freshly gathered vegetables from the garden. 'I want everything to be perfect,' she told Hobbs.

The butler nodded and automatically curled his fingers tightly around the only key to the wine cellar, which hung with other keys from a chain at his waist. 'Yes, M'Lady. Everything is in order. At what time is Mr Leighton-Harvey expected to return, M'Lady?'

'About four o'clock. We'll have tea in the garden. You did order the scones he particularly likes, didn't you?'

'Yes indeed, M'Lady. We've also got a Dundee cake.'

'That's splendid. Thank you, Hobbs.'

He could tell she was nervous by the strain in her voice and the way her hands were tightly clasped. Lady Laura's face also looked drawn, the result of losing a lot of weight during the five months the master had been incarcerated in a special nursing home in Edinburgh, although his absence was referred to as him 'being away' to suggest he might have been cruising

on the Mediterranean or some such place. This had fooled
no one in the neighbourhood and especially not the rest of
the staff, but Lady Laura had her pride and he didn't blame
her. Recently she'd referred to 'new beginnings' and 'turning
over a new leaf' – it was obvious she desperately wanted
everything to be perfect in future.

Hobbs was a realist, though. You couldn't turn a sow's ear
into a silk purse, as his old mother used to say, nor could you
hope Mr Leighton-Harvey would never touch another drop
of alcohol. People were people.

At two o'clock Laura went up to her room to change into a
white lawn dress with frills around her wrists and a long full
skirt hemmed with a *broderie anglaise* flounce that swirled around
her slim ankles. Then she tied a black velvet sash around her
waist and added a stylish black velvet choker to which she
pinned a diamond brooch. Her hair was already swept up into
an elegant chignon, but as a last touch she tore from a small
pad a little page of paper, already impregnated with face powder,
with which she dabbed her nose and cheeks.

Today, she assured herself, was the first day of a new life for
both her and Walter. The doctor had said he had high hopes
that Walter would never drink again and, as long as he was in
a stress-free setting, he should be fine. He'd learned his lesson,
the doctor added.

'I've told him that if he drinks again he will die this time,'
Dr Allen said with conviction. 'His liver cannot take any more
abuse.'

Laura had thanked him, wanting to believe more than
anything that she need never fear Walter drinking again. Now
it was up to her to make sure he wouldn't slip back. She
decided that peace and calm would pervade in the household,
with little entertaining and no alcohol at all. In future Caroline
and Neil would be the centre of their lives and, for their sakes
if nothing else, Walter must never have another drink.

When she was ready, Laura went up to the nursery to fetch
Caroline, who had just returned from her dancing class.

'Mama, I've just learned how to do the Highland Fling,' she
exclaimed excitedly. 'Can I show you?'

'Why don't you change first, darling? Put on that cream dress I made for you, the one with the blue smocking round the waist?'

'La-La, La-Le!' the child sang as she twirled around and around on her tip-toes. 'Shall I be a fairy?'

Laura smiled. She loved her daughter with every fibre of her being and was so proud of her. Caroline was pretty and vivacious, with Walter's dark sparkling eyes, and she was always smiling and chattering happily.

'I have a better idea!' Laura exclaimed teasingly.

'What is it?' Little hands tugged at her skirt.

'Dada is coming home today and he'll be here soon. Why don't you put on your dress and dance for him?'

'The Highland Fling?'

'Any dance you like, darling.'

Caroline's small face lit up as if a light inside her had been switched on. 'Dada's coming home? Today?'

Laura nodded, pleased at the welcome Walter would receive when he arrived.

When they heard the car coming up the drive Caroline flung herself out of the front door, having been sitting waiting at the bottom of the stairs for the past half hour.

'Dada! Dada! I'm going to dance for you. I can do the Highland Fling,' she boasted. 'Watch me, Dada! Watch me dance!'

Standing in the open doorway, Laura watched as Walter jumped out of the back of the car and scooped his little girl up in his arms.

For a brief flicker of a moment she saw the healthy, good-looking man she'd fallen in love with and married. The man who had swept her off her feet with his enormous charm and wit. The man with a military background: disciplined, brave and with a distinguished army record.

He caught her eye at that moment and, putting Caroline down, came towards Laura and placed his hands on her shoulders before kissing her on the cheek. She tried desperately hard to hang on to the momentary vision she'd had but it was no good. Looking into his eyes now she saw his vulnerability, his deep flaws, his shame and his apology. It made her want to weep for the man she'd lost to alcohol but she kissed him back, hoping he'd think she loved him as much as she'd used to.

'I thought we'd have tea in the garden and Caroline is going to show you how beautifully she can dance,' she said as she turned away so he wouldn't see her sense of loss, and she led the way across the lawn, where Hobbs had laid the table for tea.

This is the rest of my life, she reflected as they sat down and talked to and through Caroline, for they no longer had words for each other. Too many links had been broken and there was nothing left between them except their little daughter.

As soon as they finished their tea and Caroline had danced prettily around the garden, singing as she went, Walter rose to his feet. 'I'd better go and tackle the post that must have accumulated for me,' he said. 'Neil's coming home tomorrow?'

'Yes. Rowena is bringing him over and she's staying for luncheon. I'm afraid your desk is rather swamped by post but your affairs have been looked after by John while you were away so I don't suppose there's anything urgent. Why don't you leave it until tomorrow?'

'No, I want to see what's been happening.' Walter remained in his study until it was time for dinner and then he announced that he wasn't hungry. His face was white and he seemed to be very distracted as he paced up and down the room.

Laura watched him anxiously, filled with dread. She'd never seen him in a state like this before and she wondered if he was finding it difficult to adjust to being at home again.

'You must eat something,' she protested. 'Would you like some soup? Or a cup of beef tea?'

He shook his head. 'I'm sorry but I've got to go out.'

'Out?' She stared at him, stunned. 'Where are you going? It's eight o'clock.' Her mind flew to pubs and clubs and the bar of an Edinburgh hotel where he'd once been found unconscious.

He spoke quickly. 'I've got to see John.'

'At this hour? He'll be dining with his family. Why don't you use the telephone if you want to have a word with him?'

Walter wasn't listening. 'I'm going to drive over to see him now.'

'What is it?' Darts of growing alarm shot through her. 'Shall I come with you?'

He turned on her angrily. 'You don't need to chaperone me, you know.' Then he slammed the front door and she heard him walking round the house to where the car was parked. A few minutes later she heard the purr of the engine as it slid away. He was gone.

Hobbs was hovering in the background. 'Shall I keep the master's dinner warm, M'Lady?'

'You could do but I'm not sure when he'll be back.' Her own appetite had gone too and she felt sick. 'Will you make my apologies to Cook, please? Tell her my husband has been called away on urgent business and I have rather a headache. I think I'll go upstairs and lie down.'

'Very good, M'Lady. Is there anything I can get you?'

'No, thank you, Hobbs.' Her legs felt leaden as she slowly climbed the stairs. A strong sense of dread overwhelmed her and she decided to go to bed even though it was early. What had happened to her careful plans to give Walter a perfect homecoming? Now all she wanted was a few hours of oblivion, for her mind was in turmoil. What in God's name had made him rush off like that? She got undressed and, slipping into bed, she lay down, closed her eyes and prayed for sleep.

The cold, grey light of dawn crept through a gap in the curtains and Laura awoke suddenly as if something had disturbed her, but she was alone and Walter's side of the bed hadn't been slept in. She got up and hurried into his dressing room where he sometimes slept if one of them was unwell. The single bed hadn't been touched either.

With mounting panic she put on her *peignoir* and ran down the stairs to the telephone. It seemed to take a long time before John Osborne answered and she realized it was very early in the morning and he was probably asleep.

Then she heard his voice. 'Hello? John Osborne here. Can I help you?'

'This is Laura speaking. I'm so sorry to telephone you so early but I'm very worried about Walter; did he stay the night at your house?'

There was a long pause and when he spoke he sounded cagey. 'He was here until quite late. I imagined he was driving home when he left.'

'Can you tell me why he needed to see you so urgently?'

There was another long pause. 'I believe it would be better if you talked to him yourself about it.'

'I'm at my wits' end, John. Was he drinking again?'

'No. Definitely not. He was absolutely sober. Try not to worry, Laura. I'm sure he'll turn up. I must go now. Perhaps we can talk later.'

There was a click as he hung up, leaving Laura more worried than ever. Was he lying in some ditch having had a motor accident?

Returning to her room to get dressed, fear jolted dark thoughts into the crevices of her mind, bringing back the terrible moment when little Eleanor's body had been found on the terrace at Lochlee. No matter how often she persuaded herself that Walter would breeze into the room at any moment and scold her laughingly and say he stupidly ran out of petrol, she couldn't quell her apprehension.

There was a knock on her bedroom door. It was Hobbs. 'I'm afraid it's bad news, M'Lady. The master has been taken to the local hospital because he was found sitting in the motor. He was unconscious and they've taken him in for observation.'

Laura reached for her coat. 'Get me a carriage, please, Hobbs. And send Gordon to fetch the car, wherever it is, and bring it back here. I don't know how long I'll be so tell Nanny what's happened but say I don't want Caroline to know.'

'Very well, M'Lady.'

In a daze she put on her black fur toque, buttoned up her coat, grabbed her gloves and handbag and hurried out of the room.

The local hospital was small and the rooms were dark and pokey. There was also the strong smell of disinfectant pervading the atmosphere. A nurse standing behind the reception desk looked up and smiled in recognition when

Laura appeared. This was not the first time she'd been on duty when Mr Leighton-Harvey had been admitted.

'I was expecting you, Lady Laura,' she said cheerfully. 'You'll have heard about your husband?'

Laura nodded. 'How is he?'

'Not too bad. Considering.'

'Was he very drunk when they brought him here?' Her voice was strained and she still found it humiliating to acknowledge that William was an alcoholic.

The nurse looked down at the notes before her. 'I'm afraid he was very intoxicated. At least he'd had the sense to stop driving and pull up by the side of the road. It's possible he felt ill because the doctor thinks he may have had a slight stroke as well.'

A feeling of utter despair swept through Laura. 'He's only just come out of Saint Saviour's hospital in Edinburgh,' she said in a low voice. 'They treated him for five months to help him after his last binge.' She looked up and her eyes were filled with anger. 'How can he be so stupid? He's been warned that if he drank again it would kill him.'

'He's in his fifties, isn't he? It's not unusual for someone of his age to have a stroke,' the nurse said in an attempt to console Laura. 'The alcohol didn't necessarily bring it on. Would you like to see him?'

Laura rose wearily to her feet. 'Yes, please.'

She was led down a narrow corridor and shown into a bleak room where Walter was lying on his back, looking as if he'd fallen asleep. His face was grey and he looked like an old man. Laura dragged over a hard wooden chair from the corner and, placing it beside his bed, sat down and took his hand.

'Walter?' she said.

He didn't respond. He was still unconscious and only his shallow breathing told her he was still alive. Where had he got the alcohol from in the first place? He couldn't have got it at home, and John had sworn he hadn't offered it to him. Pubs would have been closed by the time he'd left the Osbornes' house so the only possible answer was that he'd gone to a pub on his way to see John and hidden the drink in the boot of the car. But why? Why had he gone dashing off to see John in the first place? Why had he made sure he had alcohol to drink after he'd left John?

Laura began to feel guilty that she'd placed all his mail neatly on his desk while he'd been away; it must have contained something that had obviously upset him deeply. Why hadn't she put it to one side until he'd settled at home again? How could she have been so stupid?

Worried about his future and what could have caused this lapse, Laura stayed at the hospital for several hours but Walter didn't regain consciousness and the doctor in charge told her she should go home.

'You look tired, Lady Laura. This has been a great shock for you and I recommend an early night. Don't worry about your husband. We're doing everything we can and should it be necessary we'll have him transferred back to Saint Saviour's again.'

The moment Laura stepped out of the hired carriage she knew something was wrong. There was a deathly silence, almost as if Lasswade Hall had been abandoned by its occupants. Hurrying up the front steps, she noticed the front door was wide open.

'Hobbs?' she called out nervously.

There was no response. The empty silence unnerved her.

'Hobbs?' she shouted shrilly.

At that moment the green baize door that separated the kitchen and servants' quarters from the rest of the house opened and John Osborne appeared, looking grim.

Stunned, Laura exclaimed, 'What on earth are you doing here?'

'Let's go and sit down somewhere, Laura. I'm afraid I've got bad news for you.'

'What is it? And where is everyone? Is Caroline all right?'

'Yes. Caroline is fine. I asked her nanny to take her out for the day and I'm hoping it'll be all over by the time they get back.'

'What will be all over? Have you had fresh news from the hospital? Oh, God, has Walter died?'

John looked blankly at her. 'No. Hobbs said he's back in hospital and that you were visiting him. Why? Is he that ill?'

'He's had a stroke. We think he started drinking after he left you last night and it may have . . .' She couldn't continue. Staggering into the drawing room she slumped down on to a sofa and covered her face with her hands.

John seated himself beside her. 'I'm so sorry, Laura. I came here to see you because the situation is terribly serious.'

'I know,' she replied in a small voice.

'I don't just mean about Walter's health.'

Laura looked up at him. 'What else is there? Where's Hobbs? Why are you here? What do you want to speak to me about?'

'I hate to have to tell you this, Laura,' he began and from his expression she could see he was agitated, 'but Walter is deeply in debt. He owes a variety of people a great deal of money. Not just a manageable amount of debt that could be cleared over time with careful planning, but monumental amounts. It seems he's been living on credit for a long time. He hasn't even paid for your motor. He also opened accounts at several shops in Edinburgh, including a Gentleman's Fitter where he bought a lot of clothes and handmade shoes . . .' He paused, deciding not to mention the jeweller where Walter had purchased a pearl necklace, gold bracelets and diamond earrings for Laura.

Her head was in a spin as she tried to take in what John was saying. 'I don't understand,' she exclaimed. 'He's always given me the impression he was well off,' she said in bewilderment. 'He told me he'd inherited a fortune from his parents along with this house. You've got to remember he's been in hospital for months and couldn't do anything. Aren't you supposed to be looking after his affairs when he's away?' she asked accusingly.

John's mouth tightened. 'I'll come to that in a moment.'

Laura raised her chin. 'Can't the bank lend him some money to pay off these bills? Surely he can get an overdraft?'

'I'm afraid Walter already owes the bank a very considerable amount of money by using this house as collateral but they refused and have now foreclosed his account. He found their letter on his desk last night and that was why he wanted to see me so urgently.'

'What do we do now?' Her voice rose in anguish. 'They can't do that. He's been with them for years.'

'I'm very much afraid they've done it.'

'Then we're going to have to economize. Would it help if we cut down on staff? If you count in the gardener and the chauffeur that means we have to pay the wages of eight people.' Her mind went back to the days of her youth when her parents had an indoor and outdoor staff of one hundred and seventy-six. Eight, by comparison, seemed to her a very modest number.

'We've got past that stage, Laura. There's been no money to pay their wages for the past six weeks as it is.'

Her face registered shock and incredulity. 'That's terrible. I had no idea. Why didn't you tell me?'

'I didn't want to tell you while I worked out how much all his debts came to. I even hoped I could persuade the bank to lend more but unfortunately they've refused.' John got up from his chair and started pacing up and down the room as if he didn't know how to word what he had to say next.

Avoiding eye contact, he finally continued: 'I've been paying your staff wages with my own money; they don't know that and neither should they. But I'm afraid I'm not in a position to carry on so I came here today to give them what was due to them, and told them they must leave immediately and find other employment.'

'You mean they've gone?' White with shock she leaned back in her chair, trying to take in what had happened. Her whole world had collapsed as if wiped out by an earthquake and as it dawned on her more and more with every passing minute the enormity of what Walter had done she became engulfed with anger.

'How could he have been so irresponsible?' she exclaimed. 'I'm most terribly sorry you've got involved in this mess, John, and it was so good of you to do what you've done. I'll make sure you are repaid before anyone else gets their money.'

He smiled sadly. 'With what, Laura? That's the point. There is no more money. It's all gone and Walter owes other people a fortune. To pay off your staff was the least I could do as his old friend while he was still in hospital and I didn't want to worry you. I had hoped the bank would be cooperative but alas there is no way out except bankruptcy.'

The silence in the room was profound. The word went round and round in Laura's head as she tried to work out what it would actually mean.

'He must be mad as well as an alcoholic,' she murmured.

'That's what an alcoholic is; mad when he's in the grip of binge drinking. He's very ill, Laura, and it's a tragedy. When he was a young man he had the world at his feet. His career in the army was auspicious, and then he became a very clever businessman for a while, investing the fortune he'd been left with great skill.' John sighed deeply. 'And now this.'

Laura looked at John and there was sadness in her voice, too. Her eyes were brimming with unshed tears. 'I'm not blaming you but why did nobody warn me before I married him? My sisters tried to stop me and make me wait, but Rowena could have told me there was a problem, and so could you. If I'd realized I'd probably still have married him because I loved him but I'd have insisted on looking after our finances, with your help, of course, and I'd have banned drink in the house and got him into hospital at the first sign of him slipping.' She shook her head in despair. 'It could have all been so different.'

'One is loyal to one's friends,' he replied simply. 'Walter is very much in love with you and I could see you bringing great happiness into his life. I had hoped that once you were married he'd decide never to drink again. I warned him, Laura. I told him that he'd lose everything, including you and Caroline, if he continued in this way, but it was no good. His desire for drink was stronger than for any of us.'

'So all the staff have gone . . .?' She sounded bewildered. 'What about Nanny?'

'I'm afraid so. She'll be bringing Caroline back here very shortly. She's also been paid. I've promised them all good references, so don't worry about that.'

'Oh, God, this is all a terrible mess. What happens next?'

'The house will be repossessed, but that will take time.'

Laura sat in silence. More hurtful than his drinking and his living beyond his means was the fact that Walter had lied to her about their financial state, encouraging her to spend on things for the house and pretty clothes for herself and Caroline. That she couldn't forgive.

As he rose to leave, John took both her hands in his, marvelling at her bravery. Looking into her eyes, he said, 'For the moment just sit tight while I try to work out something. Don't discuss it with anyone else.'

That night Caroline slept with Laura in her big bed, which she was told was a sort of game.

When they awoke the next morning, Laura told Caroline, 'Everyone has gone away so it's up to you and me to keep house.' She struggled to sound bright and cheerful when she felt physically sick with worry. 'We're going to have to make the bed and cook our own breakfast and pick some vegetables in the garden for luncheon . . .' Her voice broke and she looked away quickly. 'You get dressed, darling, while I put up my hair.'

'Where is Dada?'

'He's away on business.'

'Will he be back soon, Muzzie?'

Laura ground her teeth in anguish. 'I'm not sure, darling. Now hurry up and get dressed.'

While Caroline went up to the nursery, Laura sat at her dressing table, wishing she could go back to bed and shut her eyes because she didn't want to face the coming day. Wishing for complete oblivion. And peace of mind. Dressing swiftly in one of her long black skirts and a cream silk blouse, she added the gold chains and pearls she always wore. Then she was struck by a terrible thought: she did not have any money in the house. Supposing she needed to go to the village to buy food? Opening her handbag she found several shillings – her change from the hired carriage from the hospital the previous day. Instead of putting it back in the bag she slipped it into a small purse which she tucked for safekeeping into her corsets.

'Come along, Caroline!' she shouted as she started down the stairs to the kitchen. 'Let's see what we can find for breakfast!'

At that moment there was a thunderous banging on the front door. It took her a moment to move the bolts and turn the lock with the big key. The banging started again, impatiently and even louder this time.

Pulling the heavy door open she looked up in alarm at a tall, powerful-looking man with a red face, angry eyes and a mean little mouth. He flapped the papers he was holding in her face.

'What do you want?' Her manner was imperious but inside she suddenly felt afraid.

He pushed past her into the hall and then she realized there were several rough-looking men standing on the doorstep about to follow him in.

'You can't come in here! This is private property,' Laura protested vigorously. Her heart was thudding in her chest and she knew she was in a vulnerable position.

The man leered at her and flapped the papers in her face again. 'Court order,' he snapped. 'I'm the county bailiff. We've come to clear the contents of the house.'

She froze and for a moment the hall seemed to whirl around her head in a shower of black spots. She thought she was going to faint. 'No one told me you were coming,' she managed to say.

'That's the point! We don't want people like you running off with all the stuff.' He turned to the men, who she realized were furniture removers. 'Get to it, lads. It looks like it's going to take all day. Start at the top and work down. Pack the china and glass in boxes and also all the silver. Don't damage the paintings – they'll lose their value. Don't forget the attic!'

'Yes, sir,' they all chorused.

Through the open front door Laura could see a very large removal van.

The bailiff was watching her. 'I'll have that stuff off you now,' he said unpleasantly, eyeing the gold chains and pearls that hung from her neck and the diamond and sapphire ring on her finger.

'This is my personal jewellery. You can't take that. It comes from my family and has nothing to do with my husband's debts,' she pointed out, aghast.

'I don't care where it comes from; you're bound by law to hand over all your possessions.' He stuck out his large hand, palm up. 'Hurry up,' he snapped. 'I haven't got all day.'

With enormous reluctance Laura handed over her chains and her engagement ring.

'And the other!' he ordered.

'Other what?' she asked, finding it hard to believe this was happening.

He clicked his tongue impatiently. 'Your wedding ring. Nice bit of gold that.'

She shook her head. 'No. Not my wedding ring.'

He came closer, towering over her menacingly. 'Give it to me.'

As she reluctantly took it off her finger, he asked, 'Now where's the safe?'

'We don't have one,' she replied.

'Where's the rest of your jewellery, then?'

She sank down on to a nearby chair. 'In my jewel case,' she replied faintly as tears stung her eyes. 'My little girl will be down in a moment and I don't want her frightened.'

'If I were you I'd stay with her in the kitchen all day. We'll clear it last of all.'

He wandered up the stairs, presumably to find her jewel case, and Laura hurried over to the telephone. It took a minute for the operator to get John's number and then he was on the line.

'How are you this morning, Laura?' he asked immediately.

'Oh, thank God you're there! The bailiff has arrived with a bunch of removal men. How can I stop them clearing the house? He says they're going to strip everything out and he's already taken the jewellery I was wearing. Is there anything you can do, John?'

There was a long silence and for a dreadful moment Laura thought he'd hung up. Then he spoke. 'I'm so dreadfully sorry, Laura. I had no idea they'd act this quickly. I thought it would take several weeks for the Court Order to go through. I'm afraid there's nothing we can do. It's in legal hands now.'

Laura thanked him and hung up. It was impossible to take in the calamity that had befallen her without warning.

'What am I going to do?' she muttered aloud, covering her face with her hands. How was she going to explain this to Caroline and where were they going to live now?

The bailiff came back into the hall whilst scribbling on a pad.

Laura looked at him beseechingly. 'You're not going to take all our clothes, are you?'

He stuck out his bottom lip again. 'Even second-hand clothes have a value. They'll fetch a few pence.'

'Muzzie!' Caroline came running down the stairs. 'What are these men doing?'

With huge effort, Laura braced herself. 'Let's go to the kitchen and have breakfast and I'll tell you all about it.' Taking Caroline's hand she led the way, feeling as if her legs might give way at any minute. The enormity of what was happening seemed to be draining away her will to live.

Somehow she managed to rake out the ashes of the stove and see if there was coal so she could light a fire and at least make toast and hot drinks.

'What are those men doing, Muzzie?' Caroline asked again.

Laura sat at the kitchen table and drew her little girl on to her lap. 'Dada is not very well so we're putting all our things in storage for a while,' she lied, 'because I think we need a much smaller house.'

'Are my toys going in storage too?' the child asked anxiously.

At that moment Laura wished with all her heart that she had the money to pay off Walter's debts so that her child would be spared the pain of what was happening. 'Yes, because we haven't found a new home yet, have we?' God forgive me for these lies, she thought, but will Caroline forgive me when she knows the truth?

'Will it have a garden? Our new house?'

'Maybe. The kettle's boiling and we must have some breakfast so come along. Sit in that chair and I'll make you some toast.'

'Will the garden have a swing like Dada made me?'

Laura gazed at the child, envying her the smallness of her world and her trusting acceptance of what she'd been told. At the same time she wanted to scream at the persistent questioning.

'We're going to spend the day here so we don't get in the way of the busy men.' She went to the window, from where she could see the open doors at the back of the van. At that moment she caught sight of the furniture at the far end, already neatly stacked. There was Caroline's doll's house, rocking horse and her dressing table. Then they piled in her favourite bedroom chair and a table on which they flung an armful of clothes, including her beautiful sable fur coat.

It was unbearable to watch. It was like seeing her past being carted off bit by bit to God knows where and lost to her for ever. She turned swiftly away, biting her lower lip, consumed with anguish and anger in equal measure.

At five o'clock the bailiff strode into the kitchen. 'They need to clear everything in here, then we'll be done,' he announced without preamble. 'You'll want to lock up the house before you leave,' he added curtly, and with that he walked out again.

'Where are we going, Muzzie?'

Laura had been thinking of nothing else all day. She was thankful that some dreadful premonition had prompted her to keep some money tucked in her corsets, though it wouldn't get them far.

At last the bailiff and his removal men left, leaving the house an empty shell – the rooms bare, the atmosphere deserted. As Laura went from room to room blinded by tears as she checked window locks and closed doors she knew she was saying goodbye to what had been her beautiful home, her marriage and her standing in the world as a respectable wife and mother. She was the wife of a bankrupt alcoholic and a pauper now, with only the clothes she stood up in and a few shillings in her hand. The dreadful day had come to an end and it was Walter's fault.

Dry-eyed now and in deep shock, she took Caroline's hand as they walked through the front door and away down the road for the very last time.

Ten

Lochlee Castle, 1898

Beattie lounged back in her chair with her hands clasped behind her head, gazing up at the ornate ceiling in the library. 'The irony of it staggers me,' she said, half laughing. 'I always thought I'd be next to get married but no; it's not me who's sailing up the aisle next week. It sadly isn't you either, Laura. It isn't even Georgie! It's the youngest of the five of us, Diana. And she's only nineteen, for goodness sake.'

Laura smiled and nodded. 'I know. What a good marriage she's making.'

Beattie grinned. 'This time next week she'll be the wife of the very rich Lord Kelso of Cranley Court.'

'He's so nice, too,' Laura enthused, genuinely happy for her sister. 'Good looking, intelligent and madly in love with Di. He's everything she ever wanted.'

'I'm happy for her but I must admit I'm also green with envy. When are the rest of us going to meet a man who has everything? That's what worries me.'

Laura didn't answer. She'd been introduced to a lot of very nice young men at various parties and she'd enjoyed flirting with them as they danced with her and conversed over a glass of fruit cup, but none of them had made her catch her breath and none of them had touched her heart. To her Rory had been a man in a lifetime and there was unlikely to be another.

'Is her wedding dress gorgeous?' Beattie asked, breaking into Laura's thoughts. She was dying to know what it was like but Laura and Diana were keeping it a secret from everyone until the very last moment.

'I've done my best and Diana is going to look like a princess. It's a pity we don't have a tiara in the family any more but I think what we've planned will work just as well.'

Beattie stretched her arms above her head. 'Oh, well! At least I'm the matron of honour and I love the dress you've made me. What would we have done if you hadn't been able to make all our clothes? Mrs Armitage would have charged an absolute fortune and Mama says we must be careful with money in future. She's terrified of us being really poor now.'

They sat in silence for a minute, thinking deeply about their change in fortune and their standing in Argyllshire. The death duties due on the Lochlee estate had forced them to sell almost all their land. Grouse moors and woodland where they'd shot pheasant and partridge had been sold, as had the river where they'd caught salmon and tickled for trout. All sold along with the home farm and cottages. The magnificent stags that roamed the mountains like proud kings no longer belonged to them either. Nothing was left except a beautiful view that stretched for miles and to which they no longer had a claim.

That autumn the leaves of the Rowan tree which still stood near the castle had turned a stronger shade of crimson than in previous years.

'With the blood of my family,' Lady Rothbury claimed bitterly. She'd come to believe her late husband had been right all along. Their family had been cursed and she knew who had cursed them because William had told her as he lay dying. It was a secret she'd borne alone ever since, for fear it would bring worse luck if the family knew the truth. She had another reason for remaining silent; she didn't want her children to know what their father had done.

She remembered how William had spoken with anguish about 'the sins of the fathers . . .' she knew what came next, '. . . shall be visited upon the sons a thousand times.'

Those words haunted her now. There had been no news of Freddie since he'd killed the stable boy and then run off with the family jewels four years ago. Torn between maternal feelings of grief at losing her eldest son and fury and disappointment that he could have behaved so outrageously, she half longed to hear from him and yet dreaded doing so.

Freddie had shamed the family and Lady Rothbury was sure that was why Laura, Beattie and Georgie had failed to find suitable husbands. Diana's fiancée, Robert Kelso, came from Aberdeen on the east side of Scotland, whilst Lochlee was in Argyllshire, so the worst of the scandal might not have reached him, for he never mentioned Freddie and she comforted herself with the thought that perhaps he didn't realize what had happened.

Diana's wedding was the only bright beam that shone into her dark world at the moment. It brought with it a sense of hope that the other girls might have a chance to shine, too. She could picture it all. Her beloved Henry, who would inherit the earldom in another three years if Freddie couldn't be found and was then legally declared dead, was going to give Diana away. He'd be resplendent in the kilt of the Fairbairn tartan, with a burgundy velvet doublet and his father's jewelled-handled skean-dhu showing out of the top of his right high sock. She smiled at the thought of her handsome young son in the role of heir apparent, receiving the guests by her side at the reception where William would normally have stood.

Henry was the future of the Fairbairn family now. The one who would keep the line going for another five hundred years. Although they had lost all their land, at least they still had their fortress castle and within its thick stone walls they would remain safe.

On the day the church was packed with friends and neighbours and great arrangements of spring flowers and leaves softened the severe interior, creating a festive air. Down in the great hall of the castle the family stood waiting for Diana to come down from her room, where Laura was dressing her in her bridal finery.

'You look beautiful,' Laura told her with satisfaction, for she had worked hard to create the dress. 'Look at yourself in the long mirror.'

Diana turned to see her reflection and her eyes widened. 'Is that really me?' she breathed. 'I'd no idea it would turn out this well.'

'It's you who is making the dress look so good,' Laura assured her. 'Come on. Everyone is waiting.'

'What time is it?' Lady Rothbury asked anxiously. No longer

in mourning but dressed in silvery grey silk, she looked at Henry anxiously. He took out the flat round gold watch on a chain which his father had left him. 'Four minutes to eleven. Di ought to be coming down by now.'

At that moment a figure appeared at the top of the grand oak staircase and there was a stunned silence as Diana descended – an ethereal figure of delicate beauty in a dress of white satin covered with Chantilly lace, gathered at the front in a shawl effect, and a long train.

There was an awestruck silence and from the top of the stairs, holding up the train, Laura had the gratification of seeing the expressions of amazement on the faces of the family.

'Oh, darling . . .!' For once Lady Rothbury was lost for words. 'You look wonderful.'

Diana's face glowed with happiness. 'Look at my tiara!' she said, giggling.

Laura had made a headband of white satin and then embroidered it with crystal beads and pearls. It looked most effective as it held her long silk tulle veil in place.

'Well done!' croaked Henry, stepping forward to offer Diana his arm.

In the background the household staff, led by the old butler, McEwan, sent up a massive cheer and clapped as Henry led her out of the castle, followed by her seven sisters, all wearing pale blue silk dresses which had also been made by Laura.

Lady Rothbury stepped into the waiting carriage which would take her ahead to the church while the bridal retinue walked the short distance along a gravel path lined with all the members of the outdoor staff they'd once employed. There was their old ghilli, their gamekeeper and several beaters, the pony man, the foresters and ten gardeners. There was also the group of men that maintained the gates and fences on the erstwhile estate and the men who looked after the rivers. Many of them were still wearing the Fairbairn tartan and it touched Diana deeply that they'd remained so loyal to the family in spite of what had happened. Most were having difficulty finding new employment yet none bore a grudge on this day when a member of the family got married.

Henry smiled, vowing to himself that when he took his place as the Earl of Rothbury he would do everything he could to help them financially. Maybe he could find a way of buying back some of the land. Maybe he could even do the unthinkable and turn what was left of Lochlee into a profitable business where people could come and stay as paying guests and be charged extra if they wanted to shoot, fish and stalk. His father would turn in his grave at the thought and Mama would be appalled and ashamed, but Harry wanted to do what he could for these loyal men he'd known all his life.

To the music of 'Here Comes the Bride' Henry proudly led Diana up the aisle, followed by the rest of the Fairbairn girls, all so tall and elegant, all with glossy dark hair and hazel eyes. From her place in the front pew Lady Rothbury felt quite overcome with pride.

The ceremony was simple and straightforward and when Henry had said 'I do' and given Diana's hand to Robert Kelso, he stepped back and stood beside his mother.

'Thank you,' she whispered gratefully. 'Your father would have been so proud of you today.'

Back at the castle the reception was in full swing as the three hundred guests waited in line to be received and McEwan did his best to announce each person correctly. The champagne flowed as waiters skimmed around refilling glasses and offering tiny sandwiches filled with salmon and other sweetmeats.

While Lady Rothbury, Henry and the new Lady Diana Kelso and Lord Kelso shook hands with all the arrivals, the other sisters mingled with the guests.

'Let's see if we can find any husband material!' Beattie whispered to Laura with a mischievous smile.

'Now, which sister are you?' asked a warm male voice behind Laura. She turned and found herself looking up into the strong-featured face of a tall man in his late forties with a military bearing and dark twinkling eyes.

'I'm Laura,' she replied, laughing. 'I'm the second daughter.'
'Out of . . .?'
'Nine girls, but now I'm afraid there are only eight of us.'
His brow puckered in sympathy. 'I'm sorry to hear that.' He

looked around the magnificent room. 'You were born here, I imagine?'

Laura nodded. 'We all were. The local doctor and midwife practically lived with us for a few years.'

He burst out laughing. 'Let me introduce myself. I'm Walter Leighton-Harvey. I live in Lasswade, near Edinburgh, and I'm ashamed to say this is the first time I've visited Argyllshire. I was in the Scots Guards until I retired so I had to be wherever I was posted.'

'I suppose so,' she replied stupidly. Her heart was pounding in her chest and she was having difficulty breathing as she continued to look into his eyes. There was something about this man that she found deeply attractive in a way she hadn't found any man since Rory.

'Are you staying up here for long?' she asked awkwardly, and to her own surprise realized she was hoping he'd say yes.

'I'd like to go to Mull. There's a ferry from Oban, isn't there?'

She nodded. 'Mull's very beautiful.' *Why can't I say something witty and intelligent?* she thought frantically. *I can't let this marvellous man slip through my fingers before I've even got to know him.*

Lizzie passed behind him and gave Laura a knowing nod of approval.

'How long do you plan to stay on Mull?' she asked. 'Perhaps you'd care to stay with us for a few days on your way back? Friends are always dropping in for a night here or there and Mama loves to entertain,' she added, astonished at her own boldness. Her cheeks were quite pink now and she could see the admiration in his eyes as he gazed back at her.

He seemed to hesitate before answering and Laura held her breath. 'That's really sweet of you,' he began in his warm, rich voice, 'and I'd have loved to stay with you all, but the thing is my wife and I have to get back to Lasswade for our son's birthday at the end of the week, so alas! I'll have to refuse your lovely invitation.'

'Oh, of course,' she replied, a shade too quickly. 'Maybe another time,' she added with forced gaiety while her heart plummeted with disappointment.

'There you are, Walter!' exclaimed a sweet-looking woman in a large hat covered in silk roses. 'I think they're going to cut the cake in a minute.' She turned to Laura. 'You look so lovely, my dear. I hear you made Diana's wedding dress and all the bridesmaid dresses, too?'

Laura nodded, hating this woman for being so nice and so charming. 'How incredibly clever of you,' Mrs Leighton-Harvey continued in her sugary voice. 'Wherever did you learn such a skill?'

Laura shrugged as if it was nothing. 'I picked up a few tips from the person Mama used to employ as a resident dressmaker,' she replied casually.

'Well, I'm full of admiration, my dear,' said Mrs Leighton-Harvey, patting her arm. 'Isn't she a clever girl, Walter?'

'Very clever,' he replied, his eyes never leaving Laura's face as he smiled down at her.

'Come along, Walter. Let's find a good place to watch them cutting the cake.'

Walter gave Laura a little bow. 'Will you excuse us?'

As they moved away Laura saw the reluctance in his eyes. 'Goodbye,' she replied, determined to hide her disappointment.

Nearly all the guests had been received now and McEwan had put the number one footman in charge of announcing any latecomers while he gathered together those who were to make speeches by the three-tier cake that Cook had spent weeks baking and icing.

'Mr and Mrs George Thornby,' shouted the footman as an elderly couple stepped forward to be received by Lady Rothbury and Henry. 'Lord and Lady Ellison,' came a minute later. They too stepped forward.

There was a slight pause and then the footman cleared his throat to make another announcement. 'The Earl of Rothbury,' he boomed.

Lady Rothbury turned white and gripped Henry's arm. 'It can't be,' she whispered aghast. 'Has Freddie returned?'

The room fell silent, the guests not sure what was going on but sensing something momentous was happening.

Everyone looked towards the doorway, their expressions

expectant. Many were asking themselves if it was possible that Freddie had really had the nerve to come back to Scotland, knowing he'd face charges of murder and robbery?

When a tall, thin man in his early twenties with a black moustache and sideburns strolled arrogantly into the room as if he owned the place, confusion broke out. Whispering swept through the guests like incoming waves on a beach. This certainly wasn't Freddie. Whoever he was he couldn't be the Earl of Rothbury. Unless a previously unknown cousin had succeeded to the title?

'The footman must have got the name muddled,' an elderly lady presumed.

Everyone stood watching as the young man stepped up to Lady Rothbury with his hand held out. 'I don't believe we've had the pleasure of meeting until now,' he said with a strong Scottish accent.

She shrank back from him, a look of fear and horror in her eyes.

'Who are you?' demanded Henry angrily. 'Did Freddie send you here?'

'I've no idea where Frederick is,' the man replied loftily. 'All I know is he's not going to return so it's time I made an appearance. I am and always have been the rightful heir of Lochlee anyway.'

For a moment Lady Rothbury had to be supported by Henry and Robert Kelso as she staggered and nearly fell.

'Get out of here,' Henry said roughly. 'You've no right to adopt my late father's title. Who do you think you are?'

The man looked at him with sardonic amusement. 'I'm your late father's eldest son. This is where I belong. Where I've always belonged.'

Lizzie and Laura had gathered around their mother in bewilderment.

'What's going on?' Laura asked.

Lady Rothbury rallied. 'Let us talk about this in private. Robert, you and Diana stay here and talk to the guests.' Then she turned to McEwan. 'Take this . . . this person to the morning room and I will follow.'

McEwan looked stricken. 'Yes, M'Lady. I'm sorry, M'Lady, he would never have been allowed across the threshold if I'd been on the door when he arrived.'

Glowering angrily, he grabbed the young man's arm. 'This way, laddie,' he said roughly.

There was a scuffle as he protested and swore at the butler to 'Keep your filthy hands off me,' but as quick as a dart Henry bent down, whipped his skean-dhu from his sock and held the blade, unsheathed, towards the interloper's throat.

'Do as my mother says,' he growled.

The whispering had spread across the room and spilled into the great hall as two strong footmen frogmarched the man along the corridor followed by Henry, his mother, Laura and Lizzie.

'Get someone to fetch the police,' Lady Rothbury instructed McEwan, 'and we don't want to be disturbed. See that one of the footmen stays outside the morning-room door.'

'Yes, M'Lady.' For the first time in his long years of employment at Lochlee he looked flustered and apologetic.

There was a round table in the middle of the rather drab room and Lady Rothbury seated herself at it, indicating that the young man should sit opposite. Henry stood protectively by her side, his dirk still held firmly in his right hand while the sisters sat on their mother's other side.

Lady Rothbury looked stern and composed as she faced the interloper. When she spoke her voice was sharp and angry. 'I know all about you, Douglas Kirkbride – you have the blood of my family on your hands.'

'You know this man?' Henry exclaimed in a shocked voice.

'I know all about him and the misery he has caused us all,' his mother replied bitterly.

Kirkbride shrugged and his manner was insolent. 'I'm the eldest son of William Earl of Rothbury and that's an indisputable fact. Therefore I'm his rightful heir.'

Laura rose angrily. 'That's rubbish! Freddie is his eldest son. I was four when he was born and I remember everyone saying he was Papa's first son.'

He smirked. 'You were also four when I was born three months *before* Frederick. Therefore I'm the eldest son. Frederick, who is no longer around, is the second son, and this young bully brandishing his skean-dhu is the third son. I am merely doing my duty in claiming my inheritance because Frederick is probably dead, and this whippersnapper is never going to amount to much,' he added, giving Henry a disdainful look.

Infuriated, Henry sprang forward, throwing his arm out and gripping the man in a headlock. 'Who the hell do you think you are?' he shouted, resting the tip of his dirk against the man's throat. The two men struggled and Lizzie's scream of alarm caused the footman waiting outside the door to rush in.

He managed to separate them with the help of another footman, but Douglas had to be held back to prevent him charging at Henry again.

'Get him out of here,' Henry raged. 'The man's an imposter and he should never have been allowed in.'

Lady Rothbury had risen imperiously to her feet. Her eyes flashed with fury and she spoke harshly. 'My husband told me everything about you, Douglas Kirkbride, because that is who you really are. Before he died he warned me about you. Your mother was the village trollop, Dolly Kirkbride, who seduced him one night when he was drunk. He gave her money to move away when you were born but he carried the shame of what he'd done to the end of his life. My husband also told me you kept coming on to our land, threatening him unless he made you his legal heir, and when he finally thought he'd got rid of you for ever,' she paused, shaking now with extraordinary passion, 'you came back in the dead of night and cursed us all by the Rowan tree. My daughter Eleanor lost her life trying to undo that curse. You're rotten to the core, Douglas Kirkbride, and you're no doubt satisfied that the curse haunts us still and there have been a series of tragedies in the family. Let me tell you something: I hope you rot in hell and eternal damnation for the havoc you have wreaked on the Fairbairn family. Now throw him out or we'll set the dogs on you.'

'The police are here, M'Lady,' McEwan replied.

Henry tucked his dirk back into his sock. 'Good. Show them in.'

Then he turned with a look of disgust at Kirkbride. 'I'll make sure you're charged with trespass and intent to cause a disturbance, and if you ever come here again you'll have me to answer to,' he added hotly.

Kirkbride looked evenly at Henry, his shifty dark eyes glittering with malice. 'I swear you'll never become the next Earl of Rothbury.'

A cold shiver ran through those in the room and Henry turned pale. 'Neither will you,' he retorted.

A moment later Diana came rushing in, looking flustered. 'What's happening? We've got to have the speeches now. Everyone is waiting.'

'Yes. We'll all come now.' It was obvious Lady Rothbury was deeply shaken.

Diana hurried off and her mother turned to the others. 'As far as your younger sisters and the guests are concerned, that creature was a drunken lunatic. He didn't know what he was saying. Do you understand? Not a word of what you heard just now must ever be repeated.'

They all nodded, taken aback by her commanding manner and the incredible strength she'd shown in dealing with what had just happened. It was the first time they'd ever seen her like this; a lioness protecting her cubs. And the reputation of the family.

Diana and Robert had left in a flurry of rose petals and cheering guests as they set off in an open carriage drawn by two grey horses who had garlands of flowers hung round their necks.

'What a splendid wedding, my dear Margaret,' the Duke of Argyll told Lady Rothbury as he took his leave. Everyone was brimming with enthusiasm and champagne as they waved to the young couple who were going to Paris for their honeymoon.

'Imagine, Paris!' said Georgie enviously. 'I'd give my right arm to go to Paris.'

Laura, standing on the front steps of the castle, was scanning the crowds for a final look at Walter Leighton-Harvey. Then she caught sight of him, head and shoulders above the melee, talking to another couple, his wife by his side. He was laughing good-humouredly and Laura felt a pang of sadness that it was not her who stood beside him at this moment. If only he wasn't married, she reflected regretfully. As if he was aware of her gaze, he suddenly turned and, seeing her, raised his top hat and waved it. She waved back and smiled, and he smiled too. Then his wife tugged his arm as if she wanted to leave and, almost reluctantly, he gave Laura a little nod before replacing his hat and turning away.

Feeling suddenly deflated, Laura turned and went back into the castle where the servants were frantically clearing up and trying to restore the pristine tidiness of the reception rooms in readiness for a dinner party that night.

Beattie came up behind her and slid her arm around Laura's waist. 'Wasn't Di's dress a triumph! Everyone was saying how gifted and clever you are. Are you pleased with the way it all went? Our dresses are beautiful, too. I'm longing for another occasion to wear mine.'

'Thank you, Beattie.' Laura led the way up to her bedroom. 'Yes, I think it all went very well and Di certainly looked beautiful, but it's been one of the strangest days of my life.'

'How so? Because of that strange man gatecrashing the reception? What was that about? Someone asked me if Freddie had returned.'

'Come into my room and I'll tell you,' Laura replied in a low voice. 'Mama made us promise not to tell the young ones.'

Beattie's eyes widened. 'What is it?'

Laura told her about Douglas Kirkbride being Papa's illegitimate son. 'He was apparently born three months before Freddie,' she added grimly.

Beattie looked shocked. 'Then Papa must have . . . you know . . . *after* he was married to Mama?'

Laura nodded. 'Six years after he married Mama.'

Beattie gave a little snort of disgust. 'What's the matter with men? And Mama knew about it?'

'Apparently Papa told her just before he died. You know what this means, don't you?'

'In what way?'

'Remember how we heard Papa yelling at a man to stay away from us? Papa seemed in a state and then Eleanor heard a man cursing us by the Rowan tree one night?'

Beattie gave a sharp intake of breath. 'Of course. That

explains everything. And Eleanor thought she could . . .' she began and her hand flew to her mouth. 'Oh, this is terrible.'

'Now I think Papa may have had reason to say we were all cursed.'

'What a dreadful thing to say, Laura.' Beattie looked near to tears. 'You can't really believe that, surely?'

'Sometimes I do and sometimes I don't,' Laura replied with honesty. 'I don't want to believe it; Mama used to tell us only uneducated people were superstitious and all that nonsense was just an old wives' tale, but you have to admit that everything has gone wrong since this man laid a curse on us. I believe Mama thinks so too, now.'

'Who knows about this man beside you?'

'Only Henry and Lizzie.'

Beattie sighed. 'You certainly have had a strange day.'

'I also fell in love,' Laura said in a small voice.

Beattie's face lit up and she clapped her hands with delight. 'Oh, Laura. How wonderful. Who is he?'

'Don't get excited,' Laura warned in a dry voice. 'He is absolutely perfect but he's a married man.'

Her sister's face fell. 'What a shame! Oh, what bad luck! Never mind – you'll meet someone one day who will be just right for you. You mustn't give up.'

Laura rose and went over to her hanging cupboard. 'I can't decide what to wear for dinner tonight.'

Her eye caught a midnight-blue chiffon dress she'd made which was very becoming. If Walter Leighton-Harvey had been single and dining with them it was the dress she'd have chosen. 'I'll wear this,' she announced, taking a pale pink dress from the cupboard. 'It's a bit insipid, but who cares?'

That evening Lady Rothbury hosted a large dinner party for people who had travelled from afar to attend the wedding. Beattie looked delighted when she discovered her mother had placed her next to a good-looking man in his early thirties whom she had never met before.

His *placement* card said his name was Andrew Drinkwater.

'I'm afraid I'm a poor substitute for my brother-in-law,' he told Beattie self-deprecatingly after he'd introduced himself.

'I'm here to escort my sister, Amelia Watson-Brown, as her husband was unfortunately detained in London. He's a barrister and is now a member of parliament. He's a jolly clever chap. I'm just a rather boring business man.' He added, grinning, 'And I'm sorry you've been done out of a fascinating man to talk to.'

'I'm sure you're just as clever as him,' Beattie quipped flirtatiously. 'Where are you and your sister staying?'

'We're at the Craigan Hotel, not far from here.' He leaned closer and lowered his voice. 'I must say it was most awfully kind of your mother to invite us tonight as well as to your sister and Robert's wedding this afternoon. We were bracing ourselves for a dinner of Haggis with Neeps and Tatties.'

Beattie burst out laughing. 'Sorry to disappoint you! Actually we are having mashed swedes and potatoes tonight but with beef instead of Haggis, which I must tell you is absolutely delicious. I love it.'

'What exactly is Haggis made of?' he murmured cautiously.

Beattie's eyes sparkled mischievously. 'Take a sheep's stomach,' she began, but seeing his expression she took pity on him. 'No, I'll tell you another time. I wouldn't want to ruin your dinner tonight.' She took a sip of her wine. 'Where is your business?'

'In London, I'm afraid,' he replied almost apologetically, 'but I go to my place in Kent at the weekends, which isn't so bad.'

Beattie didn't think it was bad at all. She hung on to his every word throughout dinner as he talked about his Elizabethan manor house with a knot garden, and his horses and dogs and the housekeeper he'd inherited from his late parents, who ran the house for him. Beattie's brain spun with expectation like an awestruck fifteen-year-old as this charming thirty-three-year-old bachelor poured out his heart to her. It was obvious he was equally enchanted, because when the men joined the ladies in the drawing room after dinner he made straight for Beattie with the determination of a homing pigeon.

Lizzie and Laura watched this budding relationship with amusement but Georgie sat glowering, eyes smouldering, her mouth grim. No one had been even vaguely struck by her at the reception or at this dinner party, which she thought was boring anyway because all the guests seemed so old.

When the evening came to an end, Andrew Drinkwater and his sister bade Lady Rothbury goodbye, and he turned to Beattie, saying, 'I won't forget to send you that book on India.'

'Thank you, that's so kind,' she gushed, gazing up at him as they shook hands.

'*India?*' Laura giggled incredulously when they'd left. 'Beattie, when did you ever have the remotest interest in India?'

Beattie flushed with annoyance. 'Have you forgotten our great-grandfather on Mama's side was *chargé d'affaires* at the British Embassy in Lucknow during the Indian Mutiny?' Then she turned and stalked off across the great hall and up the stairs to her room.

'What's the matter with her?' Georgie asked.

'Can't you tell?' Laura laughed. 'She's just fallen in love.'

The book on India wasn't the only thing Andrew sent Beattie. In the weeks that followed there were letters, a sepia photograph of his country house, other books she might find interesting and finally an invitation from his sister to stay with her and her husband for a week in June at their Belgrave Square house.

There are several balls that week, Amelia Watson-Brown wrote to Lady Rothbury, *and of course I will chaperone Beatrice at all times, and if you are agreeable my brother, who stays at his club when in London, would be very happy to escort her to these parties.*

Beattie was ecstatic. The thought of going to grand balls in London during the height of the season had been beyond her wildest dreams.

Laura was commanded to make her at least two new evening dresses and Lady Rothbury lent her a lace fan, several pairs of long white kid gloves and a velvet evening cloak lined with ermine.

'I wish I had some nice jewels,' Beattie remarked sadly.

'Unmarried girls shouldn't wear jewellery as such,' Lady Rothbury advised reprovingly. 'One day your husband will buy you jewels but for now it would be most inappropriate.'

'I bet you she'll be engaged to Andrew by the time the

week's over,' Laura observed as Beattie left for the station in a horse-drawn carriage with her trunk strapped to the roof. 'They're a perfect match.'

'I think we can safely say it's a certainty,' Lady Rothbury replied gleefully.

Eleven

Lochlee Castle, 1899

'Three down and another five to go,' Lady Rothbury privately reflected when Beattie's engagement was announced the following month. She wasn't worried about Alice, Flora or Catriona; they were still very young, but she was concerned about Laura and Georgie. Especially Georgie. She didn't make the best of herself and she didn't try hard enough to please or attract anyone.

Beattie's wedding was to take place in September, when the Oban Gathering took place with its Highland Games and parties every night leading up to the Oban Ball, which was a grand affair. Everyone who was anyone would be in Argyllshire then.

Lady Rothbury began making her meticulous plans, as she'd done for Diana and Lizzie's weddings, which had now become a blueprint for all future family nuptials, and she was happily thinking about the choice of flowers for the church when Henry came into the room.

His mother looked up at him affectionately. 'Are you ready to give another of your sisters away?' she asked half-jokingly.

Henry looked at her seriously. 'I shan't be here for Beattie's wedding, Mama.'

'What do you mean you won't be here? Of course you'll be here. You don't go to Edinburgh University until the end of September.'

He looked her straight in the eye. 'By September I'll be in South Africa, Mama.'

Her heart skipped a beat and then plunged sickeningly. 'South Africa?' she faltered, knowing what that meant because there'd been a lot about it in the newspapers.

'Yes. I've just joined up. I'm off to fight the Boers.'

'Who *is* going to give Beattie away?' Lady Rothbury wept, knowing that wasn't the reason for her tears but too frightened to even contemplate the real cause. She couldn't bear to think of her beautiful boy being on the battlefield, facing the terrible dangers of musket wounds and cannon fire.

'Has he joined up as a regular soldier?' Georgie asked in astonishment.

'Yes. He's joined the Household Cavalry; he always did like riding. How I wish he'd discussed it with me first instead of rushing off in such an impulsive way.'

'He probably knew you'd try and stop him,' Laura said gently. 'No mother wants her son to go to war but Henry has always had a mind of his own. He'll be all right, Mama. There are thousands of soldiers from Australia, Canada and South Africa fighting the Boers. Not just soldiers from Britain.'

'I shan't have a moment's peace of mind until he returns,' Lady Rothbury spoke passionately. 'The whole future of the Fairbairn family rests in his hands; apart from which, I need him here.'

'Why don't we ask Robert to give Beattie away?' Laura suggested. 'He's your eldest son-in-law so it would be absolutely fitting.'

'I suppose I could,' she agreed with reluctance, 'but it won't be the same.'

Laura sympathized with her mother but she also knew Henry felt frustrated by the confines of the castle, especially now they'd lost their own shooting and stalking rights. He was just eighteen and thirsting for excitement and adventure, and the idea of sailing abroad to fight a war on behalf of Queen and country was something few young men would be able to resist.

Robert agreed immediately and offered any other help he could give while Henry was away. 'You only have to ask and Diana and I will be delighted to do anything we can,' he promised.

'Aren't we providing you with wonderful sons-in-law?' Diana teased her mother. 'You've got Robert and Humphrey and now you're going to have Andrew Drinkwater, too.'

Lady Rothbury smiled wanly, refusing to be cheered. As far as she was concerned it was only Henry she wanted.

Nothing could dampen Beattie's spirits, though. From the moment she'd returned from her visit to London, with a very large ruby and diamond engagement ring flashing on her finger, she had talked of nothing else but her dazzling future. Andrew was going to buy a house in London, 'in the best part in Mayfair', she added repeatedly, where they would stay from Monday until Friday, retiring gracefully to his Elizabeth mansion in Kent on Saturdays 'where we'll entertain and have guests to stay for a couple of days', she enthused.

Whilst delighted for her, Diana and Lizzie began to feel that their palatial country abodes were positively suburban by comparison.

'Imagine having two large houses to run,' Lizzie remarked.

'How exceedingly vulgar!' Georgie retorted. 'The next thing we'll be told is that Andrew is buying the Crown Jewels for her. I never thought I'd have a sister who was joining the ranks of the *nouveaux riches*.'

'Stop being so snobbish!' Laura protested. 'I think it's really rather wonderful and I know she'll be tremendously happy.'

'He's a businessman,' Georgie reminded them, as if they weren't already aware of the fact. 'There isn't a mention of him in Burke's Peerage, although there will be once he's married to Beattie.'

'You're just jealous,' Laura pointed out. 'The only thing I envy Beattie is the fact she's getting away from here. I have half a mind to leave myself.'

'Where will you go? What would you do with yourself?' Georgie demanded.

'Earn a living,' Laura countered swiftly. 'Make a life for myself.'

Georgie looked appalled. 'Get a *job*?' she asked in horror. 'Mama would never let you. Girls from our background don't work.'

'Why not? There must be hundreds of skilled women in this country who are wasting their talent just because they're only supposed to be wives and mothers,' Laura argued. 'I want to make something of my life. And I do have a talent. A natural talent, Mrs Armitage said. I want to design and make beautiful clothes and I know I can do it.'

Georgie sniffed. 'Only common women are seamstresses. You'd let the whole family down if you did that. We've never been in trade, nor has anyone else we know.'

Laura covered her face with her hands for a moment and then she got to her feet with a gesture of exasperation. 'Times are changing, Georgie. Women are fed up with being just ornamental ladies, kept in their place by their husbands and by society. Take Emmeline Pankhurst, who is working so hard for the rights of women. She's formed the Women's Franchise League so we're at least allowed to vote in *local* elections now. Within a few years we'll be able to vote in general elections and quite right, too. I don't want to be stuck here any longer, Georgie, and neither should you.'

Her sister folded her hands primly. 'Well, I don't intend to work for my living.'

'So what if you don't marry a well-off man? Are you going to stay with Mama, doing your needlework and helping to arrange the flowers until you die of old age?' Laura demanded hotly.

Georgie shrugged. 'If I have to, then I'll just have to. I certainly don't intend to work, though.'

'This is the worst day of my life,' Lady Rothbury declared as Henry bade them all goodbye as he left Lochlee to join his regiment, which was sailing to South Africa the following week. The servants had all gathered outside the castle to watch him set off, the old retainers who had known him since he'd been born with tears in their eyes, the young maids smiling and waving, hoping they could catch his eye.

Flushed with excitement, Henry kissed all his sisters before saying farewell to his mother.

'Come home safely, my darling,' she whispered as she struggled for composure. 'Take care of yourself.'

'I will, Mama,' he replied jovially, imbued with the optimism of youth.

'Good luck, M'Lord,' McEwan said gruffly as he gave a little bow.

'Goodbye, McEwan. Look after everything for me until I get back,' Henry replied as he ran down the front stone steps to the horse-drawn waiting carriage.

There was a loud chorus of 'good luck' from family and servants alike as they waved and cheered him off and Henry waved back, grinning with delight and loving his moment of glory as he set off.

'Pray to God I never see a day like this again,' Lady Rothbury murmured as she slowly climbed the stairs to her room.

'He'll be back before you know it,' Beattie assured her cheerfully, 'although I am disappointed he can't give me away at my wedding.'

Laura looked at her trunk, packed and ready to go. With a sense of mounting excitement she realized that by this time tomorrow she'd be in Edinburgh and her new life would have begun. All the months of arguing with her mother would be over and she'd be staying with a Mrs Sutherland, a cousin of Lady Rothbury, in her house just off Princes Street. Mrs Sutherland was a widow who had been left penniless and it had been arranged that Laura was to rent a room for four shillings a month.

'I will be sure to chaperone her if required,' Mrs Sutherland promised, 'and I will notify all my friends that she is a first-class dressmaker. For this,' she added cannily, 'I will expect a small commission from whatever business Laura derives from these introductions.'

Georgie had cast her eyes to heaven when she'd heard this. 'You're paying an old woman to tout for business for you?' she exclaimed in mortification. 'Mama, how can you let Laura lower herself in this way?'

For once, Lady Rothbury backed Laura's plans. 'She's very talented. All the great artists have had sponsors when they started,' she retorted, 'and Lucinda Sutherland may be very poor but in her day she knew absolutely everyone and she's managed to keep her friends.'

Her new sewing machine had been packed in a crate, and there was another box containing all the things she'd need, from pins and needles to sewing thread in every colour and sketching pads and pencils.

She hardly slept a wink on that final night in the castle. Earlier in the day she'd received little notes through the post from her sisters sending her their love and wishing her good luck. *You're so brave*, Diana added, while Lizzie wrote, *No woman in the Fairbairn family has ever done anything so enterprising!* Beattie had scrawled, *Enjoy your big adventure!* on a very elegant sheet of writing paper with her Mayfair address printed at the top.

Laura was deeply touched. The support of her siblings meant the world to her and, as a reminder of their affection, she tucked the notes in her handbag where she could look at them whenever she felt lonely.

There was no doubt she was going to miss them but they were all scattered around the country in any case. The only difference now was that they all had husbands and she didn't. She was going to have to carve out her own future, by herself.

Twelve

Edinburgh, 1899

Mrs Sutherland greeted Laura with enthusiasm when she finally arrived in Edinburgh, exhausted by the long cross-country journey from Lochlee. 'My dear Lady Laura!' she squealed in her high-pitched, tinny voice. 'Come in and welcome!' She was a small woman in her sixties, bursting with energy as she darted about, hands fluttering, her little face pointy and pink.

'I'm very glad to be here,' Laura replied, 'and thank you so much for letting me stay in your house.' As she spoke she looked around the narrow hall and staircase to the upper floors, and saw what had once been an elegant abode reduced to shabby genteel poverty.

The old lady clapped her bony hands. 'I've told lots of people that you're going to be living here to do dressmaking and I can tell you, you're going to be very, *very* busy.' She wagged a finger knowingly.

As she prattled on she led Laura into a spacious ground-floor room with a bay window overlooking the street. It was comfortably furnished with a single bed in the corner disguised as a sofa with lots of cushions, but everything looked spotless and there was a faint scent of lavender.

'This is lovely,' Laura exclaimed. It was certainly an improvement on the hall. The light was good; there was a large table in the middle which would be perfect for her work, and plenty of space in a cupboard for her personal belongings.

'My last lodger was a teacher,' Mrs Sutherland remarked. 'He was very clean and tidy.'

'So am I,' Laura assured her, laughing. 'So you think I'll have lots of customers?'

'*Clients*, Lady Laura,' Mrs Sutherland whispered urgently. 'The ladies of Edinburgh and the surrounding area are most impressed that the daughter of an Earl is to set up in business here. I told them you lived in a grand castle and they're all looking forward to meeting you. You'll get a lot of business, especially as we're so near Princes Street where they all come to shop.'

'You're most kind, Mrs Sutherland, and I'm very grateful.' She reminded Laura of a little mouse, scurrying around, hunting cheerfully for crumbs. 'I hope my work lives up to their expectations,' she added.

Mrs Sutherland looked up and her small eyes were as bright as glass buttons. 'You haven't forgotten our little arrangement? You'll give me some commission on the work I get you?'

Laura smiled down at her reassuringly, thinking how sad it must be to be old and alone and begging for little perks. 'Of course I haven't forgotten, and from what you tell me I'm sure you'll deserve some remuneration. I also have the money here for the first month's rent.' She dug into her handbag and withdrew a small white purse.

The old lady clapped her hands excitedly as she took it.

'Oh, that's very good, Lady Laura. Why don't I make us a cup of tea while you unpack?'

'Please just call me Laura,' she said, privately longing to be left alone to lie down and have a rest but fearing that might look rude. 'A cup of tea would be delicious.'

This was the start of her new life and she was desperate to succeed in making her own way in the world. Keeping in with Mrs Sutherland, she felt, was the first step.

It was after midnight and as Laura sat at the centre table stitching the hem of a pale grey taffeta dress she was making for a Mrs Insworth, she began to wonder how she was going to finish this dress and four others for different clients by the end of the week.

Mrs Sutherland hadn't exaggerated six months before when she'd said 'the ladies of Edinburgh' were excited about finding a new dressmaker who could also design. She'd been inundated with requests for garments that ranged from dresses for weddings to funerals, gala Highland balls to small dinner parties, and even simple gowns to wear about the house or in the garden. Many of her new clients also had young daughters who were longing for pretty dresses too, reminding Laura of how she and her sisters had clamoured around Mrs Armitage, driving her mad as they begged her to make things for them.

There was only one problem which made Laura think she might have to find somewhere else to live and work. Mrs Sutherland had never been able to afford to have electric lighting and so, when she worked late into the night, Laura was dependent on old gas lamps. Her headaches were getting worse from the strain on her eyes and she wasn't sure how much longer she could endure it. On the other hand, in spite of being so poor, Mrs Sutherland knew everyone because their families had been friends of her and her late husband when they'd been young and well off.

It made Laura wonder if she would continue to get so many clients without her landlady's help?

It was several weeks later when Mrs Sutherland tapped on her door before darting into her room early one morning, bubbling with excitement. 'My dear,' she trilled. 'Your reputation is spreading by word of mouth! I've received three letters this morning from very prominent ladies who will be going down to London for the Little Season, which begins in October and who want new wardrobes! Their names are . . .' She fumbled with the letters, nearly dropping them all. 'One is from Lady Grimond, who is exceedingly rich. Then there's Mrs Edward Ponsonby, who is a bit *nouveau riche* but very nice. The third one is Mrs Leighton-Harvey. I knew her mother-in-law. They come from Lasswade and have a lot of money . . .'

Laura was no longer listening. At the mention of the name her heart seemed to miss a beat and she felt herself flushing deeply. Walter Leighton-Harvey's wife. That sugary sweet woman who had clung to his arm possessively and interrupted them when they were talking. She bent down quickly to pick up a bale of lining fabric in an effort to hide her blushes, but she couldn't stop a wave of mixed feelings sweeping over her.

'Mrs Leighton-Harvey?' she repeated foolishly. 'I believe I've already met her,' she added.

'That's right! You have, Laura.' Mrs Sutherland squinted myopically at the letter. 'She says . . . Oh yes, here we are! She says she met you at your sister's wedding at Lochlee Castle. Fancy that!' Her expression suddenly changed to one of anxiety. 'I don't suppose I'll get any commission from work you do for her as you already know her?'

'Of course you will,' Laura replied reassuringly. 'It's you she's written to and I don't really know her at all. We just met briefly.'

'Splendid, splendid!' Mrs Sutherland's expression brightened. 'This is going wonderfully well, isn't it?'

Laura agreed with equal enthusiasm and then decided to broach the question of working by a gas lamp at night. 'Have you ever considered installing electric lighting?' she asked in a casual way, as if it was really not of great importance.

'Electric lighting?' The little widow looked as stricken as if Laura had inquired if she'd ever thought of holding orgies in her house. 'Oh, dear me, no! I think it would be far too dangerous. People can die from electric shocks, as they can from lightning. I believe it's very expensive, too.'

Laura nodded, as if in understanding. It was stupid of her to have brought it up. She was just going to have to struggle for a bit longer with the old gas lamps. Meanwhile, her feelings about making clothes for Mrs Leighton-Harvey were uppermost in her mind. Would her husband come too? There was no private changing room for her clients; another reason why she wanted to move, so it was unlikely he'd accompany her.

When she was alone Laura found herself putting her work down on the table while she sat and stared out of the window, lost in thoughts of 'Walter' as she referred to him in her mind. She couldn't help wondering how she was going to feel about making beautiful and seductive dresses for the wife of the man she was so deeply attracted to. Sometimes she dreamed about him, and in her dreams he was always standing with his hand outstretched, beckoning her to go with him. Then she'd awaken with a start. Would his wife talk about him? Would she refer to him as 'my husband' or 'Walter'? Would she show Laura a new piece of jewellery he'd given her?

Laura decided she must be strictly professional in her dealings with Mrs Leighton-Harvey. They might be friends of Robert's family but for her to encourage a social relationship would be a fatal mistake.

As she lay in her narrow little bed that night unable to sleep, she couldn't get the memory of his rich yet mellow voice out of her mind. Normally she didn't notice people's voices, only what they said, but with Walter it wouldn't matter whether he was reciting Shakespeare or a shopping list: his voice would thrill with its sensuality.

If only he wasn't married, she reflected over and over again, remembering how charming and handsome he'd seemed and how she knew in her heart he'd found her attractive, too. It would be perilous for her to see too much of him but for a wild moment she longed for that danger, for the excitement of mutual desire and longing when their hands touched and they looked into each other's eyes. Not since Rory's death had she felt like this about a man.

Suddenly she sat up in bed, shocked by the intensity of her feelings. Walter Leighton-Harvey was a married man with a the twelve-foot Christmas tree which stood in the great hall. Laura was the only one who had earned her own money with which to buy presents, unlike the others, who were given pocket money by Mama, and the married ones, who received an allowance from their husbands. This made Laura feel extraordinarily grown-up and independent, and she secretly relished her plans for the coming year, which she decided to keep to herself for the time being because she knew she'd be met by a barrage of opposition, especially from her mother.

Meanwhile, there had been so much to talk about during those first few precious days as the castle was being prepared for the celebrations.

On Christmas Day they all trooped merrily though the thick snow to church for morning service, after which they returned to the castle where log fires were blazing in all the reception rooms and two footmen stood with trays of champagne which was imbibed in the drawing room.

Then McEwan struck the big gong and everyone took their seats around the long table in the dining room, which had been decorated with fir cones and branches of holly thick with red berries.

'This is the happiest Christmas we've all had since Papa died,' Lizzie confided to Humphrey as the main course of roast turkey with chestnut stuffing and cranberry sauce was served with a variety of vegetables. This was followed traditionally by spicy mincemeat tarts dripping with rich brandy butter.

'Your mother is bearing up very well,' Humphrey agreed. 'I'm glad Laura is here, too. She's like a breath of fresh air.'

'Yes. I miss her so much. This is like old times, us all being together again.' Lizzie spoke almost wistfully.

He smiled sympathetically. The five eldest girls had always been close and as an only child he sometimes wished he'd had brothers and sisters to jolly him along. Lizzie was pregnant again and he was delighted at the thought of a third child.

'Why are you grinning at Lizzie in that asinine way?' Georgie asked him from across the table.

'Wouldn't you like to know,' he teased.

She shrugged. 'You used to be quite intelligent, Humphrey. Now you've become all soppy.'

very sweet wife; what was she thinking of? How could she possibly entertain romantic notions about a man who had a wife and child?

She felt ashamed of herself for daydreaming about him in that way. What would Mama say if she knew? She'd forbade her brain to even *think* about him in future. Lying down again she curled up on her side but just as she was drifting off to sleep she remembered his dark, penetrating eyes and the way he'd looked at her at Lizzie's wedding. A tear slid from her cheek and disappeared into the pillow.

'I'll never forget the exquisite wedding dress you made for your sister,' Mrs Leighton-Harvey said as soon as she arrived for her appointment with Laura a week later. 'I'm simply thrilled you're doing this professionally. We need someone like you in Edinburgh. Many of us have had to go down to London or to Paris to get our clothes.'

'I don't think I can compete with Paris,' Laura replied with a smile as she ushered Mrs Leighton-Harvey to a chair at one end of the table, 'but I will do my best.' She sat opposite and picked up a notebook and pencil in a businesslike manner. 'First of all I suggest you tell me what you require for London's Little Season, be it dinner dresses, ball gowns, or daywear suitable for luncheon parties? Maybe you'll go racing? Or join country house parties at the end of the week?'

Mrs Leighton-Harvey blinked rapidly and looked confused. 'I don't know really,' she simpered. 'Maybe I need a range of outfits which will cover a lot of different social engagements.'

'That's always wise. The same dress can be made to look quite different with the aid of accessories. Then we can discuss style and suitable colours and fabrics, and what type of fur trimming you like on coats and jackets? Sable and ermine are the height of fashion at the moment but I think the new collections will feature red and black fox fur; red fox with tweed outfits will be the essence of smartness, and of course black for daywear and white Arctic fox for the evening. Although, of course,' she continued conversationally, 'black fox in the evening worn with a black satin dress and diamonds makes a magnificent impression.'

By now Mrs Leighton-Hartley was speechless, imagining herself gliding through the grand London drawing rooms of the Duke of Westminster and the Marquess of Londonderry, turning heads wherever she went, being flattered and feted and envied by other women.

'Shall I take your measurements today and then I'll have them on record for future purposes?' Laura continued smoothly.

'That's a good idea.' The dazed blue eyes blinked again. 'A very good idea.'

'Lastly, I'll send you some sketches and you can choose which designs you favour. I'll also pin to each sketch a small example of the fabric I suggest would be the most appropriate.'

'Goodness, you're so efficient.'

'I like to be organized,' Laura replied quietly, smiling with inner satisfaction. The woman was a fool. A sweet, brainless socialite. *What did Walter ever see in her?* flashed through her mind unbidden.

'Yes. Of course. Now let me think.' Mrs Leighton-Harvey frowned as if tackling a tricky mathematical problem. 'Walter and I will be in London for the month of October so I suppose that will be quite a lot of clothes?'

'If you're going to a lot of functions, yes.' Laura spoke briskly as she made notes. 'Have you got a good milliner?'

Mrs Leighton-Harvey looked flummoxed. 'I don't know. I usually buy my hats from Fraser's in Princes Street. My friends and I always shop there.'

Laura nodded. 'I know it well. It might be a good idea to have a word with their chief milliner. We could show them the designs and the fabrics for your daywear so they could produce hats that went perfectly with the ensemble.'

Light at last dawned and Mrs Leighton-Harvey looked enraptured. 'Fancy having hats made to match your outfits!' She spoke wonderingly. 'My word, you're very clever.'

'Not at all,' Laura responded modestly. 'I will enclose a list of my prices when you receive the designs and if you agree we should get started right away. We've only got four months if your new wardrobe is to be ready by the end of September.'

'I'll let you know at once. Wait until I tell Walter! He's very

particular about what I wear.' She departed in a confused whirl of delight, leaving Laura feeling exhausted and tainted by the irony of the situation. She was about to make a lot of money as she slaved over making a dozen or more exquisite outfits for another woman to wear in order to please the one man she herself was in love with.

On a practical level one thing was certain: she was going to have to find an experienced seamstress to help her or she'd never be able to cope with the demands of the ladies of Edinburgh, who were now flocking to have her make their clothes.

Thirteen

Lochlee Castle, 1899

'How good it is to be home again, even if it is only for a few weeks,' Laura declared as the family sat down for their traditional Hogmanay dinner. She'd returned to Lochlee in time for Christmas and was given a big welcome, not only by her mother but also by Lizzie and Humphrey with their two baby daughters, Diana and Robert with their baby boy, Richard, and Beattie and Andrew, who had come up from London by train, and then Georgie. The younger sisters, Alice, Flora and Catriona, who were fast growing up, had also greeted her with shrieks of awestruck delight, wanting to know what Edinburgh was like and what did she do in her spare time?

'Spare time?' Laura laughed, hugging them all. 'What *is* spare time? It's something I haven't even heard of for the past year. She'd lost weight and her features were more delicately defined than before but, although her fingertips were always tender these days from pinning and stitching garments, she had a healthy glow and her hazel eyes sparkled with confidence. Her finances had allowed her to buy nice Christmas presents for everyone which she'd wrapped stylishly in green paper with scarlet ribbons, and they'd been placed almost reverently under

'While you've become all stroppy,' he countered good-naturedly.

'Stop it, you two!' Diana said, laughing. 'Robert is about to make a speech.'

'Oh, Lor',' Georgie murmured. 'How he loves the sound of his own voice.'

Diana gave her a warning glance as her husband pushed back his chair and rose to his feet.

'Dearest mother-in-law,' he began, bowing to Lady Rothbury before turning to the others. 'Ladies and gentlemen. On behalf of Henry, who would be standing here now if he wasn't fighting the Boers in South Africa, I would like to thank you, Mama, for giving us such a wonderful Christmas. Your generosity is overwhelming and we are all so grateful to you for inviting us to enjoy the splendour that is Lochlee Castle.'

'Here, here!' exclaimed Andrew and Humphrey in unison.

'So let us drink a toast to our hostess!' Robert raised his glass.

There was a chorus of 'To Mama!' and Lady Rothbury smiled although she felt like weeping, for she missed Henry so much. He should have been here, at home with them all, safe and well within the protective stone walls of the castle.

In the days that followed the festive air still pervaded Lochlee, and Laura realized that her three brothers-in-law were wonderful additions to the family, bringing with them a male sense of adventure. Robert went off to buy a couple of toboggans so they could have races down the hillside, and Andrew insisted they buy ice skates so they could whirl around on the large frozen pond and even have gentle games of ice hockey.

'Why did we never do anything like this before?' Laura demanded, her slender nose as pink as her cheeks as an icy breeze coming off the mountains invigorated them all into sporting activity.

'Too many girls and not enough boys in the family,' Georgie pointed out.

'Come on,' Laura called out and, gathering up some snow in her gloved hands, she quickly shaped it into a ball and threw it at Robert, catching him on the back of the neck.

His look of utter surprise made Diana laugh so much she

tripped on her skates and fell over, while Humphrey and Andrew quickly joined in the fun, so that snow balls were being hurled through the air with speed and the girls were retaliating by throwing them back as they shrieked with laughter. Even Georgie was giggling and enjoying herself so much she actually called Lizzie 'darling' before tossing a snowball at her head.

Then Andrew threw a snowball at Beattie which landed on the side of her face and, turning, she gave a howl. A moment later their arms were around each other until they slipped on the ice and rolled helpless with laughter in the snow.

This prompted Diana and Robert to link arms and he gave her a quick kiss before she too lost her balance and he had to hold her tightly to prevent her falling over again. The air was filled with merriment and laughter, and for a moment Laura stood alone, watching her sisters with their devoted husbands. A sudden deep sadness welled up within her because she had no one. Unshed tears welled up in her eyes. It seemed a long time ago since she'd been so happily engaged to Rory. By now, if they'd married, they'd have had several children and London would have been as familiar to her as her rented room in Edinburgh. The thought flashed through her mind that it would probably always be like this and she'd better get used to it. When her much younger sisters married she'd be the old maid who sat in the corner, always smiling to hide her sadness, always laughing to keep her profound loneliness a secret. She resolved to put Walter Leighton-Harvey out of her mind completely. To even fantasize about him was stupid and dangerous. His pretty, vapid wife would flaunt herself in front of him in the gowns Laura had so painstakingly made and he'd never know that there were nights when she dreamed of him only to wake alone at dawn, cold and shivering in her single bed.

'Help me to my feet, Laura!' Beattie called out, laughing. 'My hat has fallen off and this dreadful man I married has ruined my hairdo!' She ran her gloved hands through the loosened tendrils that straggled down her back and Andrew thought he'd never seen her look so adorable.

'Give me your hand,' Laura replied gaily. 'Mama is going to

be horrified when she sees us all looking such a mess. "What will the servants think?" she'll say.'

'She'll say more than that,' Diana countered. 'Mama will say, "Where's your dignity? And you a married woman?" That's what she'll say.'

'Not in my case she won't,' Laura mocked lightly.

Alice, Flora and Catriona had already returned to the castle to change into dry clothes and get warm again, and soon the whole family were congregated before the log fire in the library, drinking hot chocolate provided by McEwan, who was unsuccessfully trying to keep a straight face having caught a glimpse of the antics of the family by the pond from one of the castle windows.

Hogmanay brought even greater celebrations to Lochlee as the whole of Scotland got ready to welcome in the coming New Year. No matter what, the Fairbairns feasted lavishly on the thirty-first of December but for Humphrey and Andrew, who were English, it was a new experience.

'You two are Sassenachs!' Georgie declared disparagingly.

Andrew, new to the aristocracy and especially the Scottish nobility, looked puzzled. 'What's a Sassenach?'

'Don't worry, dearest,' Beattie, smiling, assured him. 'It's not really an insult, although Georgie seems to think it is.'

There was a mounting sense of expectation as they all gathered for dinner on New Year's Eve, the women in all their finery and Robert in his kilt, but Humphrey and Andrew in white tie and tails, much to Georgie's disapproval.

'Not a kilt between the two of you!' she scoffed. 'Let's hope Henry is back by next year to show you how it's done properly.'

The new arrivals to the family privately noticed that Freddie, the disgraced eldest son, was never mentioned these days. It seemed the Fairbairns had decided he was persona non grata and might actually be presumed dead.

As they all sat around the long, candlelit dining table enjoying game soup, pheasant and partridge pie, venison served with creamed potatoes and red cabbage laced with bacon and chestnuts, followed by an array of puddings including Charlotte

Russe, Baba au Rhum and raspberry tartlets, Laura realized how frugally she'd been living, partly to save money but also because she didn't have time to cook in Mrs Sutherland's almost medieval kitchen. Bread, cheese and apples were her main sustenance, with a glass of water or a cup of tea. As the wine flowed tonight she found herself relaxing as they waited for McEwan to perform the ancient Scottish tradition of being the First Footer.

'It would, of course, have been Henry if he'd been here,' Lady Rothbury explained, 'but McEwan is a dark-haired man, or at least he used to be, so he'll have to do it.'

At five minutes to midnight the family stood expectantly in the great hall, looked down upon by the heads of stags whose magnificent antlers gleamed in the lamp light, while McEwan stood in the drive, braving the freezing conditions until the church bell struck twelve times. Then, with a dramatic flourish, he pushed open the heavy oak door of the castle and strode across the threshold as the First Footer of the New Year, carrying in his outstretched hands a piece of coal for warmth, a small bag of salt for wealth, a piece of rich fruit cake known as a Black Bun for food, and half a bottle of whisky for sustenance. This ancient ritual based on the Pagan Winter Solstice ceremony was received by Lady Rothbury with gravity, before the family started clapping and cheering and McEwan looked suitably gratified. His role had been to bring good fortune to the family in the coming year and he felt deeply honoured.

'Well done!' Robert shouted above the din of approval. 'Give the man a stiff drink. He must be frozen half to death!'

'Thank you, M'Lord,' McEwan replied with a little bow.

'Let's all drink to the New Year,' declared Humphrey, who was particularly partial to the champagne he'd purchased in France and had brought two cases of it with him to Lochlee 'to imbibe with the family over Christmas and the New Year', as he put it.

There was a chorus of 'Here's to 1900!' as everyone kissed and hugged, but then they fell silent as Robert raised his glass and announced another toast. 'Let us give thanks for the blessings we have received in the past year and let us drink a toast to the family hero, Henry, and to his speedy and safe return from South Africa in the near future.'

'Pray to God,' whispered Lady Rothbury under her breath.

'To Henry!' Everyone raised their glasses, and Diana and Laura felt tears stinging their eyes. It didn't seem the same without Henry and his vibrant youthful charm and energy. They all missed him deeply.

Robert put his arm around Diana's waist. 'The Boer War will soon come to an end,' he said comfortingly. 'Henry will be home before you know it.' His strong, matter-of-fact tone lifted the moment that had plunged the atmosphere into darkness.

'He's right,' Humphrey warmly agreed. Then he turned to Lady Rothbury. 'Mark my words, I'll get more of this very good champagne from France and we'll give Henry the biggest welcome home party this castle has ever seen. Isn't that right, girls?' he boomed to all the others.

'I'll definitely come home for that!' Laura declared stoutly.

'We'll all come home for that,' agreed Beattie, smiling through her tears.

Laura stayed at Lochlee until Twelfth Night when, in another ritual, they all helped take down the Christmas decorations and get the groundsmen to carry the tree out of the castle and chop it up for firewood. The holly and the mistletoe also had to be removed, and suddenly it seemed the festivities were over for another year and it was time she went back to her new life in Edinburgh.

'Are you looking forward to returning to Mrs Sutherland's house?' her mother inquired as they all had luncheon together for the last time. Lizzie, Diana and Beattie were also returning to their own homes later that day.

'I'm not returning to Mrs Sutherland's house,' Laura announced.

Lady Rothbury put down her knife and fork. 'So you're going to continue your dressmaking from here?' she asked hopefully.

Laura shook her head. 'I'm expanding the business.'

'In what way?' Georgie sounded aggressive and almost envious.

'I've taken a flat in a house, very near Mrs Sutherland, and it's got a big room for my work, a small bedroom and a little kitchen and bathroom and . . .'

'I forbid you to live alone, Laura,' her mother said fiercely. 'Getting a flat? What were you thinking of? A young lady living alone in the city will ruin your reputation.'

Laura's jaw hardened. She'd known all along her mother would disapprove. 'Times have changed, Mama, and I'm in a very respectable part of Edinburgh. I need a proper workroom and a changing room for my clients if I'm going to expand. Anyway, I've already taken it and paid a month's rent in advance. There are other professional people living in the building and I'm employing a young woman who is an excellent seamstress to help me with the work. It's all arranged and Mrs Sutherland is very happy to continue getting clients for me.'

'Robert, tell her this is unseemly,' Lady Rothbury begged. 'She mustn't be allowed to behave like someone in *trade*, for goodness' sake! It's one thing to make clothes for a few friends, but to set herself up as if she were practically running a *shop*! Oh, it's out of the question. She must be stopped.'

Robert smiled gently and gave Laura a supportive nod of approval before turning to Lady Rothbury. 'My dear mother-in-law, times are changing, alas,' he said affectionately. 'Laura is a very talented young woman and it would be cruel to deny her this opportunity to express her talent.'

'But for *money*!' she wailed. 'And living alone in a flat could be misconstrued. Some men might think she was a . . .?'

'Knowing Laura, no one would think that,' he retorted firmly. 'She is obviously a very respectable young lady who makes an honest living designing beautiful clothes for the aristocracy. It's not as if she was running up garments to be sold in some cheap emporium,' he added.

'What she's doing is a let-down for the Fairbairn family, though, isn't it?' Georgie remarked spitefully.

Lizzie turned on her angrily. 'That's a horrid thing to say and absolutely untrue.'

'Yes, Georgie, and it's a pity you don't do something useful with your life instead of always criticizing others,' Beattie snapped.

Then Diana spoke. 'Why is it you haven't a nice thing to say about *anybody*?' she remonstrated crossly.

'It's all right for you lot,' Georgie shot back rudely. 'You've already found eligible men to marry.'

Humphrey's mouth quivered with suppressed laughter. 'I didn't know we men were lost in the first place?' he asked, putting on a plaintive voice while his eyes twinkled with merriment. He turned to Andrew and Robert, winking as he did so. 'Did you know we were lost, chaps?'

They grinned back, shaking their heads.

'Well, I'm very relieved to hear we've been found anyway,' Robert declared stoutly, taking Diana's hand and kissing it tenderly.

'Oh! You're all so childish,' Georgie sniped with chagrin as she got up and flounced out of the room.

'And happy, too,' Andrew said softly as they watched her departing figure.

Robert looked serious. 'I must apologize to her. It was mean of us to tease her like that. We shouldn't have done it.'

'Don't worry,' Lizzie assured him. 'Georgie brings it on herself every time she opens her mouth.' She turned to Laura. 'We all think what you're doing is absolutely splendid and good luck to you.'

'Yes, good luck,' Humphrey echoed. 'We're all very proud of you and I think this new place sounds much more comfortable.'

'I still think you should have a chaperone,' Lady Rothbury fretted. 'In my day if a girl lived on her own it meant she was a scarlet woman.' She rose stiffly. 'You're over twenty-one, Laura, so I can't forbid you, but I do not approve of what you're doing.'

The men rose and Robert stepped briskly forward and opened the door for her as she swept grandly out of the room.

There was a moment's silence, then they all turned eagerly to Laura, wanting to know more about her new premises.

Laura's eyes were sparkling as she answered their questions. 'Do you know the best thing about it?' she asked, laughing.

'What?' Lizzie enquired.

'It's got electricity! No more working until the early hours by the dim light of a beastly gas lamp.'

'Is it safe?' Diana queried. 'We were thinking of installing it at Cranley Court but then I became nervous, although Robert says everyone will have it within a few years.'

'Of course it's safe,' Laura protested. 'The first thing I saw when I went to look at the flat was this priceless notice pinned to the hall wall. It said, *Do not attempt to light with a match! Simply turn the key on the wall by the door.* So I did and the room was instantly filled with this brilliant light. I couldn't believe it at first. It's so much better than gas.'

'Jolly clever chap, Mr Edison. I wish I could come up with an invention like that,' Humphrey murmured thoughtfully.

'You'll enjoy living there,' Lizzie remarked.

Laura beamed. 'I don't care what Mama thinks, I'm going to love it!'

Fourteen

Edinburgh, 1900

Laura spent the first few days settling into her new flat with the enthusiasm of a bird getting her nest in order. She'd brought a few things from Lochlee, too, which helped to make the rooms more like home. By the time she'd laid down some Persian rugs on the polished floor, scattered several *petit point* cushions on the chairs and sofa and hung a couple of framed watercolour paintings of Loch Etive on the bedroom wall, she realized with excitement that she'd actually created a home of her own. This was not just a room in someone else's house, which was what she'd had with Mrs Sutherland, but her very own place where she could do as she liked. Energized at the very thought of being able to come and go and eat whenever she liked, it was so liberating she really didn't mind being on her own at all. In fact, she rather enjoyed it.

By the time she went to bed that night, she'd set up her sewing machine beside the large work table she'd bought and filled the drawers of a chest with all the tools she'd need, and felt ready to start. Her desk was ready for work, too, with a box of index cards filed in alphabetical order of her clients names and addresses and all their measurements. She'd had writing paper for quotes and invoices printed with her name, Laura Fairbairn Designs, and address at the top. Mama was going to be horrified if she knew Laura had dropped her title but she felt it was necessary. It was not her business to be grander than her clients.

As she lay in bed that night unable to sleep, excitement flowed through her body, as heady as alcohol. Tomorrow morning her new assistant, Helen Miller, was arriving to start work at eight o'clock and she had no doubt that by the end of the week they'd be busy because the ladies of Edinburgh would want to plan their spring wardrobes.

Towards the middle of January Laura began to feel a flutter of anxiety. Only three clients had come to see her and they'd only wanted simple house dresses which she could easily have made herself without Helen's assistance.

'It's the bad weather, my dear,' Mrs Sutherland assured her when Laura dropped in to see her. 'There's always a lull after Christmas and Hogmanay in every line of business. People are tired, they've spent a lot of money and they're not in the mood to go gallivanting off to get new clothes. For one thing it's too cold. The horses find it slippery, which is dangerous. As soon as it thaws they'll all come back, mark my words.'

'I suppose so.' Laura was worried, though. She only had a small amount of money saved and it wasn't enough to pay her rent and Helen for much longer if the icy weather continued.

Mrs Sutherland wagged a finger. 'The butcher was only saying to me yesterday that he's never been so quiet.'

'I'm sure you're right.' Laura felt angry with herself for not realizing that January was always a bleak month when even her own family was not in the mood to indulge in new clothes because there was little socializing until Easter. How had she gauged it so wrong? With hindsight she now knew she shouldn't have taken her new premises until late February or early March.

As she walked home she decided to economize on food for the time being, and rather than ask anyone in her family for money because she had her pride, she might be forced to sell one of the Persian rugs to pay next month's rent. That night she slept badly and awoke at dawn, deciding she might as well give Helen the day off because there was nothing for her to do.

Just before eight o'clock Helen came rushing into the flat, flushed and breathless as if she'd been running. 'Have you heard the news?' she gasped, clutching the *Scotsman* newspaper.

'Is the Boer War over?' Laura asked instantly.

Helen looked at her blankly. 'No,' she replied, puzzled. 'The old Queen has gone and died! Look!'

Laura skimmed the headlines in disbelief. *Queen Victoria has died at Osborne House on the Isle of Wight*, she read in heavy lettering.

For a moment she found it hard to believe. The Queen had reigned for sixty-three years and her subjects had become so accustomed to her being on the throne that it seemed impossible to believe she was no longer there – a familiar figure in her widow's weeds, which she'd worn ever since her beloved husband had died.

Laura suddenly threw down the newspaper. 'I've got to go out,' she said urgently as she struggled into her long tweed coat. Then she jammed a fox fur hat on her head, grabbed her purse and gloves and spoke briefly. 'Stay here until I get back, Helen. If anyone calls invite them in and take down their name, address and their order. Tell them I'll get back to them later. Or tomorrow morning,' she added. A moment later she was gone and her bewildered assistant heard her running down the front steps and along the street.

It was late in the afternoon when an exhausted but triumphant Laura returned, casting off her hat and coat and flinging herself into a chair.

'Whatever have you been up to?' Helen asked. 'I was getting ever so worried. No one has called but about nine or ten letters have come for you. Put through the letter box, they were. By hand,' she added, obviously impressed.

Laura gave a deep sigh of satisfaction. 'First, I went to see my bank manager,' she began, 'and when I told him what I wanted to do he agreed to lend me quite a lot of money.'

Helen made no comment. She didn't think it was her place to ask this nice employer, a real lady who belonged to ever such a grand family, what she needed the money for.

'Then,' Laura continued, enjoying drawing out the suspense, 'I got a cab and went to the wholesale company, from whom I buy all the fabrics.'

'But they're near Glasgow,' Helen exclaimed, as if they were on the other side of the world.

Laura nodded. 'Do you know what I bought, Helen?'

The girl shook her head, her eyes wide.

Laura leaned forward and her eyes blazed with excitement in her flushed face. 'I bought all the black fabric they had in stock.' She started ticking on her fingers. 'In tweed, soft wool, alpaca, velvet, silk, chiffon, lace, taffeta and crepe de Chine; hundreds of yards of fabric to make up for our clients, who are all going to be wearing full mourning for the next twelve months.'

Helen's jaw dropped. 'Because the Queen died?'

Laura leaned back, savouring the moment. 'Yes, because the Queen died. I also placed orders for grey and purple fabric for the following year, which is what many of our elderly clients will move on to for a while. You do know what this means, Helen, don't you?'

'We'll be busy,' the girl replied solemnly.

Laura burst out laughing. 'We'll be more than busy. We've cornered the market. None of the other dressmakers in Scotland will be able to obtain quantities of black fabric for months to come because I've snapped it all up! We are going to dress all the ladies of Edinburgh with everything they will need for the coming year. Coats, cloaks, day and evening dresses, skirts and blouses . . .' She paused and looked around the workroom. 'I wish I'd taken a bigger place now. We're going to need extra help, Helen.'

'Where will you store all the fabric?'

'I've already been to see Mrs Sutherland and she's very kindly allowing me to rent a big room in her basement. The whole-salers are going to be delivering the material next Wednesday.'

'You have organized everything,' Helen said with admiration.

'Not quite everything.' Laura looked thoughtful. 'We need to get in a good stock of nice black buttons, including ones made of jet, and also poppers, hooks and eyes and a thousand reels of black thread. I think I should also buy a second sewing machine.'

'What about the people who can't afford to go into mourning?'

'They always wear black armbands out of respect.' Laura paused, her mind still working feverishly. 'We'll offer to make small armbands for the children of our clients,' she continued, 'because they won't have to wear black clothes unless they're eighteen.'

After Helen had gone home, with instructions to help find two more experienced seamstresses, Laura made herself a cup of tea and then sat at her desk making some rough calculations. She'd borrowed a large sum of money from the bank and the manager, who knew her family well, had been quite happy for her to have the loan because her business plan was impres-sively well thought out and planned, but now she had to work out for herself the exact cost of materials, extra staff, a new machine and everything else she'd need for this sudden expan-sion, coupled with how much she'd need to earn to pay back the loan and hopefully show a profit by the end of the year.

Lord Rothbury had often talked about businesses that had expanded too quickly and eventually led to a financial loss, and this was at the back of Laura's mind now as she tried to forecast exactly how much business she was hoping to acquire during the next twelve months. Had she been stupidly impulsive today? Wouldn't it have been more sensible if she'd asked for someone else's advice? Andrew was a successful businessman as his father had been before him, and now she wondered if she shouldn't have consulted him first? It was too late now. Her euphoria of earlier had been replaced by anxious tiredness as her mind revolved around whether she should have gone ahead without thinking it through or not?

By three o'clock in the morning she comforted herself with the belief that by the time she'd taken advice from some experienced source another dressmaker would have gone along and bought every length of black material available from the wholesalers, and she'd be sitting here now kicking herself for having lost such a wonderful opportunity.

At present the reality of the situation was that she was up to her neck in debt. Now it was a case of sink or swim.

As dawn stole over the sleeping city and Edinburgh Castle perched high above gleamed in the first pink rays of the sun, Laura bathed and then put on the black gown she'd made for her father's funeral. She was facing the biggest challenge she'd ever had and there was no going back now.

This was a turning point in her life. If she got through this she could get through anything.

'Laura, you've got so thin!' Diana exclaimed, hugging her sister affectionately. 'Are you all right?'

Laura smiled merrily. 'I've never been better,' she laughed. 'Rushed off my feet but everything is going so well. Even better than I expected.'

'I can't wait to hear all about it! Let's order tea and then we can talk.'

They had arranged to meet in a restaurant in Princes Street because Diana had come down to Edinburgh for the day to do some shopping.

'So tell me what's happening? I haven't seen you since Christmas.'

'When the Queen died in January it became a mad house. We're partly working at my flat and partly at Mrs Sutherland's house which luckily is just around the corner. Imagine this – I've had to rent a room from her just to store the bales of black fabric I ordered. Actually there isn't much of it left. I've got Helen and two other seamstresses and we're all working night and day.'

'You must be exhausted,' Diana sympathized.

'Actually I'm quite energized. I acquired a lot of new clients and I'm hoping they'll stay with me when they want new clothes next year,' Laura said hopefully.

'I'm sure they will. I for one will be back by next February. I can't wait to get out of mourning. I fancy having dresses in red and pink and maybe primrose yellow.'

'I can't wait to get back to working with bright colours for a change,' Laura agreed. 'Tell me, what news of Lizzie?'

Diana grinned. 'She's had a third daughter.'

'She was hoping for a boy this time.'

Diana had more news to tell. 'Beattie is also expecting!'

'Already? What a family we are for having babies! Don't tell me you're expecting, too?'

Diana shook her head firmly. 'Nicolas and Louise are enough for me and as Robert has got his heir he's happy.' She leaned forward and whispered confidentially. 'I don't want to end up like poor Mama with eleven children. Have you seen how her body has been ravaged by all those pregnancies?' She gave a little shudder. 'I'd be afraid that it would put Robert off . . . you know.'

Laura nodded but didn't reply. As a family they never talked about such private matters. 'So when is Beattie's baby arriving?' she asked instead.

'In October. Goodness, Mama is going to have so many grandchildren by the time we're all married, isn't she?'

'Probably, except that Georgie and I might not get married,' Laura pointed out.

'Goodness! You haven't heard?' Diana asked in surprise.

'Heard what?'

'Georgie's met a man and he's mad about her.'

Laura's eyes widened. 'Why didn't you tell me before? What's he like? Have you met him?'

'No, we haven't met him but Lizzie has told us all about him and there is a problem.'

Laura looked cynical. 'There's always a problem with Georgie. What is it this time? Is he already married?'

'No, he's not married,' Diana declared. 'You know what a terrible snob Georgie is? How she even looks down on Andrew as being *nouveau riche*? Remember how she said you might let down the family by becoming a dressmaker?'

'I do indeed!'

'Well, this man, a bachelor of thirty-three whose name is

Shane O'Mally, comes from a working-class background and owns several pubs in Scotland and Northumberland. He's very successful and *very* rich.' Diana started to giggle. 'Georgie is mad about him, too, but she's torn between the thought of marrying for love but to someone lower class or not getting married at all! Can you imagine how tormented she is?'

Laura nodded wistfully. Georgie's lack of self-esteem had always made her feel that her only asset was belonging to a titled family and so to marry someone who wasn't listed in the peerage was unthinkable.

Diana guessed what she was thinking. 'Poor Georgie! I hope she doesn't make him feel inferior? Frankly I'd love her to marry someone who seems to be devoted to her. It's just what she needs.'

'What about Mama? What does she say?'

'I think she's rather relieved that Georgie has found someone. This is the first time she's had a man who has shown the slightest interest in her and apparently he's very nice and very kind. He's not in the least interested in her having a title and he's not impressed by Lochlee at all, so he's not after Georgie in order to better himself.'

'He sounds perfect for her,' Laura exclaimed. 'She'll be far more comfortable with someone like that than if she married someone like Robert or Humphrey.'

'Yes. It's a pity she has such an inferiority complex. You'll soon be getting an order to make another wedding dress!'

'You have come to town with a bag full of surprises,' Laura remarked. 'By comparison my news is desperately boring. Mrs So-and-so has ordered a black lace dinner dress and Lady Such-and-such wants a black taffeta cloak for the summer; not exactly riveting gossip!' She began gathering up her gloves and handbag. 'I must be getting back to work.'

'Can't you come shopping with me?' Diana asked in disappointment.

'I wish I could but I've got a client coming at five o'clock to collect some new outfits I've made for her.' Her mouth tightened. 'I've never known a woman who spent so much on herself. Thank goodness her husband seems to be very rich.'

'She sounds like the new Queen, Alexandra. Who is she?'

'Mrs Leighton-Harvey.'

Diana frowned. 'I think I've heard of her. Where does she live?'

'In Lasswade. She and her husband came to your wedding. I believe they're friends of Robert's parents.' Laura's expression had become grim and she spoke tightly.

'I remember being introduced to them. She's quite a pretty woman, isn't she?'

'Yes, and extremely vain and stupid.'

Diana looked surprised and amused. 'I can see you don't like her, but she must be a good customer? Isn't that what you want?'

'Of course it is,' Laura agreed, pulling herself together. 'I'm just a bit tired and I've still got hours of work ahead of me tonight.'

'Darling, you're exhausted. Why don't you come and stay with us for a couple of days at the end of the week? You need a rest. Do say you'll come?'

Laura thought about the sheer luxury of staying at Cranley Court and how she'd wake up in an enormous bed in the morning and have a maid bring her breakfast on a tray. What heaven it would be to relax on the terrace and instead of the constant clatter of the sewing machines the only sound would be the drowsy hum of the honey bees as they hovered over the lavender beds. The food was always exquisite too, and Diana and Robert were generous and undemanding hosts. 'I'd love to,' she said without hesitation. 'I should stay in town and work but I can't think of anything nicer than going to stay with you.'

Diana beamed. 'Excellent. Then that's settled. We've no other visitors so we can do exactly as we like. If the weather is fine we might have a picnic luncheon on Saturday in the folly. You'll arrive on Friday afternoon, won't you? And stay until Monday?'

Laura shook her head regretfully. 'I'll have to leave on Sunday. It wouldn't be fair on the others if I was away any longer.' She gathered up her fine black kid gloves and her purse. 'I must fly now but I'll see you on Friday.'

The sisters kissed goodbye and Diana watched as Laura hurried out of the restaurant, a slim, vibrant-looking young woman who attracted admiring looks from other people as she passed their tables.

If only . . . Diana reflected, if only Laura could meet some wonderful man who would sweep her off her feet and give her the sort of life she deserved.

On Sunday evening Laura was back in Edinburgh feeling refreshed and relaxed by her stay at Cranley Court, which had passed all too swiftly.

'You're not so washed-out looking,' Helen observed by way of a compliment when she arrived for work the next morning.

Laura smiled as she threaded a sewing needle with a fine strand of black silk before she began the laborious job of hand stitching it on to the cuffs of a black crepe dress. 'Washed out? What, like an old piece of faded chintz?' she teased.

Helen blushed with embarrassment. 'Oh, I didn't mean, that is, I just thought you looked, well, a bit tired,' she stammered.

Laura laughed. 'I'm only teasing,' she began when they heard knocking on the street door and then the bell to her flat rang loudly.

'It's a bit early for a client,' Laura observed, putting down her sewing. 'Can you go and see who it is, Helen? I'm not expecting any deliveries this morning.' She rose to her feet while Helen scurried down the stairs. A moment later she recognized Mrs Sutherland's voice and she sounded quite agitated.

'Terrible news, Laura,' she exclaimed, pushing past Helen into the workroom. She looked upset and her tiny frame was trembling.

'Come and sit down,' Laura said in concern. 'What's happened?'

'Mrs Cavanagh called in to see me first thing this morning. Oh, it's too shocking for words! They were great friends, you know.'

Laura frowned. 'Fetch Mrs Sutherland a glass of water,' she told one of the junior seamstresses as she led the old lady to a chair. 'Is Mrs Cavanagh all right?' she asked, knowing they were old friends. She'd also become one of Laura's regular clients, too.

'She's all right. She said it was an accident. They found her body at the bottom of the staircase. Stone cold, it was.' Mrs Sutherland's bony hand covered her mouth in anguish. 'Have you ever heard anything so dreadful?'

Laura stared at her in bewilderment. 'Whose body?' she asked.

'I'm trying to tell you, my dear.' Tears welled up in her faded blue eyes. 'She was such a good customer, wasn't she? I was terribly shocked when I heard what had happened. I knew you'd want to know.'

Laura sat down beside Mrs Sutherland and took her hand. The old lady seemed deeply shocked and she was still shaking all over. Speaking slowly, as if she was addressing a small child, Laura said, 'What was the name of her friend? Do I know her?'

From the wrinkled face two button bright eyes snapped with impatience as she turned and glared at Laura. 'I *told* you! Mrs Leighton-Harvey! They think she tripped and fell down the stairs in the middle of the night. Her neck was broken when they found her this morning.'

Laura felt her own head spin and her heart contracted painfully as she took in what it could mean, but then in an instant she was overcome with shame. A woman in her late thirties had died as a result of a tragic accident and a devilish voice in her head was saying, *He's free now. He's not married any more!* And the voice was getting louder and louder.

She struggled to her feet while the wicked thoughts that had sprung to mind like a sudden forest fire raged in her head. They must be crushed and stamped out before they took hold. How could she live with herself while a part of her grappled with the appalling thought that because his silly little wife was dead she stood a chance of having him for herself?

'I'm very sorry to hear that. How tragic,' she heard herself say, but it wasn't really her speaking. Dear God! What was she really thinking of?

Helen and the two other assistants were showing all the right emotions: gasping with shock and exclaiming 'how terrible' and 'she was such a sweet lady' and 'we're really going to miss her', all the time Laura was fighting to quell the spring of hope that had opened up in her heart.

'We must send a nice wreath, Lady Laura, mustn't we?' she heard Helen say.

Laura nodded in agreement. 'Of course we must.'

Mrs Sutherland dabbed at her eyes with a damp handkerchief. 'Perhaps you should write a little letter to Mr Leighton-Harvey. Offering your sympathy,' she added.

There were nods of agreement from the others and Laura felt her face flush red and grow hot. How could they know what they were asking of her? she reflected, but at the same time terrified that they'd guess. Rising from her chair she covered her face with her hands for a moment before saying firmly, 'I'll send him a letter from us all because we all had a hand in making Mrs Leighton-Harvey's clothes.'

'That would be more seemly,' Mrs Sutherland agreed, perking up a bit, and she left soon after in order to spread the sad tidings, which she considered her duty to do.

When she was alone that night Laura composed the letter to Walker Leighton-Harvey with infinite care, stressing how 'they would all miss' his wife and offering both him and his young son their profound condolences in their terrible loss. It had taken her several hours to strike just the right tone, but at last it was done and, slipping it into an envelope, she addressed it to Lasswade Hall, Lasswade, Midlothian, Scotland. An address she knew by heart and wondered now if she would ever see.

'A letter for you on the mat, Lady Laura,' Helen announced cheerfully a week later as she arrived for work.

Laura knew instinctively even before she'd seen the large, generous handwriting that it was from him. That's how she thought of Walter now. Him. Whom she loved but would never have. And might not even see again. Opening the envelope her eyes skimmed the page and there was nothing there to raise even her faintest hopes. He thanked her and her staff for their kind thoughts and added he was taking his son abroad 'for a change of scene' and didn't know when they'd return to Scotland. He ended by wishing her well and his sprawling signature covered the bottom of the sheet of thick black bordered writing paper.

Laura laid it on the work table so the others could read it too. There was nothing to hide from them because nothing of importance had ever existed between them in the first place. Except in her heart.

'He sounds like ever such a nice man,' Helen commented when she'd read it.

'Yes,' Laura agreed distantly. 'A very nice man.'

Fifteen

Lochlee Castle, 1901

'Mama, have you seen today's newspapers?' Georgie asked excitedly as she rushed into the study where her mother was sitting at her late husband's desk.

'I haven't had time,' Lady Rothbury replied without looking up. 'I've got all the bills to pay and it's such a lot of work. I miss your father dreadfully, for he took care of everything like this.'

Georgie hurried to her side. 'Look! Apparently the Boer War is about to come to an end.'

Her mother rose to her feet, relief melting away the deep frown lines on her forehead. 'What does it say?'

'*The Times* has quoted a communiqué from Pretoria dated the twenty-ninth of April – that's yesterday – in which it seems representatives from Great Britain and the Boer States are in talks about signing a Peace Treaty. They're calling it the *Treaty of Vereeniging.*' She looked up in delight. 'That does mean the war is ending any minute now, doesn't it?'

Lady Rothbury sank back into the chair and clasped her hands together. 'Thanks be to God,' she prayed. 'I feared it would never end. That's the most marvellous news.'

'So Henry will soon be back,' Georgie declared, still gazing at the news print as if she couldn't believe her eyes.

'The journey home will take several weeks,' her mother pointed out. 'Henry might not be able to get leave to return here until June or even July.'

'Then in that case I'll postpone my wedding in May and Shane and I will wait until Henry's here so that he can give me away,' Georgie said firmly.

'Would you really do that?' Lady Rothbury asked wonderingly. Six months ago Georgie would have fought tooth and nail to stick to her plans for her marriage to Shane O'Mally, yet here she was, prepared to postpone her big day in order to wait for Henry's return. She'd been very opposed to her daughter marrying the young man who came from a different background, but recently she'd become quite fond of her future son-in-law because he not only adored Georgie but also knew how to bring out the best in her.

'It wouldn't be the same without Henry,' Georgie said simply. 'I'll let the rest of the family know we're postponing the date.'

'Shouldn't you discuss this with Shane first?'

Georgie looked surprised. 'Why? He always goes along with what I say.'

Lady Rothbury gave a wry smile. So perhaps Georgie hadn't changed all that much after all.

The news of impending peace in South Africa spread fast. The mood of the country lightened and families began planning welcome home parties to greet their husbands, sons and brothers who had fought valiantly for three long years.

Georgie lost no time in postponing her wedding arrangements and she wrote to Laura saying there was no immediate hurry in making her wedding dress.

'I'm looking forward to meeting Henry,' Shane said warmly. He'd agreed that they should delay their own plans until Henry returned and suggested they have a bigger wedding than originally planned.

'Why don't we ask all your neighbours to join in the fun? And the people who work for you? I can supply barrels of beer by the dozen and we could roast a couple of hogs and maybe a couple of calves in the yard and give everyone a real party. Your piper could play for dancing in the barn and we could have a real knees-up! My family are going to expect a real show! Not a poncey gathering where people sip wine from tiny glasses and keep their gloves on all night.'

Georgie's eyes widened. What would her mother say to these outlandish suggestions? Even her sisters would be slightly appalled if her wedding resembled that of a rough farmer's daughter, with beer and dancing in the barn. 'I think it might be rather *avant-garde* to have that sort of wedding,' she said cautiously.

'Avant-whatever, we're doing it, Georgie! Come on. Do you want to be stuck in the last century or not?' As he spoke he slid his arm around her waist and pulled her hard against his hip. Georgie felt dizzy with desire. Shane's gentle roughness always filled her with longing for their wedding night, although she secretly feared she'd probably faint clean away with excitement when the moment came.

The gong sounded announcing luncheon at that moment and Shane reluctantly loosened his grip as he and Georgie made their way across the great hall to the dining room where Lady Rothbury was already waiting to be seated. It was several minutes later that Alice, Flora and Catriona scuttled in like hungry mice, late as usual. Making murmured apologies they took their places at the long table.

'Don't you girls ever keep an eye on the clock?' their mother remarked irritably. 'How often have I told you it's rude to be late?'

'Sorry, Mama. Catriona's hair was a mess and we were helping her to pin it up,' Alice explained.

'Catriona should have made sure her hair was neat and tidy twenty minutes ago,' her mother said severely.

'Better late than never, that's what I say!' Shane exclaimed breezily as he tucked his table napkin into his collar. The family ignored this faux pas and listened as he proceeded to describe his wedding plans in detail with the footmen pretending not to hear as they served the first course of *consommé à la Julienne*.

Georgie held her breath, fearful her mother would say something snobbish like 'we do things differently here', but before she could comment McEwan appeared in the dining-room doorway. For a moment he stood rigid, holding a silver salver in his white gloved hands, but his normally ruddy face looked as white as candle wax.

As soon as Lady Rothbury saw him and what he was holding she seemed to crumple and grow small and old. There was fear in her eyes and her hand trembled as she reached for the buff envelope that rested so innocent-looking on the tray.

'No! Oh, God no!' she moaned in a low voice. 'Oh, please God, no.'

McEwan said nothing as he stood, head bowed by her chair as she grabbed the envelope and ripped it open.

Watching, Georgie and Shane knew instantly by her lost and pitiful expression as she read the telegram that nothing at Lochlee would ever be the same again for any of them.

'What's the matter?' Flora asked in a small, scared voice.

'Not my boy, not Henry. Please God, not Henry.'

Then Lady Rothbury collapsed, half fainting, while Shane jumped to his feet to support her, muttering 'Get the brandy,' to the stunned footmen who stood awkwardly about, not knowing what to do.

'What's *happened*?' shrieked Catriona as she looked wildly around at the others.

Georgie knew. 'This is too cruel,' she sobbed tearfully as she picked up the telegram from where her mother had thrown it down on the table. 'Killed in action . . .' she read aloud, 'and just as the war is ending,' she added pitifully as she held her table napkin to her mouth.

The room was filled with the sound of crying and sobbing as the four sisters tried to console their mother though they were in need of being comforted themselves. Their beloved brother would not be returning to Lochlee now, and they all felt the loss profoundly. He wasn't just the only son and heir, he was the light of their lives and adored by everyone who knew him. Lochlee had no heir now and with Henry's death the title had become extinct. Five hundred years of history wiped out by a single bullet.

'You need all the family to be here,' Shane announced pragmatically as soon as Lady Rothbury had been helped up to her bedroom where her younger daughters were administering to her needs while her lady's maid ran to fetch the family doctor. 'Would you like me to send telegrams to your other sisters?' Shane asked Georgie.

She was clinging to him like a child. 'Yes, please,' she said in a muffled voice. 'You'll stay here a bit longer, won't you? I don't want you to go.'

Holding her in his arms, Shane looked unflinchingly into her eyes. 'I promised I'd stay with you now and for ever,' he said passionately. 'I've got managers to run the pubs and I don't pay dogs in order to bark myself. I'll look after you, Georgie, and I'll do everything I can to look after your family.'

'Thank you,' she whispered gratefully. 'I don't know what I'd do without you.'

During the next twenty-four hours Shane held the reins of Lochlee in a cool and businesslike manner. Once he'd notified the rest of the family he ordered the housekeeper to have the necessary bedrooms prepared, checked with Cook that she had sufficient supplies to feed up to twenty guests for at least a week and gave her *carte blanche* to order anything she needed at his expense. Then he asked Georgie who the family lawyer was so that he could contact him, too.

Shane didn't mention the words 'death duties' to Georgie. That would become the lawyer's job in due course, but he privately feared the Fairbairns hadn't only lost their beloved son and heir, but that they would also lose Lochlee Castle in order to pay the inheritance tax on what was left of the estate.

By the following afternoon Laura, Lizzie and Diana had arrived with Humphrey and Robert and Beattie had telegrammed to say she'd be coming on her own the next day, as Andrew was regretfully caught up with business affairs but would be arriving at the end of the week.

The girls went straight to their mother's room where they found her prostrated in her bed, incoherent with grief. The doctor came twice a day to give her a sedative but it soon wore off and nothing anyone said could comfort her.

Meanwhile, Shane talked to Humphrey and Robert as they drank whisky and smoked cigars in the study.

'It's the irony of the situation that is so appalling,' Humphrey said dolefully. 'The Peace Treaty was signed only a few hours after Henry was killed? How devilish is that?'

Robert shook his head. 'Damned bad luck.'

'I suppose there's no chance of the eldest son showing up now, is there?' Shane asked. Georgie had told him about Freddie and how they hadn't heard from him since he'd disappeared with all the family jewels seven years ago.

'I wouldn't have thought so,' Robert replied in surprise. 'You've heard . . .?'

'Yes,' Shane cut in. 'Georgie told me everything. So technically had Henry become the eldest son?'

Humphrey nodded. 'Yes, I believe so. Lizzie told me at the beginning of the year that Freddie had been legally declared dead.'

'So . . .?' Shane hesitated before continuing. 'Does that mean that Henry had already become the Earl of Rothbury? Sorry, but I don't know much about the titled aristocracy.'

Robert smiled. 'My dear chap, titles are a minefield which most of us trip up over, even if we're listed ourselves. But yes, poor Henry had already become the Earl of Rothbury, the last Earl of Rothbury now, and that's sad in itself.'

'There are no distant cousins or anything?' Shane persisted.

'We'd have heard if there had been. Our mother-in-law would have winkled them out from the pages of the peerage years ago,' Humphrey remarked dryly. 'Can you imagine it? Nine daughters and only two sons? Talk about the family being cursed.'

'I'm trying to think of ways for the family to avoid paying more death duties than they need,' Shane explained, 'but Henry's death now means they'll have to pay inheritance tax for the third time in seven years. First Georgie's father dies. Then Freddie is declared legally dead earlier this year, so the Inland Revenue must already be working on what is owed. Now with Henry's death, will there be anything left?'

The three men looked at each other in stunned silence.

'I see what you mean,' Robert said hollowly. 'It's pretty devastating, isn't it?'

'It's a flaming disgrace,' Shane growled, 'and I blame the government.'

'What will they do?' Humphrey asked. 'It'll kill the mother-in-law if she has to leave here and she still has three daughters to look after, too.'

'I don't want to push my way in,' Shane said, smiling slightly self-deprecatingly, 'and I'm new to the family, unlike you two gentlemen, but I can afford to buy a very big house and offer Lady Rothbury and the younger girls a home as soon as Georgie and I are married. That might ease the situation a bit.'

Robert and Humphrey stared at him, feeling both embarrassed and ashamed. They'd joked with Lizzie and Diana about Georgie's 'lower class' boyfriend and how unlike her it was when she was such a snob, and now here they were, realizing he was a thoroughly decent and compassionate man, making a generous offer which should really have come from one of them.

'My dear chap,' Humphrey said, determined not to sound patronizing, 'that's most awfully good of you but let's hope it doesn't come to that . . . What I mean is,' he floundered, his cheeks turning red, 'I'm sure there will be enough money left to house them on the land here and we'd all chip in anyway, wouldn't we, Robert?'

'Naturally,' Robert agreed, helping himself to more whisky.

Later that day Laura came slowly down the stairs from her mother's room and found Humphrey standing alone in the great hall, gazing up at one of the many family portraits of past Earls. He looked up when he heard her footsteps. 'How are you, Laura, my dear?'

'Desolate,' she replied in a small voice.

'How is your poor mama?' he asked as he followed her into the drawing room.

Laura looked at him, her face pale and drawn and her hazel eyes deeply troubled. 'I don't think she'll ever get over this. She's suffered so much tragedy but this is different. Henry wasn't only her favourite child. He was the future of Lochlee and all it has stood for, for generations. She was so sure he'd marry and have lots of sons.' Laura looked down at her clasped hands. 'Now he's gone.'

Humphrey watched her struggling with her emotions, not knowing what to say that would bring comfort.

Laura raised her head and looked at him sadly. 'Before Henry left he told me his plans when he returned were to make money by having paying guests stay here, like a sort of private hotel, so he could earn enough to buy back some of our land – at least enough to enable the guests to go shooting and fishing. Mama would have been strongly opposed to the idea, of course, but Henry was determined.'

'I'm sure Henry could have pulled it off,' Humphrey agreed. 'I believe that one day a lot of people with stately homes to run will be forced to commercialize their estates in one way or another.'

'Do you think so?' she asked, surprised. 'Henry thought it was the only answer. Now we'll never know.'

'I think your mother is stronger than you realize. Are you able to stay here for a while?'

'Yes. I've left one of my staff in charge and she's very capable. I can stay here as long as I like because there's really nothing to keep me in Edinburgh,' she added poignantly.

Humphrey glanced swiftly at her face. Some deep inner pain had come to her mind as she'd spoken and he felt sure it had nothing to do with Henry's death.

'Do you have much time for a social life?' he asked ingenuously.

'No time whatsoever,' she replied with finality as she rose from her chair. 'Now I'm going out to get a breath of fresh air before I go back to sit with Mama again.'

Georgie strolled slowly by Shane's side in the formal garden on the south side of the castle where, in spite of the sometimes harsh weather, a profusion of plants flourished. Exhausted by a mixture of grief and stress, she was depending more and more on Shane, who was the only person who could soothe her. 'I wish you'd known Henry,' she told him.

He smiled down at her. 'In a way I feel as if I did. I've heard so much about him from you and the others and I've seen his likeness since he was a child; I think we'd probably have got on all right.'

'Oh, definitely,' Georgie agreed. 'He loved this place so much and he had so many plans. We used to play croquet on the lawn over there. Henry always won and Freddie got so angry one day he threw his mallet down on the ground and it broke. Papa was furious with him.'

'Never played it myself,' Shane admitted. 'Darts is more my game.'

As they strolled round to the other side of the castle, Georgie stopped suddenly and gave a cry of shock.

Shane looked at her and then at where she was staring, her expression both surprised and fearful. 'What is it, love? I don't see anything,' he said.

'It's gone! Dear Lord, it's gone! What does that mean?' she exclaimed fearfully.

Shane stepped forward but she pulled him back. 'No, don't go that way,' she said hurriedly. 'Not until we've found out what happened to it. It's either good or terribly bad.' She spoke falteringly, leaning heavily on his arm. Then she whispered, 'Surely nothing more can happen?'

'Sweetheart,' Shane said firmly as he turned to face her. 'How can I comment when I don't know what you're talking about? *What's* gone?' Georgie looked at him with glazed eyes. 'The Rowan tree, of course. It's been cut down.'

'Have you heard?'

There was as much commotion in the servants' hall as there was in the drawing room. Talk of dark forces in the night, or perhaps even the ghost of Eleanor trying to lift the curse was spoken about while others muttered that Henry's spirit had removed the tree.

'It was definitely there yesterday,' Laura said, 'because I remember seeing it through the window.'

'Let's have a closer look,' Robert suggested, marching towards the front door. 'Perhaps it's just been blown down by the wind.'

Shane went with him. 'I wanted to look closer but Georgie was in a dreadful state and she wouldn't let me go near. Why is everyone so interested?'

Robert looked at him. 'You're Scottish? And you don't

believe in the Rowan tree's ability to cast both good and bad spells on a family?' he asked half-jokingly.

'I'm Irish,' Shane protested. 'Shamrock is the nearest we get to good luck. Unless it's an Irish-bred horse running in the Grand National.'

'It is hard to take seriously,' Robert conceded, 'but the Fairbairns have certain tragic reasons for believing they've been cursed by an illegitimate relative who has a grudge against them all.'

Humphrey caught up with them as they walked to where the Rowan had previously stood. 'Lizzie said we were to look for clues as to who might have hacked the tree down,' he panted breathlessly.

'What sort of clues?'

'Gardening tools, I suppose, or maybe farming tools?'

Robert started pacing around the grass some ten feet from the terrace that surrounded the castle on the west side. 'It stood about here, didn't it?' he asked in a puzzled voice.

The grass seemed undisturbed and there was no sign of wood shavings or broken branches or twigs anywhere. It looked as if the tree had simply vanished into thin air, leaving no trace behind.

'It was on this side of the castle, wasn't it? Are you sure it wasn't on the east side?' Humphrey asked uncertainly.

'Don't ask me, I've never noticed the flaming thing,' said Shane.

'It was definitely here,' Robert insisted, rattled. 'It can't just have simply disappeared. It doesn't make sense.'

At that moment one of the upstairs windows in the castle opened and Laura leaned out.

'This is the right spot, isn't it, Laura?' Humphrey called out.

'It grew about six or seven feet to your left,' she called down.

The three men wandered in a small, bewildered circle, studying the grass and testing the ground with their polished brown brogues.

'Laura, how can you be so sure?' Shane asked with mild frustration.

Laura was very sure. She was standing in what had once been Eleanor's bedroom and remembered how she'd looked down in anguish at the Rowan tree, which grew exactly in line with the window, the day they'd found her sister's body on the terrace below.

'I know that's where it was,' she replied firmly. 'Whoever destroyed it must have partly uprooted it, too. I can see from up here that it's new turf you're all standing on.'

The men moved swiftly to one side, as if they'd been told it was hallowed ground.

'One of the gardeners must have done it after we'd all gone to bed last night. I suppose he didn't want to upset the family,' Humphrey said as they wended their way back inside the castle.

Robert nodded. 'Yes. The guest rooms are all on the other side of the building so that's probably why none of us heard anything.'

'So who sleeps on the side overlooking where the tree used to be?' Shane inquired.

'It's Eleanor's room but it's never used now, and next to it is Freddie's old room.'

'Did you go into Freddie's old room?' Diana whispered urgently to Laura, whom she had cornered in the library.

Laura looked at her blankly. 'Freddie's room?' she repeated in surprise. 'No. Why should I? And why are you whispering?'

'Robert wondered if Freddie had secretly returned. Maybe he got rid of the tree to break the spell of bad luck once and for all.'

Laura looked at her incredulously. 'You can't mean it? Freddie here? I hope to God you're wrong.'

'I don't know whether Robert's right or not. He hasn't said anything to Humphrey or Shane but as you were in Eleanor's room he just wondered . . .' Her voice faded and she shook her head. 'What do you think we should do?'

Laura rose. 'Let's go and look in his room now,' she said firmly. 'I suppose Robert also thinks Freddie magically made the tree disappear in the night too?' she scoffed.

'Well, his body has never been found,' Diana shot back. 'If he managed to get into Scotland without being recognized this is the one place where he could hide without ever being discovered. Some of the rooms on the top floor haven't even been opened up for years.'

As they climbed the stairs they met Georgie on the landing. 'Where are you off to?' she asked.

'We thought we'd sit with Mama for a while,' Laura replied evenly.

As soon as Georgie had gone down to the drawing room they hurried up another flight of stairs and then along a corridor past Eleanor's old room until they came to another door.

Diana wavered nervously but Laura grabbed the handle and, turning it, pushed it open with a flourish before striding fearlessly into the room. Diana followed on tiptoe and looked around anxiously.

'It looks pretty empty to me,' Laura said, taking in the smooth brocade counterpane on the bed, the oak dressing table and bookcase, still filled with Freddie's books. There was a faint, musty smell but the window was closed so that was to be expected.

Suddenly Diana gave a shrill cry of fear as she pointed to the lower shelf of the bedside table. 'Look!' she choked.

Laura bent down swiftly and picked up a copy of the *Scottish Herald*. Her eyes flew to the date. April 30th, 1901.

'Put it back!' Diana whispered in panic.

Laura replaced the newspaper but she was in no hurry to leave the room.

'Come *on*!' Diana pleaded from the doorway.

'Why should we be frightened of our own brother?'

'You know what he's like! Look what he did to the stable boy! He'll go mad if he finds out we know he's here.'

Laura left the room, slowly closing the door behind her, deep in thought. 'I wonder how long he's been back? He must have heard about Henry by now. I suppose, knowing the place as well as he does, he's been living a nocturnal life, helping himself to food and drink and anything he wants while we all slept.'

Diana shuddered. 'I want to go home with Robert. I'll never be able to sleep here tonight. Are we going to tell the police? That would be the best thing to do, wouldn't it?'

Laura paused halfway down the wide staircase to the great hall and looked out of the window at the mountains in the distance on this warm May day. 'Could you live with yourself if you did that?' she asked. 'Sent your own brother, your own flesh and blood to the gallows after all these years?'

Diana looked at her, concerned. 'You're not thinking of keeping it a secret, are you? After what he did? After he beat Hamish to death and then stole the family jewels, breaking Mama's heart and bringing shame on the family? Freddie was rotten to the core. He was a cruel boy who put Henry down all the time because Henry was more popular.'

Laura turned to face Diana. 'You're talking about the Freddie who was only seventeen when he committed those crimes and who was so frightened he ran away. He'll be twenty-five now and he may have repented. We must talk to him before we go rushing off to the police, or,' she added, gripping Diana's wrist, 'before we tell anyone he's here.'

'I must tell Robert,' Diana said instantly.

'Give me twenty-four hours,' Laura insisted. 'That's all I ask. Think about it, Di. Do you want to have to live with the thought for the rest of your life that you sent your brother to his death, when he may well have repented and made amends?'

Diana hesitated. 'If he'd made amends then why is he here? In hiding?' she asked grudgingly.

'That's exactly what I want to find out.' Tears rushed to Laura's eyes. 'We've lost Henry. Just think how wonderful it would be, especially for Mama, if Freddie had returned full of contrition for his past sins.'

'All right,' Diana replied uncertainly, 'but I don't like having secrets from Robert.'

Laura wrapped a black shawl around her shoulders and slipped into Eleanor's room, leaving the door open a fraction. It was nearly midnight and everyone had gone to bed, including the servants.

The silence and stillness were almost palpable and all she could hear was the beating of her heart. Freddie had been violent and brutal and after being on the run for nearly eight years he might be even more so. Nevertheless the situation had to be resolved. One thing was certain: in spite of what he'd done she didn't want to be the one responsible for the law to seek just retribution.

A footfall suddenly alerted her and at that moment she saw a flicker of candlelight pass through the open crack in

Eleanor's door. Jumping up she flung the door wide, whispering, 'Freddie?'

Stepping into the corridor she saw he was standing rigidly with his back to her, holding the candlestick aloft. In silhouette he appeared to be wearing a long, heavy coat.

'Freddie! It's me. Laura,' she whispered urgently.

He raised the candle higher and then, turning very slowly, stepped towards her. For a moment she thought he was going to strike her and she braced herself, looking up into his bearded face which she could see more clearly now. Then her heart started hammering faster than ever.

This man wasn't Freddie. This was a tall, powerfully built stranger who was standing menacingly before her, glaring into her eyes.

'Who are you?' she asked, fear making her voice shrill.

He pursed his lips and raised his forefinger to them. 'Hush. I won't hurt you. I'm not here to do any harm,' he whispered. 'Freddie, as you call him, he asked me to come here.' His accent was French and he was smiling down at her now. 'We can talk? *Oui?*'

Dumbfounded, Laura backed away. 'Who are you?' she repeated, hoping she sounded haughty now. 'What are you doing here?'

'I tell you. Your brother wanted me to come to this castle to do something for him. He gave me instructions. In great detail.'

Laura started walking towards the stairs which led down to the great hall, from where she would be able to raise the alarm by striking the old brass dinner gong.

'So he's sent you to rob the place for him, has he?' she asked angrily, as she gripped the banister in case she fell in the darkness. The shock of coming face-to-face with this strange man had numbed her feelings, making her fearless.

He followed her closely, still holding the candle aloft as they descended together.

'Rob?' he queried.

'Steal. Take what doesn't belong to you,' she said harshly.

'*Au contraire!*' he retorted loudly. 'I have brought you something. It is a long story. Can we sit somewhere? I want to explain.'

Once down in the hall Laura lit an oil lamp and set it on a table near the gong before seating herself on a carved bench. Only then was she able to have a good look at this weird intruder who was being so polite.

To her surprise he looked clean and tidy, and his hair and beard were neatly trimmed. He had the ruddy complexion of someone who works outdoors and his hands gave testimony to the fact he was a manual labourer. What would Freddie be doing with a man like this?

'Let me introduce myself,' he began with strange formality under the circumstances. 'My name is Pierre Dussord and I'm a gardener. I work in the Tuileries Garden in Paris; the most lavish gardens in the whole of France.' His dark eyes beamed with pride as he spoke and he gesticulated with his hands as he added, 'And you are Lady . . .?'

'Laura,' she replied. This encounter was taking on a dream-like quality. Was she really sitting in the hall in the middle of the night making polite conversation with a French gardener who'd been secretly living in the castle in Freddie's old room?

'How do you know my brother?' she asked suspiciously.

'He liked to sit in the gardens. He said they reminded him of Lochlee.'

'So he's living in Paris?'

Pierre frowned. 'You did not know? Did no one tell you?' he asked uneasily.

'Tell us what?'

'M'Lord Fairbairn – he died several months ago.'

The flicker of hope that Freddie was still alive dissolved in a heartbeat at that moment. 'He's dead? How did he die?'

He spoke haltingly and averted his gaze. 'He died of syphilis. I promised him before he died that I'd come here and carry out his last wish.'

Laura blanched. 'What, in secret? Creeping around the place in the middle of the night? Why couldn't you have come as a guest?'

'He wanted me to . . . how you say? . . . create magic? He said the family had been cursed and he wanted me to lift the curse.'

Laura leaned forward. 'So it *was* you who removed the

Rowan tree?' Her eyes were sharp with enlightenment. 'Of course. You're a gardener. You knew what to do and how to lay fresh turf where the tree had been.'

Pierre nodded. 'He insisted it must vanish and leave no mark, no trace. He also drew me diagrams of the castle so I'd know which was his room and where I would find food.'

Her eyes widened with amazement. 'So when did you arrive here?'

'Two days ago. I go back to Paris tomorrow but I have something to give you first. I was going to put it in an envelope and leave it on the hall table over there,' he gestured again, 'but I will give it to you now, to return to your mother.'

He groped in an inner pocket of his coat and drew out a small leather pouch. 'This is all that he had left and he asked me to bring it back here.'

Laura took the worn and grubby pouch and opened it with shaking hands. Then she pulled out a small pearl brooch which she remembered her mother used to wear, pinned at the throat of a cream lace blouse. It was such a simple, innocent-looking piece of jewellery compared to the dazzling emeralds and diamonds that had been handed down from previous generations, and it brought tears to Laura's eyes.

'This is all that was left?' she asked brokenly.

Pierre nodded. 'He was destitute at the end. Everything had gone because he'd lived the high life around the capitals of Europe. Especially Paris.' He paused, as if wondering if he should continue.

'Go on,' Laura urged, wiping away the tears from her cheeks.

'Freddie, he was filled with remorse at the end and feared he'd go to hell,' Pierre said quietly. 'He knew he'd sinned and he was truly sorry. I know he wanted to return here but he feared he'd be spotted and so he sent me instead.'

Laura sat weeping for the baby boy she'd seen lying in his cot as the family celebrated the birth of their first son and she wept for the bright-eyed little boy who'd played at being a soldier on the ramparts of the castle and had later grown into an accomplished rider to Papa's delight. When had it all gone wrong? Had Mama spoilt him by telling him he was the heir to all that surrounded them? Had he become jealous when

Henry had been born? Maybe having nine sisters had over-whelmed him and made him feel smothered by femininity?

'I'm sorry I upset you,' she heard Pierre say gently. 'Perhaps I say too much.'

'I wanted to know,' she assured him as she sat up and straight-ened her shoulders. 'Thank you for telling me everything. My mother will never know the details of Freddie's death but I shall give her this,' she continued, opening her hand to reveal the pearl brooch lying in her palm, 'and I shall tell her Freddie sent it to her, with his love.'

'Very good,' he replied, and there was warmth in his voice, 'because that is the truth.'

Laura stood up and held out her hand. 'Thank you also for removing the Rowan tree.'

He rose too and gave her a little bow as they shook hands. 'It was nothing. It was just a little bit of magic and I hope your family enjoys *bonne chance* in the future.'

Wending her way upstairs to bed Laura could hardly believe how the night had unfolded in such an extraordinary way. Would Diana believe a word of what she had to say? The pearl brooch was her only real proof of her strange encounter. That, and the fact that a Parisian gardener had expertly removed the Rowan tree and repaired the damaged soil with fresh turf.

Laura felt that for those who believed in the evil curse only time would tell whether it had been banished or not. She was one who believed that people on the whole make their own good or bad luck and nothing would change that. There was no need to tell anyone the cause of Freddie's death either; she felt she owed him loyalty about how he'd lived his life during the past few years, but she would stress how he'd repented for the terrible sins he'd committed. It was a life that had been wasted and that was the saddest part of it all.

Laura dreamed of Freddie that night. Dreamed he'd returned to Lochlee, fit and well, and he'd heaped all the stolen jewel-lery on to the middle of Mama's bed.

Sixteen

Although two years had passed since the death of Queen Victoria, the ladies of Edinburgh were still flocking to Laura to have their clothes made, especially since official mourning had come to an end. Now they wanted dresses in blue and burgundy, primrose yellow and pink, and for a change the workroom was a riot of brightly-hued fabrics and trimmings.

During the day Laura was too busy to think about the tumultuous changes that were happening to the family back at Lochlee as she, Helen and their two assistants machined and hand-stitched, made delicate buttonholes and added final trimmings to garments from early in the morning until six o'clock in the evening.

The girls chattered and gossiped throughout the day and Laura half-listened idly, but mostly she concentrated on thinking up new designs for her demanding clients. The day seemed to pass swiftly and then the others couldn't wait to get home to their families or, in Helen's case, her husband.

That was when Laura felt both lonely and sometimes even abandoned. From a busy little hive of activity her flat suddenly seemed utterly deserted. The silence was almost palpable. She was alone and coming from such a large family this was something she wasn't used to. Sometimes she visited Mrs Sutherland but mostly she read, favouring the historical novels of Sir Walter Scott, particularly *The Legend of Montrose*, which she was reading for the second time. In comparison to Lizzie, Diana, Beattie and Georgie, who had recently married Shane in a quiet ceremony, her own life was barren.

At twenty-nine there was little chance of her meeting anyone now and she had long since banished her foolish fantasies of Walter Leighton-Harvey falling in love with her. She'd heard nothing of him since his formal and polite reply to her letter of condolence and she figured he'd probably met someone else by now anyway. Looking around her flat she realized it was a work place, a tiny, highly productive factory, and not a home. Not that she blamed anyone else. She'd wanted to be independent and earn her own money and she'd succeeded beyond her wildest dreams. She should be proud of herself and thankful she was not dependent on her family, but she couldn't help wondering if the price she was paying was too high? No husband. No children. No beautiful home to which she could invite her sisters and their families.

Work had prohibited her from socializing too, and by the end of the day she was usually too exhausted to go out anyway. How could she expect to meet and marry some wonderful man when she was wedded to her chosen career? She'd made her bed and she must lie in it, she told herself fiercely, determined not to sink into a well of self-pity.

Deciding to make herself a cup of tea and get back to enjoying *The Legend of Montrose*, she suddenly heard her doorbell ring.

Fond though she was of Mrs Sutherland, she wasn't in the mood for gossip this evening, and for a moment she hesitated, wondering whether to go down and open the door or pretend to be out. There was silence and then the bell rang again, followed by the knocker being gently tapped. Laura sighed. There was nothing for it. She looked a mess; her hair was falling down her back and around her shoulders, but Mrs Sutherland wouldn't mind. The old lady might have found her a new client, or be just plain lonely, like herself.

'I'm just coming,' Laura called down the narrow stairs. When she reached the hallway she opened the front door. 'Oh!' she exclaimed, stepping back with shock.

'Have I come at a very inconvenient time? I'm so sorry.' Walter Leighton-Harvey was smiling down at her and there was a hint of apology in his voice.

'No, not at all,' Laura replied, flustered, conscious that she looked a mess. 'Come in. I'm afraid the place is upside down because we only finished work a short time ago and the others have just left.' She paused, realizing she was prattling on inanely.

'I've just made some tea. Would you like some? I'm afraid I haven't anything stronger.'

'I don't want to put you to any trouble,' he replied, following her up the stairs.

'It's no trouble at all,' she assured him, suddenly feeling breathless. 'I've already made some for myself.' She led him into the workroom.

'This is where we make the clothes,' she continued. 'I could do with double the space but for the time being we can manage.'

He looked around with interest, especially at the sewing machines. 'Priscilla used to tell me how busy you all were and I can see what she meant. You've even got two machines!' He referred to his late wife as if he was talking about a mutual friend.

For a moment Laura didn't know how to respond, then she said in a rush, 'I was very sorry to hear she was no longer with us. My assistants greatly enjoyed making clothes for her.' As she spoke she watched him closely to see his reaction.

'She enjoyed coming here,' he replied matter-of-factly. His expression was serene and when he looked at her his eyes had the same glint of intimacy she'd noticed when they first met. 'So how are you?' he continued, gazing into her face. 'Neil and I only got home a couple of weeks ago. We went to the South of France where one of my sisters live, so Neil had fun on the beaches with her children, but I'm glad to be home again.'

'Where is he now?' As she spoke she handed him a cup of tea.

'With my other sister, who is staying with me.' His eyes never left her face and she felt her cheeks grow hot.

'How old is Neil now?'

'Six.' He leaned forward and suddenly spoke impulsively. 'Would you think it very presumptuous of me if I asked you out to dinner one evening? If you prefer we could invite Mrs Sutherland to come too, as a chaperone?'

Laura almost burst out laughing. Did he know how old she was? 'I don't think that's necessary,' she replied, smiling. 'I'm a working woman and quite grown-up now.'

'And very beautiful too,' he said earnestly, his eyes never

leaving her face. 'You've been on my mind for a long time, you know. Would tomorrow evening be convenient? If I called to collect you at seven forty-five?'

His keen yet diffident manner reminded her of a young man who was inviting a girl out for the very first time.

'That would be perfect,' she replied almost reassuringly. 'I'll look forward to it.' Her heart was racing and her head was in a spin but she tried to look calm and sophisticated. Was this really happening to her? Could her wild fantasy be turning into reality?

Walter left shortly after, thanking her courteously for the tea and saying he would look forward to seeing her the following evening.

When he'd left she flopped into a chair, kicked off her shoes and hugged herself with delight. Happiness had transformed her in the past forty minutes and she felt quite different. Before Walter's unexpected arrival she'd felt tired and depressed but now she felt ecstatic and in love with life itself. On a whim she reached for the silver-backed hand mirror she'd brought from Lochlee and peered at her reflection. Her expression was radiant, her skin gently flushed, her hazel eyes shining with joy. The last time she'd felt like this was when she'd become engaged to Rory at seventeen. Was it really possible that Walter had confirmed her wildest dreams just when she'd resigned herself to being an old maid, on the shelf and destined to be childless and spend her last days of her life on her own?

When she awoke the next morning a dreadful wave of doubt engulfed her. Had she read too much into his dropping in to see her the previous evening? Maybe he had a whole string of women friends whom he flattered, entertained in restaurants and regarded as pleasant companions and no more? Perhaps he was still grieving and lonely? Was she being foolish in presuming he'd come along like a knight in shining armour to rescue her from her lonely life? He was probably only being polite and just hated eating alone?

'Lady Laura, are you all right?' Helen asked with concern as she watched Laura trying to pin a lace frill to the cuffs of a blouse with shaking hands.

Laura's worried frown deepened. Their two assistants had

gone over to Mrs Sutherland's house to fetch some fabric and, as they could talk undisturbed, she told Helen what had happened.

'I've cared about him for years but now I'm wondering if he really feels the same about me,' she concluded.

'Sounds to me like a romantic novel,' Helen said enthusiastically.

'That's exactly what I'm afraid of,' Laura pointed out. 'It's been such a long time since I was wooed I've almost forgotten what it was like and now, suddenly, I doubt his sincerity. I don't want to make a fool of myself.'

'Lady Laura, you're worth a dozen of the stupid little woman he was married to. He'd be mad if he didn't ask you to marry him before someone else snaps you up.'

Laura looked surprised. 'I thought you liked Mrs Leighton-Harvey? You were always very flattering, telling her how beautiful she looked when she was fitted for a new gown?'

'Don't we flatter all the ladies when they put on our clothes?'

Laura nodded, smiling. 'I suppose we do.'

'You'll have a wonderful time tonight, mark my words!'

Helen stayed late to help Laura get ready. First she smoothed some pomade into her hair, made of a mixture of lard, olive oil and a few drops of perfume, so that her chignon would look smooth and shining, and then she dabbed her face with powder and her lips with raspberry juice mixed with Vaseline.

'You'll give Queen Alexandra a run for her money!' she said triumphantly. Then she helped Laura into a pale aquamarine taffeta dress which showed off her shapely figure and small waist.

'My goodness, Lady Laura!' Helen exclaimed, standing back and clapping her hands together. 'Now I can really see you're the daughter of a lord! Whatever are you doing working alongside the likes of me until your fingers bleed when you could be waltzing with royalty at Buckingham Palace?' She sounded quite scandalized.

Laura laughed out loud. 'Because I love doing what I do.' She paused for a moment. 'Perhaps I also wanted to make a point about women having a career and not just sitting around waiting to get married,' she added.

Helen gave her a knowing look. 'You'll make a point all right tonight and that's for sure.'

The front doorbell rang at exactly seven forty-five and, picking up her fur wrap and purse, Laura made her way down the stairs. When she opened the street door Walter was waiting expectantly for her.

'Hello,' she said shyly as he gazed at her with undisguised admiration.

'Hello,' he echoed in a low voice. Then he helped her into the waiting carriage. 'I've got these for you,' he murmured, handing her a corsage of white wax-like gardenias.

She held them to her nose and closed her eyes for a moment. 'How did you know that is my favourite scent in the world?' she said appreciatively, drawing in a deep breath. 'It's better than roses. Thank you so much.'

'May I?' He took the spray from her and in his other hand he held a gold pin with which to fasten it to her dress.

'Yes, of course,' she said a touch too quickly, for she could feel his breath on her cheek and his hands were touching her bare shoulder.

'It that all right?' he asked when he'd pinned on the corsage. 'They're like your skin. Pure white and unblemished.'

'Thank you,' she replied, blushing.

They hardly spoke on their way to the restaurant, which lay in the shadows of Edinburgh Castle, because she felt overwhelmed by the magnetic presence of this dominant man, who at the same time was gentle. He, in turn, appeared awestruck, and he kept looking at her profile as if he could hardly believe she was sitting beside him.

Once seated at a table in a discreet corner of the restaurant, Walter ordered champagne while Laura looked around with interest. All the other diners were beautifully dressed and the women exquisitely coiffured and bejewelled. This was obviously a top restaurant.

On impulse she leaned towards Walter and spoke in a low voice. 'Does this place resemble the Café Royal in Regent Street?'

Walter looked at her in surprise and then burst out laughing.

'What's so funny?' she asked.

He was still shaking with laughter. 'It's just such a funny question, and the answer is I don't know! I haven't the faintest idea because I've never been to the Café Royal in my life! It's rather *recherché*, isn't it?'

Laura started laughing, too. 'I don't know. I've only heard about it.'

They were looking into each other's eyes, enjoying the merriment of the moment and the joy of shared laughter.

'Let's decide what we're going to eat, then I want you to tell me all about yourself,' Walter suggested.

'There's really very little to tell, and you've already met my family, when you came to Lochlee for Diana's wedding,' she replied, sipping her champagne.

'Ah, Lochlee Castle – I remember it as being both rugged and beautiful at the same time. Don't you miss living there?'

'Yes,' she replied sadly. 'Especially as it looks as if we're going to be forced to sell it to pay the death duties incurred since my brother was killed in the Boer War.'

Walter looked at her sympathetically. 'My dear Laura, I had no idea. What a terrible blow to lose Henry. He was so young, too. You'll miss Lochlee, won't you? How long has your family owned it?'

'About five hundred years.'

'Can nothing be done to save it?'

'The Inland Revenue is not noted for having a heart,' she replied dryly.

They continued to talk as they enjoyed an excellent dinner and they were still immersed in conversation when they suddenly realized they were the last people in the restaurant, apart from three waiters who looked like they were longing to go home to bed.

'When can I see you again?' Walter asked almost urgently as they left the restaurant. 'I can't remember when I had such an enjoyable evening,' he added, taking her arm as they strolled along the road to where their carriage awaited them.

Laura knew they were past the moment when they had to conform to the niceties of polite society and she had to play hard-to-get. They'd both accepted during the long evening that they had a very special bond, though how and when they would openly acknowledge it, even to themselves, remained to be seen.

'When can we meet again?' he repeated.

'At any time,' Laura replied simply.

'Can you come and spend a couple of days at the end of the week at Lasswade Hall? My sister is staying with me at the moment to help with Neil and act as hostess, and I know she'd be delighted to meet you.'

Laura looked into his dark eyes and knew this was a man she could trust implicitly. 'I'd love to,' she replied.

'I'll send the carriage to collect you on Saturday morning? Would that be convenient?'

It was all happening much faster than she'd imagined. Walter was a persistent man who was rushing her along. It was like being on a helter-skelter but she was excited by the momentum and loving every moment of it. She could think of no reason to say 'no' or even 'maybe'.

Instead she smiled and said, 'Yes.' Amazed by her easy acceptance and reckless readiness to agree to whatever Walter suggested, a vision of her mother's disapproval floated across her mind and was instantly dismissed. She was no longer a young girl. She could do as she liked.

That night she lay awake for hours, going over and over every detail of the evening, and everything they'd said to each other. Most striking was that they'd both felt able to share, with complete honesty, the details of their past lives. Laura had told him all about Rory and he'd told her that sweet though Priscilla had been, her limited intelligence had hampered their mutual enjoyment of books and music, works of art and an interest in politics. In affectionate tones he'd referred to his late wife's main interest as being clothes and shoes.

There seemed to be nothing she didn't know about Walter now, and he in turn had been made aware of the various tragedies that had befallen the Fairbairn family.

'Maybe the removal of the Rowan tree has cleansed Lochlee of evil spells?' Walter had suggested hopefully, but she hadn't replied. The future of her beloved castle was something she didn't want to think about.

★   ★   ★

The carriage ride from Edinburgh to Lasswade took nearly two hours along winding roads, and when they stopped at high wrought-iron gates Laura knew with mounting excitement that she'd arrived at Walter's house when she saw him standing in the open doorway to greet her arrival.

'How are you, my dear Laura?' he asked warmly. 'How was the journey?'

Stepping carefully out of the carriage, Laura looked into his eyes and had the strangest feeling of coming home, of returning to a familiar place where she was always welcome. 'I'm very well,' she replied as he took her hand to help her down. 'We passed through some beautiful countryside.'

'Come inside; my sister is looking forward to meeting you.'

At that moment a middle-aged woman with the same dark, intelligent eyes as her brother stepped forward, and Laura had the distinct feeling she was being examined from top to toe.

'How do you do? I'm Rowena Marshall and I'm so glad you could come and stay.' Her tone was brisk and businesslike. 'This is Neil, my nephew.'

A small, dark-haired boy in a white sailor suit stepped dutifully forward. His expression was sour.

'Hello, Neil,' Laura said, smiling encouragingly.

'Say how-do-you-do-Lady-Laura,' his aunt prompted sharply.

Neil mumbled something and extended a small, limp white hand which she held gently for a moment.

'I've been longing to meet you, Neil. I've heard so much about you from your father,' she continued, bending down to his level.

Neil continued to stare down at the carpet and remained mute.

'He's shy,' Walter remarked jovially. 'I was the same at his age. Let's all go into the garden and have a cool drink before luncheon.'

Rowena led the way and Laura followed, taking off her gloves and opening her travelling cloak as she did so.

'Allow me,' Walter said, taking her things and handing them to a waiting butler.

Stepping through French windows, Laura found herself on

a large lawn that stretched away to trees down one side and a tennis court on the other.

'Let's sit in the shade,' Rowena suggested, but as soon as they were settled in wicker chairs under a Cedar of Lebanon tree that spread out its great horizontal evergreen arms, she murmured something about checking with Cook to make sure luncheon would be ready at one o'clock. Neil immediately followed her.

'It's so wonderful to see you here,' Walter said as he poured her a glass of chilled elderflower cordial. 'I've been longing to show you the house.'

Laura smiled, feeling comfortable and relaxed. 'It's lovely to be here. Have you lived here for a long time?'

'It used to belong to my parents. My two sisters and I were born here so we're quite attached to the old place.'

'How wonderful that you were able to keep it on.'

Walter looked at her sympathetically. 'Is your family really going to give up Lochlee?'

'I don't think we have any alternative.' Her expression was sad.

'You'll continue to live in Edinburgh, will you?'

She nodded. 'That's where my work is and that's where I'll remain.'

'Won't you miss the countryside?'

'Of course, but I can always stay with Diana, who is quite near or Georgie, who recently married a man who lives in Northumberland.'

Walter looked at her in silence, as if wondering what he dared say next. She knew what he was thinking and so she added in a casual voice, 'I also have some friends with whom I can spend a few days relaxing or going for walks on the moors.'

His eyes lit up. 'I hope you'll look upon this as a place you can visit as often as you like.'

Laura couldn't help being amused by his careful and very proper approach to wooing her. Rory had been much more impetuous and outspoken, declaring his feelings for her almost immediately. The difference was Rory had been only twenty-two at the time. Walter, she guessed, was in his late forties.

'I'll come as often as you ask me to see you, not the house particularly,' she told him gaily. 'I see you've got a tennis court? Can we have a game after luncheon? I'm probably very rusty as I haven't played for ages but it's one of my favourite things.'

Walter started to relax from that moment on and the next two days flew past as Laura realized this was more than just having a romance with an attractive man. As far as Rowena was concerned, Laura felt she was being sized up to see if she would make a suitable wife for Walter and an exemplary stepmother for Neil.

Laura was grateful for the moments she and Walter had on their own because now that her fantasies looked as if they were turning into reality she needed to find out if she really cared enough for Walter to step into his dead wife's shoes, with all that it would entail. She and Priscilla were very different in every way; would she fit into Walter's life? He was so different to her own father, who cared only for his dogs and horses. He forgot his children's birthdays and had sometimes even forgotten their names, while he lavished his love and devotion on his animals. To find a man who cared so much as Walter obviously did for Neil was a revelation. She also had to remember that she would be moving into another woman's house and from the fussy way it was decorated it looked much more like the handiwork of Priscilla than it did of Walter.

'You're a wonderful father, Walter,' she told him frankly as they sat talking on the Sunday evening after the little boy had gone to bed. This was a side of him she found deeply touching and attractive. 'Neil is a lucky little boy,' she continued. 'I believe my Papa only married and had children to secure an heir for Lochlee. Imagine the irony of it? Nine girls and only two boys, and both of them dead in their early twenties. He'd probably have had a much happier life if there'd been no title and no inheritance, and he could have worked as a simple gamekeeper.'

Walter nodded thoughtfully. 'Those who envy the very rich and exalted don't realize what a heavy burden it can sometimes be. I'm sure your father really loved you all but the responsibility of owning a place like Lochlee must have weighed heavily

on him. Why people seem to love their animals is because
dogs and horses can't talk. They can't nag and ask questions
or make demands.'

Laura raised her eyebrows. 'Is that what people do?' she
asked quizzically.

Walter blushed, then grinned. 'Some people.'

'Women in particular?' she queried, smiling.

He laughed outright. 'You're very astute, aren't you?'

'I'd better not be too astute or you'll never invite me here
again,' she quipped spiritedly.

He instantly reached for her hand and held it tightly.
'Intelligent conversation is wonderful. Foolish prattling can
become wearing,' he said, suddenly looking serious. 'You're
not given to chattering inanities and frivolous nonsense.'

He's thinking of Priscilla, she thought, remembering how, from
the moment Priscilla Leighton-Harvey had arrived to order an
outfit, she'd talked non-stop about nothing in particular until
the moment she left. It had driven her and Helen mad.

Laura squeezed his hand and wished he'd take her in his
arms. 'Men can talk balderdash, too,' she informed him
playfully.

'Can they indeed?' Then he suddenly leaned forward and
kissed her.

A moment later she slid her arms around his neck and at
once felt that this was where she belonged. As he drew her
closer she closed her eyes, all doubts swept away.

This was the man she'd marry and live with for the rest of
her life. She'd really known it from the moment they'd met at
Diana's wedding and it felt right as she lay in his arms.

As if he knew what she was thinking he drew back and
looked down into her eyes. 'I fell in love with you the
moment we met, you know,' he said with sudden passion. 'I
want you in my life now, Laura, more than I've ever wanted
anything.'

They were the words she wanted to hear and they'd been
a long time in coming. 'That's all I want, too,' she whispered,
hardly able to believe her good fortune.

Seventeen

Lizzie and Humphrey persuaded Lady Rothbury and the rest of the family that if they had to leave Lochlee Castle they must do so with a memorable ball, the likes of which hadn't been seen in the county for half a century.

'We'll all pitch in, won't we?' Humphrey asked his brothers-in-law. Robert, Andrew, Shane and Laura's new husband, Walter, all agreed. It would be a splendid affair with pipers and fiddlers, fireworks and flowing wine. The castle would be filled to capacity with all of Lady Rothbury's children and grandchildren, the eldest of which would be allowed to stay up until late. Hundreds of guests would also be invited to bear witness to what was the end of a noble era.

They'd dance Highland reels all night and forget that the valuable portraits of past generations would in future be looking down on strangers. The family would also use the best silver for the very last time before it was sent to be auctioned. The reception rooms were already half-empty; not so that guests had the space in which to dance but because the best pieces had already been carted off to the sale rooms.

Three days after the ball the new owners, an American railroad millionaire and his family, would take possession and try and pass off the family portraits as their own ancestors, whilst vulgarizing the castle with extravagant drapes and French furniture. None of the family wanted to think about that now. This was the last time they'd all be together in the family seat and they all wanted it to be a happy, unforgettable occasion, although they knew many secret tears would also be shed on both sides of the green baize door. Only those who toiled on the land were happy because Lochlee's new owner had also managed to buy back the surrounding acres, providing employment for everyone in the neighbourhood.

Henry's dream come true, in fact, but under the auspices of another family.

Laura found that Henry was very much on her mind when she arrived a few days before the ball with Walter and a nanny to look after their six-week-old baby, Caroline and little Neil.

'All this makes me feel that Henry's really gone for ever,' she said as they walked around the echoing rooms.

Walter slipped his arm around her waist. 'It's strange how things work out, isn't it?' he said, looking around. 'Who would have thought the day we first met that Lochlee would no longer belong to your family? I imagine you thought there would be Fairbairns living here for the next five hundred years?'

'We all took it for granted that Henry would marry and have at least one son and that Mama would live in the west wing for ever, and we'd all come home for Hogmanay.' Her voice broke. 'It really hurts to realize that after these next few days none of us will ever come back.'

Walter held her close. 'Alas, nothing is for ever,' he said sadly. 'But you have a new home now, my darling, and I promise Lasswade Hall will be yours for ever and ever.'

'I know it will and I'm so thankful. It's a beautiful house and I feel so safe when I'm at home.'

Walter quickly averted his eyes. 'And so you should be,' he replied stoutly.

Laura's sisters may have been opposed to her marrying Walter because she hardly knew him; they may have begged her to wait because she knew nothing about him, but she had refused to listen to their disquiet and now she was thankful she'd gone ahead and married him. They'd slipped away for a quiet wedding on what was the happiest day of her life, and then he'd taken her to Paris for their honeymoon.

Laura had never realized such happiness existed. To add to her joy she'd become pregnant almost immediately and now she had Caroline.

She knew that even to this day they weren't sure he would make her happy. She'd known all along, though, that Walter was the right man. Yet she could tell by the careful way they looked at her that they wanted to be sure she was all right. It was because they cared for her; she knew that. They feared she'd seized the chance of getting married before it was too late; she knew that, too. It might take time but one day they'd all realize she'd married the most marvellous man.

'What are you two talking about?' asked Beattie, coming down the stairs with Andrew. In her arms she carried her small son, named after Henry. 'Isn't it strange us all being back together? I've just been talking to Di and she says it seems like years since she left here.'

'It *is* years since she left here!' remarked Georgie, joining them in the hall. She patted her heavily pregnant stomach with pride. 'None of our children are going to believe we were all born and brought up in a castle. At least mine aren't! Surrounded by the constant smell of ale they'll think they were born in a brewery!' she added, laughing loudly. These days she almost boasted about living in a house attached to one of Shane's pubs, as if it was much smarter than anything she'd previously been used to.

Diana in particular had found this extremely amusing. 'She practically apologizes for being titled these days, and mocks the way the rest of us live,' she whispered to Laura.

Robert came in through the front entrance of the castle at that moment. 'What's this? A mother's meting?' he remarked jokingly. Then he looked around. 'Where are the other chaps?' He dropped his voice. 'We've got things to discuss and I want to tidy up some loose ends before the ball, as we're all heading back home the next morning.'

Laura and Diana looked at each other and their expressions were momentarily bleak. They didn't want to think about what happened after the ball was over and they didn't want to be reminded that when they departed the morning after, they would be leaving Lochlee for the very last time.

Walter spoke. 'Shall I send out a search party for Shane and Humphrey?' he asked. 'Then we can get the business over and done with and start enjoying ourselves,' he added, squeezing Laura's hand and speaking jovially.

Georgie, Diana and Robert glanced at Walter with disapproval, his flippant manner jarring them at a tense time like this.

★   ★   ★

The lawyers had looked after everything and had reported regularly, at Lady Rothbury's request, to Humphrey and Robert as the disastrous financial details of valuation, probate and finally the amount due in inheritance tax to the Inland Revenue unfolded. It was a long and complicated business, involving the deaths of three Earls of Rothbury in quick succession.

'The bottom line,' Robert had announced, thinking it only right that Andrew, Shane and Walter should also be kept informed, 'is that the Fairbairn family face ruin. Everything will have to be sold and I've never known one family to be hit so hard financially.'

After lengthy discussion and a failed court appeal in which they had hoped to avoid paying death duties on Freddie's inheritance, seeing as he'd fled the country and never taken up his father's title, they found there would be enough money left to buy the manse, a large house three miles from the castle, formerly lived in by the late minister and his family.

Here Lady Rothbury, Alice, Flora and Catriona would live, looked after by the faithful McEwan, one footman, the house-keeper, the cook and a scullery maid, two chambermaids, a parlour maid and a lady's maid.

'The total of their salaries will cost two hundred and seventeen pounds a year, plus their board and keep,' Robert told them now as they sat in the depleted library to discuss Lady Rothbury's future expenses. 'She can also afford a coachman; they only get eighteen pounds a year, but she'll have to hire odd job men to do the garden,' he continued. 'Gardeners these days want a cottage to live in for them and their children, as well as a good salary,' he added in a scandalized voice.

'How absurd,' Humphrey exclaimed. 'Why can't they live in their own houses like the rest of us?'

Shane was frowning anxiously. 'Do you think the old dear is going to be all right?' he asked.

Their faces registered mild hostility. The countess may have fallen upon hard times in the twilight of her life, but she could not be referred to as 'the old dear'.

'Lady Rothbury will be fine,' Robert assured Shane evenly.

'I don't mind putting my hand in my pocket if she needs anything,' Shane insisted.

Walter turned and smiled at Shane. 'That's really kind and generous of you, old chap,' he said warmly. 'I think we should all watch the situation closely without worrying her. She might be offended if she thought she was a charity case, don't you think?'

Shane slapped his thigh in hearty agreement. 'She's proud, like my ma. Obviously we wouldn't slip her a few pounds across the table if she was needy, like.'

Humphrey rolled his eyes and Robert looked at Humphrey sternly. He was aware Georgie was blissfully happy with Shane and as a result was nice to everyone these days; for that alone they should be thankful and remain civil to him.

Robert spoke firmly. 'The really important thing is that our mother-in-law should be surrounded by staff who are well known to her. In reality, apart from the fact she'll be occupying much smaller rooms, nothing else will change for her. She'll have the same lady's maid, Cook will still prepare her favourite dishes and McEwan – God bless him! – will still be at her beck and call. That's the most any of us can hope for when we get old.'

There was a sober silence as the others took in his words.

Then Shane slapped his thigh again. 'We're not old yet so let's have a stiff noggin to cheer ourselves up, shall we?'

'So speaks the landlord of The King's Head!' exclaimed Humphrey, giving Shane a forgiving smile and a friendly thump on the shoulder.

The sisters had congregated in the big day nursery on the top floor to help the various nannies give the children tea, but they'd soon drifted into corners to enjoy the pleasure of chattering to each other once again.

'Have you stopped dressmaking altogether, Laura?' Lizzie asked as they sat side by side on the familiar old ottoman.

'Yes. I sold my business to Helen, whose husband had a little money squirreled away. I just make my own clothes now, and of course Caroline's layette,' Laura replied, glancing down fondly at the sleeping baby in her arms.

'She must be the best-dressed baby in Lasswade! I often wish I wasn't dependent on Humphrey for every penny.'

Laura gave a roguish smile. 'Oh, but I've spent all of mine.' She dropped her voice. 'I've redecorated the house. Priscilla had the most appalling taste. The fabrics she chose were dreadful and as for the wallpaper . . .! Walter didn't mind at all. He understood I needed to put my own stamp on the place.'

Lizzie also dropped her voice. 'And you're really happy? Walter is quite rich, isn't he?' She'd never liked him and couldn't hide her critical tone when she was talking about him. 'Was it his father who left him a fortune?'

Laura nodded. 'I believe so. One never discusses these things, does one? We can certainly afford to live very stylishly.'

'Hmm,' Lizzie retorted.

Beattie came over and joined them, sitting in a nearby chair and plonking little Henry on the floor between them. 'What are you two old witches whispering about?' she teased.

'Our lovers, of course. What else?' Laura countered swiftly with a straight face. Diana and Georgie standing nearby burst out laughing when they heard her.

'Of *course*!' Georgie echoed cheekily. 'Trouble is Shane won't let me work behind the bar so I don't get much of a chance.'

For a moment the five women were like young girls again, convulsed with laughter at each other's remarks and overcome with giggles.

Nanny Fairbairn looked up from the central tea table where the small ones were strapped into high chairs as they stuffed jam sandwiches into their mouths while the older ones sat in shy silence nibbling Dundee cake.

Nanny had known the Fairbairn girls since they'd been little and as she listened to Lizzie, Laura, Diana and Beattie and the much-improved Georgie, she knew this room in the castle would never again ring with such joyful merriment.

The last few precious days before the ball passed all too swiftly, and although everyone was putting on a good face and being resolutely cheerful, a creeping dark dread was invading Lochlee, in spite of the dozens of workers who were preparing the raised platform for the musicians, the long tables for the buffet supper and the bar which would serve a range of drinks all evening. This had been organized by Shane, who proudly pointed out how much they were saving by buying the liquor through him at wholesale prices.

'He's a useful chap to know,' Humphrey had pointed out *sotto voce.*

Lady Rothbury came down from her private quarters from time to time to see what was going on, but it pained her to see gaps where there had once been furniture, and she grieved at the impending loss of every stick and stone of the place. She'd come here as a bride and she was leaving it as a widow who had also lost two sons.

As the time to go drew nearer her misery increased so much that she wished it was all over and done with. She longed to just go straight downstairs and out through the front door on to the drive where she could keep on walking without looking back. Having a ball was a big mistake and she should never have let the family persuade her otherwise. It was prolonging the agony instead of pretending it wasn't happening, and it was rubbing salt into the grievous wound.

Pressing her fingertips to her mouth to suppress the sobs that were rising in her chest, she prayed to God to give her the strength to control her emotions during the next twenty-four hours. How often had she told her daughters that ladies don't cry because it embarrasses the servants?

Had anyone ever seen a member of the royal family cry? she asked herself fiercely. Of course they hadn't! Ladies didn't cry. She'd wear her new ball gown and she'd hold her head high and she'd expect her daughters to do the same. No matter how hard it was.

Flaming torches lined the long drive and lanterns were lit in every window so Lochlee resembled a castle in a fairy-tale book as the guests were driven up to the entrance in their carriages.

Inside the great hall Lady Rothbury, magnificently dressed in silver-grey satin, greeted the guests with the help of her eight daughters and their husbands. Instead of a formal line-up she decided they should group themselves informally and that each guest would be immediately offered a drink by a waiting footman. From the ballroom came the lilt of music and the scent of flowers and, beyond in the dining room, guests caught a glimpse of a magnificent buffet supper fit for a royal palace laid out on large silver entrée dishes.

Soon the castle was filled with a whirling mass of colourful ball gowns and men in velvet doublets and the kilt as a piper played for reels. For those who didn't want to dance there were chairs in the library, where Shane was soon holding court in front of the bar as he recommended different makes of whisky to the male guests. The older ladies gravitated to the drawing room where it was less noisy and they could marvel sympathetically at their hostess's bravery in moving to the manse the next day.

'It will be cheaper to run,' one murmured hopefully.

In the great hall the younger guests jostled with the Fairbairn girls who, Lady Rothbury proudly admitted to herself, looked outstandingly beautiful, all being tall and slender, with fine profiles and lustrous dark hair.

It would not be long, she reflected, before Alice, Flora and Catriona also had husbands to whirl them around ballrooms.

'It's going very well, isn't it?' Laura said to Robert as they came off the dance floor, having danced an energetic foursome with Beattie and Andrew. 'When are we having the fireworks?'

'I thought we'd have them just before the ball ends,' Robert replied.

She nodded in approval. There was so much noise of people talking and the fiddlers or the piper playing that she had to shout to be heard. It was two o'clock in the morning and the revelry was at its height. The castle seemed to shake with music and activity and laughter, and Robert decided this was the perfect moment to set off the firework display before everyone got tired and started drifting away.

An announcement was made and the guests all surged into the garden, pouring out of the front door and on to the lawn, huddled in great enthusiastic groups, some carrying glasses of wine, others holding hands. Suddenly the clear dark sky was splintered into a thousand sparkling lights and there was a loud crack. Gasps of appreciation followed and clapping, and that was only the beginning. Laura, standing beside Walter, had never seen such an incredible display of colour

and lights, as sparkling fountains burst above their heads and
arched over the castle's ramparts, or whizzed straight up into
the air and exploded high above them. There were burning
waterfalls of gold that fell out of the sky and whirling will-
o'-the-wisps cartwheeling over the tree tops. Then there was
a final display when the ground shuddered as if in an earthquake, releasing several rockets which whizzed up into the
sky before bursting into giant starry pom-poms which hung
above the silent crowds for a moment before fragmenting
slowly and drifting down like sparkling apple blossom in a
summer breeze.

Laura looked at Walter but he was staring in the direction
of the castle. She turned and saw a fiddler standing on the
ramparts with his bow raised. A moment later he was joined
by another man whose lone voice floated poignantly from the
ancient battlements.

> *Should auld acquaintance be forgot*
> *And never brought to mind?*
> *Should auld acquaintance be forgot*
> *For auld lang syne.*
> *For auld lang syne, my dear,*
> *For auld lang syne,*
> *We'll tak a cup o'kindness yet,*
> *For the sake of auld lang syne.*

The party was over. By tomorrow the family would have
gone, bringing to an end five hundred years of Scottish history
and for the Fairbairn girls a lifetime of memories.

Eighteen

Cranley Court, 1910

'Laura? Is that you darling?' Diana called out when she heard footsteps coming down the stairs. She hurried out of the breakfast room and placed her hands on her sister's shoulders as she reached the bottom step.

'There's someone here to see you,' she said in a quiet voice.

Laura's hazel eyes widened nervously. Sleepless nights had taken their toll in the last two months and, although staying with Diana had been the essence of comfort and tranquillity, she still felt shaken to the bone, her very being jarred by what had happened.

'Debt collectors?' she whispered anxiously.

Diana smiled reassuringly. 'No. Walter is here. He's come to see you.'

'He's here?' For a moment Laura looked distraught and then she started trembling. 'Oh, God! What's he doing here? I'm not ready for this.'

'I think he wants to make amends. He's in the study. Why don't you go and see him; Robert and I will keep out of your way for a while.'

'I'm still so angry,' Laura confessed, her mouth tightening. 'Caroline doesn't know he's here, does she? I don't want her upset.'

'She's having breakfast in the nursery and I've sent a message up to Nanny to keep all the children up there for the time being.'

With a quick nod Laura turned and marched towards the study.

'Good luck,' Diana whispered sympathetically. 'Call me if you need me.'

Walter was standing with his back to the fireplace, and as soon as he saw Laura his face lit up and he was smiling, his eyes wide and clear. His expression reminded her of a child who has been very naughty but is certain of adult forgiveness.

'Hello, Laura,' he said eagerly, coming forward as if to kiss her, but she sidestepped him and with furrowed brows looked at him coldly.

'Why are you here?'

He dropped back, looking crestfallen. 'I thought you'd be glad to see me. I'm well again, darling. The doctors said I've made a wonderful recovery. I very much wanted to see you, too.' He lifted his chin, rallying again. 'I've been staying with Rowena, who has been looking after Neil, which you so obviously didn't want to do and she . . .'

'That's unfair,' Laura shot back. 'He's happier with his aunt than he ever was with me. He's never liked me because he resented me taking his mother's place in his life and you know it. Why do you think he set fire to my bedroom? Then the drawing room? He's badly disturbed by his mother's death and your drinking; the poor child is much better off with his aunt, who can give him stability.'

Walter looked surprised, as if he was unaware of his son's feelings. 'I believe he's very fond of you,' he protested. 'I'd like us to all live together again as a real family. You, me, Caroline and Neil, and Rowena is quite happy to put us up in her house.'

Laura blinked. It was as if the events of the past had been no more than an inconvenience caused by his 'illness'.

'What? Live with you and your sister? Sponge off her and her widow's pension until you bleed her dry? Until you drag her down as you did me, until she loses everything too?'

Walter's expression was one of incredulity. 'What do you mean?' he asked, offended. 'I wouldn't dream of sponging off Rowena. I shall get a job. You've become very bitter, Laura. I'm surprised at you. I didn't think it was my money you were after.'

Laura sank on to a chair, shaking her head in disbelief. 'Walter, I don't think you realize the trail of utter chaos you leave in your wake. I don't even think you know how much you've hurt people. There are times when you take to drink that you become another person.'

'You were in love with me when it suited you,' he grumbled resentfully.

'That's true, but I'd never have married you if I'd realized there was another side to you,' she admitted with a touch of sadness. 'If you think I can forget all about losing our home and every single possession we ever had, which left me with Caroline and only enough money to get two train tickets to travel the short distance to come here, otherwise we'd have been on the *streets* . . .' her voice rose in anguish, 'then you're completely in denial about the reality of life. Diana and Robert have saved Caroline and me from the workhouse!'

'But I'm all right now. It won't happen again, I promise you.' Laura covered her face with her hands in utter exasperation. 'You say that every time, Walter. You promise you'll never touch alcohol again, but you always do. Now you've squandered every penny and there's nothing left. We had everything when we were first married but you've neglected your affairs, spent money like water and ended up bankrupt. What do you think that has done to Caroline? To watch the bailiffs throw her toys into a van? To come here with only the clothes we're standing in?'

'I can't help it.' He sounded like a lost soul.

She fought back the tears. 'And I can't help you.'

'Can I see Caroline?'

'Not today. It's too soon and it would make her very unsettled. I'll bring her over to Rowena's at some point; you can see her then.'

Walter stood up abruptly and she saw the tears in his eyes as he turned away and charged out of the room, slamming the door behind him.

Laura wiped away her own tears. It was time she went back to dressmaking professionally so she could support herself and Caroline. There was no other way.

Diana raised her eyebrows when she heard about Laura's decision. 'Dressmaking?'

'It's the only thing I can do. Caroline and I can't stay with you and Robert for ever. I'm going to have to earn money. Caroline has to be educated and given a chance in life, and Walter isn't going to be able to provide that. I'm going to have to bring her up on my own.' She spoke with sudden confidence. Seeing Walter again had made her realize she was the stronger of the two.

Diana looked appalled. The idea of having a husband who didn't provide for his wife and children was unthinkable. 'How will you manage? You must live with us, Laura. You can always work from here if you want to do some dressmaking and Nanny can look after Caroline while you're sewing, but you can't possibly fend for yourself.'

'You sound like Mama,' Laura pointed out. 'I have two options. I can ask Helen if I can join her in business; that is if she'd have me. Or I can get the bank to lend me some money so I can start from scratch.'

'How can you be so brave? You've just lost everything, Laura. *Everything!* You're destitute, darling. Don't you understand?'

Laura nodded. 'I don't need you of all people to rub it in. I know none of you thought I should rush into marriage with Walter, and you were right.'

Seeing Diana's sympathetic expression, she continued, 'I'm not the first woman to be left destitute! I'll get back on my feet. I started my own business before and I can do it again.'

Diana looked pained. 'You were on your own then, with no one but yourself to think about, knowing you could always go back to Lochlee if the worst happened.'

'I'll never forget the ghastliness of what happened and I don't know if I can forgive Walter, but I do know that life must go on, if only for Caroline's sake. It's made me more determined than ever to rebuild my life. I promise you, Di, I'll make a success of my business all over again.' Laura held her sister's gaze, her eyes full of resolve. She was ready to face the future, no matter what it might hold.